T0358801

THE SEVENTH SPELL

THE SEVENTH SPELL

Davis Bunn

SEVERN
HOUSE

First world edition published in Great Britain and the USA in 2024
by Severn House, an imprint of Canongate Books Ltd,
14 High Street, Edinburgh EH1 1TE.

severnhouse.com

British Library Cataloguing-in-Publication Data
A CIP catalogue record for this title is available from the British Library.

ISBN-13: 978-1-4483-1329-7 (cased)
ISBN-13: 978-1-4483-1413-3 (e-book)

All Severn House titles are printed on acid-free paper.

MIX
Paper from
responsible sources
FSC® C013056

Typeset by Palimpsest Book Production Ltd., Falkirk,
Stirlingshire, Scotland.
Printed and bound in Great Britain by TJ Books,
Padstow, Cornwall.

Praise for Davis Bunn

"Impressive . . . Bunn keeps the suspense high"
Publishers Weekly on *The Rowan*

"A wild ride"
Kirkus Reviews on *Island of Time*

"Swiftly paced with a deep look at how a transition can help heal past personal traumas, Bunn's latest will interest sf readers"
Booklist on *No Man's Land*

"A fast-paced, retro-feeling sci-fi mystery. Bunn offers readers a sure guide through his far-future setting . . . A pleasure.
This is good fun"
Publishers Weekly on *Prime Directive*

"I absolutely loved this story! *The Rowan* is a powerful political thriller that delves both into sci-fi and fantasy. The result is a mesmerizing page turner"
David Lipman, producer of the *Iron Man* and *Shrek* films

"Bunn's imaginative thriller combines propulsive plotting with sharp observations"
Publishers Weekly on *Burden of Proof*

About the author

Davis Bunn's novels have sold in excess of eight million copies in twenty-six languages. He has appeared on numerous national best-seller lists, and his novels have been Main or Featured Selections with every major US bookclub. Recent titles have been named Best Book of the Year by both *Library Journal* and *Suspense Magazine*, as well as earning Top Pick and starred reviews from *RT Reviews*, *Kirkus Reviews*, *Publishers Weekly* and *Booklist*. Currently Davis serves as Writer-In-Residence at Regent's Park College, Oxford University. He speaks around the world on aspects of creative writing. Davis also publishes under the pseudonym of Thomas Locke.

ONE

Adrian Capstan was born in Desert Hot Springs, the nowhere city across I10 from the moneyed resort of Palm Springs. His father supplanted a mechanic's pay by dealing, until he was sent away for a third and final time when Adrian was eight. His mother cleaned houses and stayed hooked on the drugs she could no longer obtain from her ex.

Adrian escaped first by way of the Nevada court system, which sent him into foster care three years later. He stayed clean, worked hard, earned a scholarship to U Nevada. There he served in the cafeteria, cleaned hallways, saved every penny. An accounting degree led to a second scholarship, this one in hotel management at UCLA. From there he entered the five-star Ritz-Carlton chain. Adrian moved slowly up the management ladder and continued his spartan existence. Holding fast to his secret quest.

Three days before his twenty-eighth birthday, Adrian knew it was time. The chrysalis was about to open. The true man revealed.

Quarter to seven that morning, Adrian was seated outside the general manager's office when Dorothy Henning arrived for work. She was a large woman with ebony skin and no sense of humor whatsoever. Dorothy eyed him sourly and declared, 'And here I always thought you were a smart one.'

Adrian rose and followed her into the office. 'I've come for my last paycheck.'

'More likely you won't live to spend it.' She was born in Nassau, left for Miami when she was six, but still carried a hint of the islands when angry. She opened her top drawer, lifted the envelope, looked ready to tear it up. 'I feel like I'm handing over a nail in your coffin.'

Adrian saw no need to respond. They had been having pretty much the same conversation since he gave his notice three months earlier.

When he did not reply, she almost shouted, 'Mars is a boiling pot! Do you even watch the news?'

'Every day.'

'Then you know! The place is on the verge of civil war!'

'The Mars Ritz-Carlton has offered me a position—'

'You think that will make you safe? Did you not see what they did to the spaceport?'

'I did, yes.'

'Then tell me why. You owe me that much.'

It was too much a temptation, too great a burning desire to keep inside any longer. 'I've been aiming for this since I was nine. It's all I've ever wanted.'

'Then wait! A year, maybe two, things will settle. Mars needs Earth more than we need them.'

It was a phrase used by every recent politician; one Adrian suspected was more propaganda than truth. Earth desperately needed the rare-earth minerals that were abundant on Mars. Earth also made substantial profits from shipping manufactured goods to the red planet. The technology to refine Martian ore remained on Earth, as did the manufacture of most high-end goods. Adrian thought Mars had been right to revolt, and the current political settlement solved nothing.

He rose to his feet and pulled the check from her fingers. 'My ship leaves in two days.'

He cashed the check, closed his account and exchanged most of his dollars for UCs, universal credits. He stopped by his favorite food van for a final meal. He wasn't hungry so much as using the Asian-fusion salad as a punctuation mark. Sitting at one of their scarred picnic tables, watching the traffic and the day. When he was ready, Adrian returned to his car and set off.

The drive to the Nevada launch site took seven hours and skirted the Sedona highlands and the Hopi reservation. After crossing into Utah at Kanab, the highway jinked west around the Escalante range, then turned north again and flew past Bryce and Canyon City. The shimmering desert landscape formed a magnificent setting for his farewell to life on Earth. The heat, the harsh light, the wavy asphalt highway, all reminded him of those awful early years. Back before he became aware of what now defined his existence.

Eventually he joined the Veterans Memorial Highway, until the old cracked and ribbed road became transformed into something so totally different it could almost have been alien.

The state road was now a six-lane expressway that shimmered silver in the afternoon sun. The junction at Beaver was a wild sweep of sculpted concrete, welcoming the traveler to grand off-world vistas. The old desert town was now a booming metropolis, as were all the other former flyspecks – Milford, Frisco, Malone, Black Rock, Minersville. Adrian continued on past his destination for the night, up a rise, around the final curve in the nearly flattened hillside, all the way to the final turnaround point, three hundred meters above the main gates. He pulled into the massive lookout parking area, joining all the other gawkers and OneEarth protesters and meal vans and campers and noise. This close to launch date, the site was jammed. Adrian walked to a relatively empty space by the perimeter fence and tried to come to terms with what he saw.

The start of something new.

Perhaps.

At long last.

The WLA Depot, Western Launch Array, known to locals as the Arena, completely overwhelmed what had previously been the Minersville State Park and Campground. The warehouses, support structures, launch pads, and desalination plants formed a gleaming crescent around the southern rim of Sevier Lake. For over a century prior to the WLA's arrival, Sevier had been an on-again, off-again body of highly noxious water. The salt content alone was three times higher than the Pacific. Plus there were the mineral run-offs from surrounding hills and the desert floor. The lake's original sources, the Sevier and Beaver rivers, had long since been diverted. All that changed when the federal survey determined this empty and super-heated region was ideal for their future needs. Now the lake dominated the region's water table. New dams were built; other rivers had their flows diverted. What the WLA wanted, it took.

The enlarged Sevier Lake was framed by vast solar farms and desert lowlands – a hostile, dusty, windswept inferno. All of which added to its choice as a launch site. OneEarth protestors constantly surrounded and often invaded the spaceport at Canaveral. Here they were safely kept miles away. Those who managed to break through the perimeter fences were often caught on security cameras, literally begging to be rescued and imprisoned.

When he was ready, Adrian retraced his route, dropped off his rental car and checked into the Black Rock Hilton. He paid the exorbitant rate for two nights, in case liftoff was delayed. After a lifetime of hoarding pennies, the cost was an absurd final luxury. He found genuine satisfaction in needing to pay cash for his room, since all his earthly accounts were closed. The hotel was overbooked and filled with the chaotic clamor of families both excited and dreading the day ahead.

Adrian dined in the overpriced rooftop restaurant on the last steak he would hopefully ever eat. Grilled asparagus with shaved parmesan, a vegetable not available on Mars because of the amount of water required in cultivation. Ditto on the single glass of cabernet, and the molten chocolate cake for dessert.

That night he had the dream.

The same one that had launched him in this crazy direction four days after his ninth birthday. It had been a Saturday, after his mother had forced him to start cleaning houses. Putting her son to work meant extra money, food on the table, rent, drug of choice. All through that endless Saturday, his mother had remained so hungover she could ignore her son's pleadings and tears.

That first night, nine-year-old Adrian had put the dream down to wishing he could be anywhere else. Even death was better than being trapped in this hellish life. Just the same, he had woken up feeling energized. Lifted up. As if even this temporary nighttime glimpse of freedom had left him able to hope for better things to come.

Only that very same dream had returned the next night.

And the one after. For a month. Thirty days in a row. And off and on ever since.

That first incredible night, his father gone and his old lady stoned, Adrian assumed he was dying. Frightened, but also welcoming it.

The dream started when he opened his eyes, only they were *different eyes.* He knew this because he was lifted free from his body, then swung partly around so he could see himself lying there, covers bundled into a tight knot so he could hug them, a habit from his earliest days. Like he would take comfort wherever he could find it. A brief instant spent looking down, then he was swept up, up, up. And away.

He could actually see the awful town of Desert Hot Springs and headlights sweeping along the I10. Further up, he saw how Palm Springs looked so much finer, the houses and condos further apart, the palm trees and the lawns shimmering under streetlights that worked.

He flew.

There was time to wonder at the sensation of being drawn forward by gentle hands. Or a person. Something. The experience so potent he didn't have room to feel frightened. He wasn't alone, and the guiding hands were doing this for his own good. He didn't require logic. Nor did he even need to understand. The sensation was that strong.

Even when he flew beyond Earth's atmosphere, could see the globe's curvature, then further and faster until he swept past the moon . . . Fear remained a distant issue. Like it belonged to the kid still sleeping in his bed. Back where the bad things could still strike. Not here.

He flew.

Not even time could touch him. Adrian had no idea how long the bodiless journey lasted. Forever, as far as he was concerned. The feeling was that splendid. All the pains and miseries of his earthly existence, gone. There was only this exquisite moment.

Then up ahead, his destination gradually took form. Growing larger and larger . . .

Mars.

He entered the main dome of Mars's capital city. How he knew this was inconsequential. There was no room for such questions, because his arrival carried not a message, not a thought, not a hope.

A conviction.

This was where he belonged.

This was where his real life began.

He flew above a broad thoroughfare. He halted in the middle of a grand circle, a plaza surrounded by structures that held the planet's government. Directly in front of him was a building of red sandstone. The emblem carved above the broad entryway showed a bold phoenix about to take flight.

Adrian was not told what the emblem meant. He *recognized* it. As if he was drawing on information that had been waiting for his arrival.

The Mars Wizards' Council. Headquarters of the Wizards' Guild.

Adrian watched as the emblem burst into flames. A silent explosion of force, so potent it pushed him away, back across the space between planets, back into the life he hated. The return journey was only bearable because of the word that resonated long after he had leapt out of bed and stood gasping for breath.

COME.

By the time the dream reduced in frequency, settling into a routine of once every three or four weeks, Adrian's life plan was set in stone. Forget the fact that he was a nine-year-old kid. A felon for a dad, stoner mom, wrong town, wrong life. None of that mattered any more. He was going to make that dream real.

Journey to Mars. Become a wizard.

It was only a matter of time.

Adrian's pre-dawn dream in the Black Rock Hilton was mostly the same. With one small difference.

Of course, given the fact that the dream had not altered one iota during the past seventeen years, it was hard to class any change as minor.

This time, the dream ended with a different word.

FINALLY.

TWO

Adrian went for a pre-dawn swim, then watched the sun rise from a chaise lounge pulled up to the hotel's eastern boundary wall. Back in his room, he spent almost half an hour in the hottest shower he could stand. Adrian emerged par-boiled and smiling. As he dressed he wondered if he'd miss the commonplace luxury of so much water.

The answer was a definite affirmative.

Did it matter?

Absolutely not.

As often happened, liftoff was delayed and delayed again. Passengers without second-day bookings filled the downstairs lobby, pool, restaurant and bars with a swarming, querulous mob.

Adrian hunkered down in his room and worked up a five-star room service bill. Three more meals, each time going for items he was unlikely to ever have again – lobster, salmon, grouse, and a bottle of vintage champagne he nursed through all three feasts.

Three fifteen the next morning, the alert finally came through.

Because of his status as member of the pod crew, Adrian was assigned to the first departure group. Which required him to maneuver through hordes jamming the lobby and hotel forecourt. Climbing into his bus meant entering an island of silent sanity.

The other bus passengers were mostly older. Before the troubles, the boundary ages for pod crews ran from thirty-five to fifty. Then the Mars rebels brought down a cold-sleep pod on landing approach, killing all on board.

The revolt was finally ended by Earth's governments reluctantly accepting a new status quo. The practice of sending so-called ambassadors to govern Mars on temporary assignment was halted. Mars was to be ruled by locals only. New cold-sleep transports were restricted to essential personnel – mechanics, miners, medical, and so forth. Quotas were limited to numbers approved by Mars's new regime.

While at university, Adrian had tried for medical, then engineering, and failed at both. His talents lay elsewhere. Not to mention how he would never sign a seven-year contract. He wasn't trading one life bound by invisible cages for another.

So he took aim for the only other option available. Pod crew.

The forty-three-mile journey from hotel to launch site was wondrous, exciting, endless. Their papers were checked and faces scanned twice. The bus remained mostly silent, and mostly happy. Despite the troubles, everyone on board was living some form of lifelong dream. He suspected almost all of them had made this journey before. The pay was excellent, room and board on Mars was free, they could spend five months on a different planet and return. For pod crew members making multiple runs, the current troubles were simply part of the package.

Gradually the massive pods grew closer, the lights shone brighter, Adrian's heart hammered louder. The pods were nothing to look at, really; metal structures that had seen innumerable take-offs and landings, their sides battered and scarred. Each was larger than any of the surrounding buildings, great metal beasts resting on arc-like structures, waiting.

A single terminal fed all four pods, a massive empty warehouse with roped-off lines and signs in multiple languages. His IDs were checked and retinas scanned a final time, then a bored guard lined them up against the side wall, droning the same words, 'Take a number, find a space, wait your turn. No talking.' Over and over.

Being this close to realizing his dream, still uncertain over his fate, left Adrian a half-step from total meltdown.

Finally Adrian's number was called. He entered the small side chamber, and found himself standing before all four pod chiefs and their aides. Each pod was run by a pod master and two assistants, also called chiefs. They were all a hard-core lot, seven men and five women. Their spokesperson was the senior woman – gray hair, broad shoulders, gravelly voice. 'What's a pretty boy like you doing here?'

Make all responses direct and short, the final training video had instructed. Be honest and crystal clear. Keep it fast. Speed was essential.

Make them understand how much this chance means.

'I've worked all my life to get here,' Adrian replied. 'Heading to Mars. I have a job waiting. But I'm not signing a seven-year contract. No way. I've worked for people I hated. I'm not doing it—'

'Pod work is hard-core, pretty boy.' This from a younger version of the barrel man, seated next to the pod master. 'You're a janitor, and you're on duty twenty-four seven.'

'What we need doing, you do,' the barrel said. 'No argument, no complaints.'

'I've been a janitor before,' Adrian replied. 'Twice.'

'Details,' the senior woman snapped.

'I started helping my mother clean houses when I was nine. Worked my way through university as a cafeteria custodian.'

Barrel junior looked at the senior woman. 'What are we doing here anyway? No way pretty boy here is thirty.'

A woman on the group's other side spoke for the first time. Lean, very still, blonde hair going grey, clear skin, bright eyes. 'They've lowered the age threshold.'

'You're having me on.'

'Twice. Which you'd know if you'd lay off the pipe.'

'Pretty boy's gonna be trouble,' the barrel said. 'I'll put money on it.'

The senior woman flicked through pages on her tablet. 'Your last job was hotel manager?'

'Assistant manager. I started at the bottom there too. Maintenance.'

All four senior masters showed tight interest. The senior chief said, 'Again, details.'

'Phoenix Ritz-Carlton. My first duty was changing the room air filters. Four hundred and eleven of them.'

The youngest chief was slightly removed from the others. Two hard-edged women were seated between her and the group. She pointed at Adrian. 'I claim him.'

The two men scowled. Barrel said, 'He's maintenance. We need—'

'I've got two hundred and seventeen in cold storage. And first-time cargo. It's my bid. I claim him.'

The senior woman confirmed, 'Her call.'

Barrel crossed his arms. Angry now. 'This is nuts.'

The woman clearly liked her win. She held out a wristband. When Adrian accepted it, she ordered, 'Pod Three. Ready-room is aft portside. Go get yourself settled. Be ready for the incoming tide.'

THREE

Adrian told himself it was crazy, the way he felt. But he couldn't help it. The actual things themselves, what he saw, were nothing. The connecting tunnel was a long collapsible tube blasted with cold, almost frigid air. Every few paces was a tight little window splashed by just another desert sunrise. Up ahead walked a man and woman with skin the color of amber, golden and brown, dark hair, both of them lean and solid and silent. Carrying cases that weighed in at eleven kilos, the maximum pod crews were permitted for the nineteen-month journey – seven out, five on Mars, seven back. Then the tunnel ended, and Adrian passed through the massive entry portal . . .

He couldn't see anything clearly. His eyes were filmed by tears. Then he bumped into the man. 'Sorry, sorry.'

'You're a first-timer.'

'Yes, yes, I am.'

'Follow us.' As they walked, the man said, 'I am Hassim, my wife is Sandhu.'

'Nice to meet you.' He cleared his throat. 'Adrian Capstan.'

'Only first names, Adrian. That's the rule.'

'One of many,' Sandhu said.

'You are lucky to be taken by Master Freya.'

'You must call her Pod Master until Freya says otherwise,' Sandhu said.

'So very lucky,' Hassim went on. 'Some of the other masters, they work the new people very hard, then downcheck them a month or so before landfall and ship them to cold-sleep. Claim half the salary as their own.'

He wanted to be alone, take his time, drink in the fact that he had made it this far. Just the same, their words helped anchor him to the moment, clear his mind, prepare him for whatever came next. Adrian followed them along the starboard passage. To his right was the pod's exterior wall. To his left was a vast open space. The steel pathway clung high to the side wall. From here it was possible to glimpse the pod's vast interior. Big as a covered arena, a hundred and fifty meters long. The bow area held the miniature pilots' quarters, used only during liftoff and landfall. Pod pilots were local to their planets. Once their duty was completed, they transited back, slept in their own beds. Adrian would have considered that a fate worse than death.

The stern was dominated by a blank steel wall, behind which lay Engineering and the pod's mini-ion drive. Directly in front of the shield-wall, multiple cold-storage units were stacked like blocks. In between stretched the vast cargo hold, segmented by temporary walls whose tops were painted with Day-Glo numerical IDs.

They entered the pod crew's ready-room and Hassim pointed him to the corner berth. 'That cabin is assigned to the first-timer. It is small and fairly terrible. Bad smells from the freshers gather there. No one knows why.'

'Doesn't matter.'

'That is the right answer,' Sandhu said, patting his arm. 'Something tells me you will be fine.'

'Use the fresher, dress in coveralls.' Hassim pointed to plastic pouches stacked on the central table. 'Sandhu, this young man's size . . .'

'Extra large, slim fit.'

'Hurry now. We must be in position when the hordes arrive.'

FOUR

Adrian had hoped to be positioned on the outer portal, there to hurry the incoming travelers, check their tickets, point them toward the correct unit. But Freya assigned him duty in the thick of things. Which was how Adrian found himself checking for illegal underwear.

Cold storage created such an extreme state of muscle relaxation that any tight-fitting garment threatened circulation. In early days, unauthorized undergarments had resulted in emergency amputations. So Adrian stood to one side of the access channel, Sandhu the other. He peered inside the standard-issue cold-storage garments of each incoming male, making sure they wore nothing else.

The first horn sounded for liftoff, but it didn't seem to Adrian that very much changed. He had been trained in pre- and post-launch responsibilities – a binder, endless videos, three exams. He wore his armband and ear comm-link, kept his onboard mini-tablet fastened to his belt, an illuminated baton in his left hand. All the lessons showed a calm and orderly process, smiling passengers, polite pod workers directing people to their welcoming capsule.

Ha.

Babies squalled, kids screamed, parents yelled, hungover loners moaned. The noise echoed off distant steel walls. Parents kept shouting questions and complaints his way. He had no idea what they were saying, nor did it matter, since he doubted he'd know the answer.

Each cold-storage unit was brought into loading position by what to Adrian looked like a giant escalator. A steel box-like structure was drawn forward, the door opened, the next group filed inside. Thirty-six cold-storage capsules per box.

Beside each capsule was a narrow fold-down seat where passengers were directed to sit, tighten the belts, stay. If kids kicked up a fuss, they were strapped in forcibly. Infants remained with one parent. Families stayed together, which meant sometimes a clutch of wailing kids and frantic parents were jammed tight behind Adrian, allowing others to fill the final seats before the next compartment was swung into position.

Athena, one of the assistant pod chiefs, worked with Hassim inside the unit, arranging the newcomers. Once everyone was strapped in, they passed out gel packs marked 'Nutrients One' and sized adult/child/infant. They took their time, ensuring every passenger ingested a full dose.

Watching them calmly work their way around the jammed unit, Adrian found himself gripped by a tension years in the making. Fearing this might never happen. Standing where he was. Surrounded by controlled chaos. Inside a pod. Go for launch.

There was no real pleasure to the moment. He knew Hassim and the assistant chief could see how his hands trembled. He knew they assumed he was frightened. Adrian wasn't the least bit scared. There was no word for how he felt.

Nineteen years.

Whatever nutrients the packets might have contained, they definitely also held a powerful calming agent. By the time Hassim and Athena made their way back to the portal, even the most terrified mother was serene. Every shrieking kid was silent. The passengers sat calmly, secure in their padded seats, looking around the steel-clad chamber that would be their home for the next seven months. Compliant, floating, silent. Happy.

When all the passengers were secured and silent, Hassim and Athena stepped back onto the loading platform. Athena pushed the red button on the railing that closed the unit's portal and drew the next into position.

When the final box was sealed and the passageway empty save for pod crew, Hassim leaned in tight and said, 'Freya and the ship's medic come by later and ready them for cold-sleep. Our work here is done.'

Athena didn't speak. She merely glanced over, took in Adrian's unsteady state, and smirked.

All the former taglines for leaving Earth – blastoff, explosive force, heavy Gs – no longer applied. The development of inexpensive room-temperature, ambient-pressure superconductors had resulted in a new first-stage flight that was, as pod pilots liked to describe, as exciting as driving an elevator.

Once the pods reached Earth's exosphere, their miniature ion drive took over until they linked with the mother ship. The pods docked nose first, forming a slowly rotating pinwheel. There were sixteen pods per ship – four from the Utah blast site, plus additional foursomes from Brazil, Australia and Kenya. Each pod remained an isolated unit throughout the voyage, as did the cockpit and stern drive. Once the docking maneuvers were completed, pod pilots shuttled back to Earth, content to go no farther from their homes than low-altitude orbit. Ion drive provided a steady, simple, cheap, almost endless propulsion, doing away with many limitations on what could be sent into space. The mother ship was little more than a metal skeleton, with a sealed cockpit area in the bow and massive propulsion unit in the stern. The mother ship was enormous, cheap to operate, utterly safe, and slow. Even when Mars and Earth were at their closest point, like now, the great lumbering beasts required seven months for the journey.

A month passed. Six weeks. Adrian worked his shifts, clocked his overtime when ordered, stayed mostly silent. He was the only newcomer in Freya's pod. The others did not ostracize him, but he was also not part of the group. Hassim and Sandhu remained his instructors, his go-betweens. The others referred to him as new guy, or pretty boy, or ignored him altogether.

The ready-rooms were aft, just ahead of the cold-storage compartments. The mother ship's rotations maintained a G-force at thirty-eight percent of Earth's normal, more or less that of Mars. This allowed newcomers like Adrian to move about in relative comfort. He was not sent into the forward compartments until Freya was certain he wouldn't toss his lunch.

The only troubling factor about those initial weeks was, the dreams stopped.

Adrian tried to tell himself this was merely a transition, he was on the right track, the nighttime confirmations weren't needed.

But he *did* need them. It became all too easy to give into fear, especially at night, locked in his smelly cubby, the dark laced with worry that he might have gotten it all wrong.

They were just beyond lunar orbit when it happened.

Adrian only knew their position because Hassim told him there would be an end-of-watch celebration. It was a long-standing tradition, dating back to the first Mars transports, marking the ship's entry into deep space.

When all the crew gathered, Freya and her two aides served. The food was excellent, hot, plentiful. A rare ease settled among the group, most of whom Adrian only knew through brief glimpses, coming on and off shift. There were twenty-three in all, one less than a full quota. Two of Freya's old standbys had reported for duty so stoned they could scarcely remain upright. Adrian was the only newcomer Freya had chosen.

While Freya and her aides cleared up, Matilda and Athena kept smirking in his direction. He had to assume something was coming, but he had no idea what it might be until Freya retook her seat and said, 'OK, new guy. You're up.'

'Excuse me?'

'Tradition holds the new pod members stand up and tell us something we don't know.'

The two aides had taken up position by the opposite wall. Athena said, 'It has to be personal and it has to be secret.'

'The darker the better,' Matilda said. 'And in case you're wondering, Earthbound laws can't nab you out here.'

'What you tell us stays with us,' Athena said. 'When we make landfall, it's gone. Forgotten. Lost to deep space.'

Freya glanced at her two smirking aides, then turned back to him. 'Adrian, right?'

'Yes, Chief.' It was the first time she had ever spoken his name.

'Stand up and go.'

As he rose to his feet, it felt like a giant's forefinger and thumb compressed him front and back.

The words were expelled, the secrets he had never shared with anyone. 'I've been training to become a wizard since I was nine years old.'

The aides both lost their smiles. Matilda demanded, 'That's it?'

'All there is,' Adrian replied. 'All I am. All I've ever wanted.'

Now Freya was the one smirking. 'A good start, Adrian. Now unpack it. Especially how you can train on Earth where there's no magic.'

Hassim added, 'And heading to Mars, when magic is soon to be outlawed.'

His wife showed him surprise. 'And you are knowing this how?'

'I keep in touch with our friends. They say it is coming. Not yet, but soon. The new regime is restricting all magic not directly related to mining.'

'Nothing the Mars government does is going to stop me from practicing magic,' Adrian replied. 'I've been working toward this too long.'

Freya said, 'Back to my question.'

'I think, I hope, magic was once present on Earth as well. There are too many spells that transcend borders and languages and ages.'

'Listen to pretty boy,' Athena groused. 'Transcend.'

Freya looked at her aide. 'His name is Adrian.'

Athena went back to scowling.

'Say it, Athena.'

'Adrian just cost me three days' pay.'

Freya liked that enough to explain, 'My ladies bet me you fled something nasty.'

'Murder, mayhem, running contraband,' Matilda said. 'Stands to reason.'

'Sorry,' Adrian said.

'I love being right,' Freya said. 'So you've been reading up.'

'For sixteen years,' Adrian confirmed. 'I did languages at university. Masters in Aramaic. One of Earth's original mother tongues.'

It might as well have been just the two of them. 'I know for a fact what Hassim hears is correct. As a first stage, the Wizards' Guild has stopped licensing new members.'

Adrian nodded. He'd heard that too. 'I'm hoping they'll make an exception.'

FIVE

Adrian retreated to his cubby, sealed the portal, and lay on the pencil-thin mattress. Thinking.

He was so relieved to have this first affirmation since departing Earth, he almost didn't mind revealing his long-held secrets. The only response he could come up with was, That was then and this was now.

But something else, a far more pressing issue, dominated his mind.

The force that had carried him through nineteen years of dream-state transports was what had pressed him to speak in the ready-room. There was a distinct flavor, or something, that held him even now, hours after the experience was over.

The mystery was simple enough. Why now? And what did it signify?

The only answer he could come up with was, entering deep space meant the force was available. Perhaps.

He rose from his pallet. Did his best to ignore the odors seeping through the wall behind him. He shut his eyes, clenched them along with every muscle in his body. And reached out, further and further and further. Following the same path he had traveled through count-less dream-states. He hoped.

He bonded. With Mars.

The sensation was as real as the bunk, the cubby, vivid as the odors. He was both there and not there. Forget the distance between the ship and their destination. They were in interplanetary space, which apparently meant . . .

Magic was real.

Not somewhere far up ahead. Here and now.

Adrian wanted to shout, scream, climb the walls, release fire from his fingertips. Something.

And yet.

This was too great a moment to be wasted.

All through those grueling years of searching and learning, Adrian experienced seven stand-out moments. Seven spells that were not words on some page, or embedded in texts he struggled to understand. For these seven, he practiced the spells out loud, doing the hand movements over and over until they felt fluid. Prepping for the day when it actually might *mean* something. *Do* something.

The practice periods for those seven spells often held a very special significance. On those occasions, Adrian stopped *saying* the spell, and started *living* it. The whole thing just came alive.

Then he finished speaking or waving his golf club or weaving hand motions over some candle, whatever. And it all faded away.

Poof and gone.

But he knew. Those experiences carried the same confirmation as his dream-states. This was real. All of it.

Now Adrian stood in the middle of his tiny room. Hoping that this bonding with Mars meant he could now genuinely work magic.

Adrian cast the first spell that had set his world to playing like a tuning fork.

An *extended-awareness* spell.

He decided it would be easier to maintain focus, fight down his racing heart and trembly limbs by focusing in a specific direction.

The question was, where?

Adrian had no desire to inspect another pod. And Mars might be a tempting target. But what if he got lost and could not find his way back? It might be silly, given how the bonding force was apparently emanating from there. But still.

So Adrian took aim at the forbidden zone.

The cockpit was effectively a spaceship in and of itself. The ship's crew was sealed off from the pods. The only communication was the rare few words exchanged between a ship's officer and one of the pod masters. Ship's crew could go out, and often did. Contact with Engineering back in the aft quarters was fairly constant. They traveled a central steel track, riding crawlers linked to metal rails, necessary because that central channel only had the ion drive's one-tenth G. All these areas, cockpit and mid-ships channel and ion drive, were strictly off-limits to everyone but crew.

The mother ship's crew members had their own ways of referring to Adrian's kind. Pod people. Minions in dungarees. Space serfs.

It gave Adrian a major sort of kick to use his newfound magic and enter the forbidden zone.

Shame that good feeling couldn't have lasted a few milliseconds longer.

Three minutes later, Adrian stood outside Freya's cabin.

He knocked. Waited. Knocked again.

A third time, then the woman appeared. Not angry. More like, ready to rain down fire if necessary.

Adrian said, 'The ship is in terrible danger.'

SIX

'Let's go over all this again,' Freya said. 'From the top.'

When Adrian had first started relating his experience, Freya had stopped him long enough to call in her two aides. Now Athena and Matilda sat in catlike ease to either side of the pod master. Gradually others filled the ready-room, all save the four on duty. They lined the back, watchful and silent. This was definitely a new one for all concerned.

'Just so I've got this totally straight,' Freya went on. 'You connected. With Mars. Which is still, what . . .'

'Five and a half months away,' Athena offered.

'This is a total first for me,' Adrian replied.

'But you're sure enough about this to risk upsetting the skipper?'

'I am. Yes.'

'Tell me why.'

'What I think happened is, when we passed lunar orbit, we also moved beyond the reach of Earth's energy sphere.'

Freya nodded slowly. 'Makes sense, in a kind of crazy, magical way. So you reached out . . .'

'It started earlier,' Adrian said. Now was not the time for secrets. *That was then.* 'When you told me to reveal myself, that was the first moment I experienced the force, and realized the conduit might be available. What happened afterwards was my trying to make the connection myself.'

'Pretty boy talks nice,' Athena said.

'He's Adrian now,' Freya corrected.

'Conduit. Experiencing forces nobody else has ever heard about,' Athena persisted. 'Lotsa nice words.'

Freya said, 'So you just, what, plucked a spell from your back pocket, and poof.'

'No, not like that.' Adrian knew what was coming. The test. And didn't mind. Not really. Either it worked or it didn't. Such issues were beyond his control. Besides, he was ready. The experience of what had just taken place inside his cubby still fizzed his bones. 'There are certain spells I've connected with.

They've helped see me through the years of waiting. This time . . .'

'What.'

'It was the first moment where the spell actually worked.' He smiled at the memory. 'Boom.'

But Athena wasn't so easily satisfied. 'How do we know this isn't some bogus tale he's telling us?'

Matilda's smile held no humor whatsoever. 'Lady's got a way with a point.'

'I happen to agree with my aides,' Freya said. 'So before I contact the skipper. Which is totally off the charts, by the way. Strictly forbidden, except in the case of a life-threatening emergency. I need something that shows me this is not just the new kid's idea of a scary dream.'

'Seeing as how none of us has ever actually met a real live wizard,' Athena said. 'This had better be good.'

'Beyond excellent,' Matilda agreed.

'Worth half a week's pay,' Athena said.

Adrian nodded. And began.

There was no question which to cast. The second spell he had bonded with was there. The ancient script illuminated behind his eyes. Dancing with the same energy that sparked his every breath.

The *reveal* spell was intricate, convoluted, and required a myriad of hand motions. Not to mention the words, which were in Devbhasha. The spoken form of Sanskrit. Considered one of the world's oldest formal languages. And which held the origins of almost all the current languages used throughout the Indian subcontinent.

He reached out, and there it was, the bond. Only this time there was a subtle change. The bone-deep resonance had a center now. A focal point, located just below his rib cage. The core of what the Earthbound masters of hand combat called *chi*. The individual's life force.

The sensation raised a torrent of questions in his brain. All of which Adrian forced to one side. Later. Right now, he needed to *focus*.

Soon as he started the incantation, speaking the words out loud because it helped him maintain that steady flow required by this spell, Sandhu gasped.

Hassim murmured, 'What tongue is this one speaking?'

'Quiet now,' Freya snapped.

He had the strong sense of power trailing behind his hands as they weaved the spell's physical portion. But he couldn't tell if it was something he alone could sense, or if it was visible to everyone. Whatever else, the room remained silent, so still they might as well have stopped breathing.

He was done.

Each of the figures in the room now possessed an illumination similar to what he had witnessed trailing behind his fingers. A shimmering brilliance, an energized portal inviting him to dive in and . . .

Know everything.

Speaking now in the common tongue required genuine effort. 'One of you must grant me entry.'

Athena demanded, 'What's he talking about now—'

'You stand up and speak the word, enter,' Adrian said. 'But you need to understand, you will then be fully exposed. I will know all there is to know.'

'This is beyond spooky,' Matilda said. She nudged Freya. 'Go on, boss. Step up.'

'Not on your life.'

Hassim kissed his wife's open palm. Stepped forward. Said, 'You may enter.'

The connection was instantaneous. 'Your birth name was Daksha. Your lineage is Khasi, an ethnic group of the Meghalaya hill peoples. You were betrothed to Sandhu when you were eight.' It felt to Adrian as if he read from a secret script. As familiar to him as any of the spells he had practiced until they were part of him. Any other point in time, he might have freaked out, seeing his second spell come alive. But the force connecting his center to the distant planet carried a calm as powerful as the vision. 'Your betrothal ceremony took place in Ludhiana, in the Punjab. It was the last time you saw each other for nine years. Your family moved to Delhi. When you were sixteen, you fell in love—'

'Enough, enough,' Hassim cried. 'This man cannot know what he knows.'

Sandhu demanded, 'This is true? You loved another?'

'No, my wife and life partner.' Hassim faced his wife straight on. 'A gangling teenager experienced a momentary and fleeting desire for what was forbidden. Nothing came of this, except I was made ready for our union.' When Sandhu remained uncertain, unsteady, Hassim continued, 'I honored my family's name. I am where I am meant to be. Nothing else matters.'

'OK, enough. Matilda and Athena, on me. Everyone else clear out.' As the room emptied, Freya told Adrian, 'Time for round two.'

SEVEN

'If this is some kind of convoluted time-waster you've cooked up, I'll have you dragged off in chains.' Though Freya still stood beside him, the ship's captain focused exclusively on Adrian. 'You don't know hard time until you've served a few years on Mars.'

Adrian had stood beside Freya through her entire report. He thought she did an excellent job of describing the impossible. Despite the fact that reporting to the ship's captain left her severely rattled.

Freya had initially requested contact with the senior medical officer, but when the junior officer who opened the comm-link heard why Freya was linking in, the officer ordered her to stand by. Fifteen seconds later, the skipper appeared and ordered her to report.

One of the videos Adrian had been required to watch had shown Captain Otieno's warm and smiling welcome to all on board. But the Kenyan skipper was not smiling now. He did not show Adrian rage, not really. The skipper did not need to. Even on the console, Captain Otieno was a force of nature.

'If I am wasting your time,' Adrian replied, 'I probably deserve it.'

Otieno muted his voice control, then turned away and spoke to someone unseen. Then he turned back and asked, 'How long before this supposed crisis of yours strikes?'

'Four Earth days. From now.'

'Gestation of the Gamma virus is forty-eight hours.'

Adrian could hear someone murmuring in the background now. He felt no need to respond.

The skipper went on, 'We were all tested pre-flight. My crew checked out. Our vaccinations and booster shots are up to date and run through our scheduled return to Earth.'

Adrian waited.

'I'm not going to allow some first-time pod crew member into my cockpit on something this flimsy.' But the skipper seemed to be retreating even further from rage. As if something, a tiny fraction of doubt or worry, was already infecting him. 'If that was your idea, you can forget it.'

'Sir, I asked to speak with you now so you would call me the instant it strikes.' He heard someone mutter to the skipper, and waited until the comm-link went silent to continue, 'Your medic goes down on day two. It would help if she had a day to train me before that happens.'

'Our medic is a male.'

'Sorry, sir. That's not true.'

A tightening of the man's dark gaze, then, 'You know what I'm going to say next.'

Adrian was ready for that as well. 'You want something to confirm this is real.'

'Go on, then.'

After releasing Hassim, Adrian had spent the reveal spell's final few moments taking aim at the cockpit. More specifically, the captain. 'You have an old-fashioned photograph of your great-grandfather in a silver frame. It stands on the shelf beside your bed. You were named after him. Vincent. He was the first Kenyan to ever train with NASA—'

'All right. Enough.' He examined Adrian a moment longer, then turned to Freya and said, 'My threat of incarceration is hereby retracted. You clearly have a far-seer among your pod crew.'

Freya's voice became somewhat unsteady. 'Understood, Skipper.'

'If the Gamma virus does not strike my own crew, this conversation did not happen.'

'Roger that.'

He turned back to Adrian. 'You say you've had the Gamma. When was that?'

'Two years and two months ago, sir. Just before the Phoenix lockdown. Not long after I was named assistant manager of the Ritz-Carlton. When I recovered, I served as nurse's aide. The hotel was used for non-critical overflow for almost a year.'

The skipper nodded, thinking. 'Anything else you can tell me?'

'Yes, sir. So long as I'm there to help out, all your crew survive.'

Another slow nod. 'Very well. I will be in touch. Or not.'

The screen went blank.

EIGHT

Adrian spent the next three watches cleaning the forward compartments and the pod's mini cockpit. It was basically make-work, light duty done twice each journey. Adrian requested the assignment because he wanted to use what time he had to prep for low gravity. The ship's cockpit relied on the ion drive's one-tenth G, nothing more. Barely enough to notice.

Freya fitted him out with null-G boots – canvas slippers with thin magnets fitted into the soles. Walking in them felt like he was treading through treacly mud, but they granted him a minimum of traction.

That first day, Adrian was beyond miserable. Constantly sick, cramped, dizzy. He ended his shift with an empty belly and splitting headache. That night, once he managed to eat a few forkfuls and retreated to his bunk, he sorted through the list of seven spells. Searching for something that might help ease his misery. Came up blank. With time and three doses of the medicine Athena brought him, Adrian's headache eased a trifle, his stomach stopped cramping, and eventually he managed to sleep.

Walking the pod's central passage his next shift left Adrian queasy long before he reached low-grav. The nausea waited for him in the same place as yesterday, six meters from the cockpit entryway. The door loomed like a monster's mouth, ready to gnaw his belly and head.

He stopped where the cramps began and reached out. Bonded. Just drew the energy in. Nothing else.

It was enough.

His comm-link clicked on, and Matilda asked, 'Adrian?'

'Yes.'

'You OK?'

'I am. Yes.'

'I saw you stopped, I was just wondering. You looked pretty rough after last duty. Nul-grav sickness is no joke.'

'I'm OK. Really. Matilda, do you see anything around me?'

'Say again.'

'I just bonded. Now I feel like there's a shield surrounding me. Like an illuminated net.'

'Man, I gotta say, hearing those words totally spooks me.'

'I take that as a negative on the shield.'

'I have no idea what you're talking about.'

'OK. Thanks. I'm back to cleaning the cockpit. And Matilda, thanks. You know. For keeping an eye on me.'

Twice during Adrian's shift the nausea and cramps returned, or started to. He reached out and found himself not just settled and shielded, but also enormously reassured. The bond was both real and *there*.

When his watch ended, Adrian returned to the cubby feeling ready for whatever lay ahead.

The next two shifts, Adrian began considering his days and life that awaited him once they arrived on Mars. The very concept left him, well, mentally weightless. Drifting. Almost frightened. His world became reshaped by a word he had never actually applied to himself.

Transition.

Behind him stretched a long hard time of preparation.

The question he faced wasn't really about what lay ahead. He would find that out soon enough. The struggle came down to asking something much harder to face, a question posed by the only woman he had ever loved: would his future be sullied by his past? The hardship, the pain, frustration, rage. Was he destined to view the life ahead through that tainted lens?

His sleep was fractured by chains from which he would probably never escape.

NINE

The call from Captain Otieno came on day five.

There was a nice formality to the way the chiefs helped him suit up. One person would have been enough. But all three were there, offering advice and pointing out all the items he wouldn't need for the brief transit.

When they started to fit his helmet, Adrian told Freya, 'The money your aides lost, betting on me.'

Athena and Matilda both tightened. Freya smirked. 'What about it?'

'Take it out of my pay.' To the pair, 'You both treated me well from the very first moment. It's not right I cost you.'

The pair were clearly flummoxed. Finally Athena said, 'How are we supposed to stay angry with this guy?'

'Working on it,' Matilda said.

Freya personally saw him forward, helping him into the airlock and sealing him through.

Waiting for the air to cycle out, Adrian turned and waved through the airlock's small portal. 'Thanks, Freya. For everything.'

'Word to the wise, sport. Don't screw this up.'

When the outer portal opened, Adrian basically crawled his way forward, gripping the rail with both hands, forcing his magnetized boots off the ramp, stepping, pulling himself toward the vehicle's open door. Adrian only allowed himself a single tight glimpse of space between the pods. Even though he had bonded again before setting out, the spinning stars and dark nothingness left Adrian half a millimeter from tossing his cookies. Which, he had been assured by both of the assistant chiefs, was a definite no-no while suited up.

The vehicle driver watched Adrian's baby-crawl in silence. Sitting there with his or her hands on the controls, making no effort to help, not saying a word. Why should he, or she? Adrian reflected. After all, this was just some nearly worthless pod serf who had the crew member playing gopher.

Finally, at long last, he clambered inside. As the door slid shut,

Adrian glanced through the driver's faceplate. Definitely a her. Highly attractive, in an intelligent, pinched-face, snippy sort of way.

The vehicle's acceleration pressed him back into his seat, offering Adrian's muddled head a temporary sense of up and down. He settled and enjoyed his brief moment of playing tourist. The vehicle was mostly glass, probably designed so the operator could check the ship's integrity while speeding along the central passage. The view was entirely awesome. Freya's pod was located furthest aft, which meant they sped past four astounding rows, with the silver-black sky as a rotating backdrop. All sixteen pods were docked nose-first, gargantuan beasts tethered to the central structure. Up ahead the cockpit grew to where it dominated Adrian's view. A central portal opened at their approach. They sped in, only decelerating as they approached the second portal. The first sealed, the second opened, they entered a massive transit bay.

When they halted, his driver opened Adrian's door, then climbed out of her side. She pointed him to what at first glance looked like a half-finished robot.

Adrian watched the crew member step on a narrow plate and turn her back to a second skeleton. She spread out her arms and spoke the first words since Adrian had joined her. 'Clear to unsuit.'

Nice voice, Adrian thought. Shame about the attitude.

The robot stripped off the woman's suit in no time flat.

She stepped off the plate, stood there in her sky-blue singlet, hands on hips. Glaring. Waiting.

Adrian stepped into position, raised his arms, repeated her words. He found himself revising his initial impression. The woman was beyond attractive. Short hair that floated like black frosting. Lovely face. Eyes to match her singlet.

He had been around enough beautiful female hotel guests to keep his eyes from drifting south. Trim and fit was as far as he let himself go.

But that attitude. Poison.

'Let's get one thing straight. Whatever sleight-of-hand you pulled with the skipper, it doesn't wash with me. Not for an instant.'

The personality, the anger, the fact she had allowed herself to be volunteered to pick him up, it all came into focus. 'You're the medic.'

'What is that, more of your hoodoo-voodoo?'

'Just a guess.'

'Save it for the crowd interested in your magic show. Because I am totally—'

The intercom clicked. 'Leighton.'

'Skipper.'

'Stow the comments and escort our guest to the bridge.'

'Aye, Captain.' The burning gaze suggested she had not been aware the chamber's comm-link was open. Leighton pointed to a sky-blue stack of clothing in a side cubby. 'Find your size and let's go.'

'If you will permit, I think it's best I stay as I am.'

Captain Otieno demanded, 'Explain.'

'Medic Leighton is correct, Captain. I'm nothing unless I'm needed.'

The woman snorted.

Adrian went on, 'Keeping to my pod gear will hopefully show your crew that I accept my status as outcast.'

A pause, then Otieno said, 'Doc, show our guest the sickroom on your way topside.'

Leighton hated that order most of all.

TEN

The term cockpit referred to what was essentially an entire space-going vessel in and of itself. Everything about the cockpit was of a totally different order compared to the pods. Even the corridor linking the aft departure chamber to the rest of the structure was buffed, polished, gleaming. Not new so much as built without concern over cost, and carefully maintained ever since. The railing Adrian gripped to keep himself from floating free was either real wood or the best artificial version he'd ever seen.

The medic was bitterly impatient with his awkward progress but did not speak until they stood in the sickbay's main entryway. Adrian found himself staring at a small but functioning hospital. Both side walls held berths shaped like spacious bunks with roll-out pallets. Two of the berths were blocked by translucent privacy curtains. The rear glass wall showed pharmacy and operating theater.

Leighton stood in the doorway, clearly ready to body-block any attempt he might make to enter her domain.

When it happened.

A young crewman, singlet stretched taut over sculpted muscles, staggered up and announced, 'Doc, I really don't feel . . .'

He went down mid-sentence. Just did a slow-motion float in the general direction of the floor.

'No, no, no.' Leighton moved lightning-fast, gripping the young man's collar and propelling herself into the sickbay.

Adrian asked, 'Can I help?'

She glared at him. Only there was something new to her gaze. Uncertainty, perhaps. She settled the crewman into an empty berth, said, 'Comm-link. Sickbay to bridge.'

The captain himself answered. 'Otieno here.'

'Skipper, we've got another. Van Hues just passed out at my feet.'

'Looks like another two are on the verge up top.' Otieno's voice held to a steely calm. 'Have Adrian remain there, you hustle to the bridge.'

'But . . . Aye, sir.' She fitted a strap loosely around the crewman's chest, pushed off, and flew past Adrian. 'Don't touch anything.'

Adrian simply waited until she was out of sight. No way was he going to hang about. Not with this new arrival in the throes of his first fever spike. Which Adrian had repeatedly witnessed back in Phoenix. Helplessly watching people go through the same agony this crewman was about to enter.

Not this time. Not if he could help it.

A narrow glass cabinet held a number of over-the-counter pain and inflammation medications. He stuffed bottles of aspirin and paracetamol in his trouser pockets. On a ledge beside one of the curtained alcoves, Adrian found the nul-grav equivalent of a plastic water pitcher. He shifted over to where he stood before the softly groaning crewman. Gathering himself.

Healing spells did not heal. Not really. Which was a major reason why the whole magical healing tradition left Adrian cold. Despite his reservations, all wishes to the contrary, two of his seven spells dealt with an individual's state.

There was no telling what might happen if or when modern medicine was combined with spell empowering. Maybe they were already doing this on Mars. Earthbound healing spells basically ground to a halt back when herbs were all the rage, and the best magic could do was magnify their potency.

Magic-related information coming from the red planet was reduced to online rumors, much of which was quashed as soon as it appeared.

The pitcher had a double-opening top, similar to an airlock. Adrian inserted a fistful of aspirin, then the same of paracetamol. Bonded. Reopened the top lid and added a handful of anti-inflammatory capsules. A third time for over-the-counter sleep meds. Then Adrian began his incantation.

Of course, the sickbay contained no herbs that he could see. Which meant everything he did at that point was different from what this third spell called for. That also risked everything he was attempting might prove totally useless.

But he had to try.

Adrian used both hands to swish the pitcher's contents. His actions were enough to pry his feet from the floor. Adrian released one hand, gripped the pallet's leading edge, and pulled himself back down. In the process he stopped mid-spell. He wanted to start over, but the crewman's teeth clenched with the coming pain-spasm.

The man, Van Hues, was also watching Adrian.

The crewman spoke in two gasping, broken segments. 'You're. Him.'

Adrian decided a confession was necessary. 'This is so twisted I don't have any idea if it will work.'

It was a very poor warning and no apology at all. But the crewman understood enough to gasp, 'Try.'

'I need a cup, straw, something . . .'

The crewman used his chin to point Adrian back to the central table, which held an oddly shaped plastic baggie. On closer inspection he saw a long tube that fitted into an aperture on the pitcher's top. Adrian drew some of his liquid into the sack, shifted back over, said, 'Tiny sip. A few drops. No more.'

He continued the spell and watched as the crewman pinched the tube where it joined with the pouch. Adrian doubted he could swallow. Nor did it matter.

The medic appeared in the doorway and yelled, '*Stop that immediately!*'

'Hush now.' Adrian held the tube's connection point and squeezed more drops onto his fingertips. He put his fingers under the crewman's nose and said, 'Breathe in.'

'It hurts. So much.'

'I know.' He whispered the spell's final elements. Hating that he now had witnesses to what he feared would be a total failure. The spell called for a bronze or copper pot, the herbs crushed and dropped into boiling water as the spell was spoken.

Just the same . . .

The man released a heavy sigh. 'Oh man oh man oh man . . .'

Adrian asked, 'Better?'

'Don't stop, please, don't . . .'

Adrian squeezed out another few drops. Repeated the final words as he held his fingers by the man's nose and mouth. Then for good measure he touched both temples, the throat where muscles could contract to the point where Gamma patients often suffocated . . .

The crewman sighed a second time and drifted off.

Adrian gripped the pitcher to steady his trembling hands and turned to where Leighton and two gaping crew members held the incoming patients. 'The first fever spasm often carries an almost unbearable pain.'

'I know that.' But Leighton was muted now. Wondering.

'How many?'

'Three. Another went down just as I arrived on the bridge.'

Adrian stepped away and watched them settle the crew members. He told the medic, 'Someone should set up an overflow for more new patients.'

She breathed against her first comeback, said, 'Of course, I can—'

'Not you. You need to prep me while there's still time.'

She watched Adrian begin the spell-casting, then dismissed the hovering crew. When it was just them and the patients, she asked, 'What did you mean, while we have time?'

He offered the pouch to each patient in turn, touched their temples and throats, watched, breathed around the enormity of what was happening. 'You need to show me around the equipment. And the drugs. I was almost defeated by the pitcher.' Once the last new patient had received treatment, he straightened, met the angry uncertainty in her gaze, and said, 'You go down next watch.'

Holding back her arguments cost Leighton. 'I've had all the vaccines, boosters, tests, the works.'

Adrian indicated the new patients. 'They have too, correct?'

She glanced over. Fear mounting to where her arguments were stifled.

Adrian studied her, decided that if it were him, and he was a pro, he would want to know. 'You go down hard.'

ELEVEN

Time became just another factor pressing Adrian to move faster.

Watch gongs sounded in the distance, marking periods that held little meaning, save that he could scarcely keep up with what needed doing.

More crew members went down every watch. Three days after Adrian's arrival, there were just four plus the captain still functioning. The eight with the most severe symptoms occupied all but one of the sickbay's bunks. Every time Adrian entered the primary care unit, the empty berth yawned like a hungry mouth.

Leighton, the medic, reluctantly came over to his side. Her careful introduction to the ship's pharmacy meant Adrian could add a sleep inducer and muscle relaxant to his concoction.

As he had warned, Leighton became ill twelve hours after Adrian's arrival. But when her symptoms did not worsen she remained snippy, caustic, wary of trusting him entirely.

Adrian saw no need to tell her it was only a matter of time.

This third spell became more clearly defined through practice. As he had always suspected, it was never designed to heal. It lessened pain. Decreased inflammation. With the addition of modern medications it also decreased fever. The potency of this *soothing spell* lasted between ninety minutes and three hours. The duration seemed to depend on how frightened the patient – how frantic, how hard they fought either the illness or him. He did not try to convince them to give into what relief he offered. If he had been trapped in their status, he would have struggled just as hard. Harder.

When the captain came aft for his third visit, perhaps the fourth, Adrian was able to confirm, 'They all remain able to take food and water.'

Otieno knew enough to accept this as good news. 'That's a great relief.'

Adrian thought the news went far beyond that. Borderline incredible, more like. He stood beside the skipper as Otieno surveyed the sickbay patients, about half slumbering, the others watching and listening as the skipper said, 'The medical records I've seen predict over a third of Gamma patients require IVs for fluids and nutrients.'

Leighton occupied one of the sickbay bunks. She had objected, of course. Adrian had pointed out this was the only way the ship's medic could keep tabs on the sickest patients. Reluctantly, she had agreed. Leighton quietly added, 'Half of those on IVs require respirators. We only have three on board.'

Otieno asked Adrian, 'What do you need? I'm asking you personally.'

'Tea would be good,' Adrian replied. 'Warm, not hot, heavy on the milk and sugar.' He indicated the patients. 'I'd like to up the frequency of their meals. I need help with that. A few mouthfuls every time they're able. Something warm and easy to digest.'

'More salt,' Leighton added. 'We'll sweat it out.'

'I'll assign another crew member to assist in the galley.' Otieno hesitated, then asked, 'How long?'

Adrian assumed the skipper already knew, so he gave it straight. 'First cycle lasts between three and six weeks.'

Two of the awake patients groaned a soft protest.

'Three cycles is generally the rule,' Adrian went on. 'But the first is almost always the worst.'

Otieno started to leave, then asked, 'Are you getting enough rest?'

'Trying,' he lied.

'We can't have you going down from exhaustion. How are you handling low grav?'

'Tell the truth, sir, I've been too busy to let it bother me.'

And for Adrian the duty never stopped. Otieno offered to assign an able-bodied crew member to assist. But there was so little anyone else could actually do, and their presence was desperately needed elsewhere. Between fever spikes, most of those afflicted could still move around a bit and feed themselves. Adrian slept an hour so at a time, ate when food appeared, then started yet another round.

The bonding with Mars as his power source became second nature.

Adrian had long suspected the convoluted weaving and warbling was not crucial to casting a successful spell. So much of the ancient script appeared florid, boring and ego-driven. How great the writer was at this or that talent. How hard it was to find a decent apprentice. What a burden it was to be the only adept for miles. Yada. As the watches and the patients' needs continued unabated, Adrian started paring down. Reducing the motions and spells to what he thought were the crucial elements. Working on the fly. Entering a chamber, treating all the patients lining bunks and pallets, moving on.

Which made him more or less ready when the virus's secondary impacts began appearing.

One crewmate complained that her eyesight was blurry, another's hearing went dim, another had an outbreak of shingles. Tongue thickened, taste lessened. Two started having terrible sore throats. All of which were treatable with antivirals if caught early. Adrian began taking more regular stops by Leighton's bunk, summarizing the latest developments, taking her suggestions as commands from on high.

At the end of the next watch, Leighton offered a soft complaint, spoken when all the other sickroom occupants were asleep. 'My muscles have started hurting.'

There were all sorts of reasons why this might be happening. Especially since Leighton had scarcely moved for several watches. Which she knew. But there was also another possibility. One they both clearly dreaded. But the pain at that point was not specific, which was symptomatic of worst-case scenarios. So he began treating her more often, and for a time it seemed to work.

Two watches later, though, she confessed, 'It's become very specific. And I'm getting tremors.'

It was the news he had feared. Such attacks of muscle spasms, preceded by intense pain, was one of the worst secondary effects that remained untreatable with current antivirals. 'Where?'

'It started in my thighs about an hour ago.'

'Both together?'

'Yes. Quadriceps femoris first. Then the abductors . . .' She clenched her teeth. Hissed a tight breath. 'Now it's everywhere.'

He had been hoping against hope it was shingles. But that generally attacked one side or the other and tracked from one joint to the next. This was far worse. 'I'm so sorry.'

'Can you help?'

'Possibly.' He had spent mealtimes and moments before sleep pondering this very issue. He had also prepared a concoction, taking special care over the spell, casting it three times in the end. Just in case.

He offered, 'You know the standard treatment is to knock you out.' Anesthetize the patient. Use the respirator. Risk severe muscle loss. Impacting mental faculties. Or worse.

'I'm the medic, remember? I hate that idea. So much.' Pacing her words between gasps of pain. 'Tell me what . . .'

He waited through the first spasm. 'You know it's not your muscles that are aching.'

'My nerves. Misfiring. I know. I read. Articles.'

'So you also know the theory about nerve inflammation leading to energy blockage. Halting the normal flow of currents. Leading not just to intense pain . . .' Adrian settled a hand on her shoulder, hating how the spasm was worse this time. Added to that was the terror. How she knew what was coming. How the next spasm or the one after would cause cramping so intense she might dislocate her own limbs, or fracture her own bones.

When the spasm eased, Leighton gave him a look without barriers. A first. 'Whatever it is you're thinking. I want you to do it.'

But he wanted her to understand fully. 'I'm in uncharted territory. One of the spells I connected with deals with energy flow. But it was written back before nerves were a thing. So I suggest you let me make one try, and one only. If it doesn't work, we put you on the standard treatments.'

Muscle relaxants. Anesthetics. IV for fluids and nutrients. Respirator.

Six weeks. Minimum.

Then the next spasm began mounting. Adrian accepted the tight head-jerk as all the response she could offer.

TWELVE

Adrian had taken one of the executive rooms and turned it into a just-in-case treatment chamber. He knew the bedroom was free because the exec was currently in one of the sickbay bunks. The wall opposite the entry was now lined with everything a critical-care patient might require – drugs and monitoring gear and IV stand and nutrients pack and hypodermics already filled with the initial injections. And the dread respirator.

Otieno had stopped by while Adrian was shifting in the necessary equipment, watched for a moment but apparently had not seen any need to question. That level of trust warmed him enormously.

The central table also held a plastic pitcher he had been working on since Leighton first mentioned her muscle pains. It contained a goop whose odor was so pungent it defied the sealed top and tainted the room.

The next spasm struck as he settled Leighton onto the room's only bed. He became caught in a momentary panic, trapped by uncertainty over the simplest of things. He couldn't strap her in and still manage the next required step. And anchoring himself by her side, on his knees, proved impossible. The slightest motion and he was floating. So he remained standing, crouched, feet tightly wedged beneath the bed's leading edge. She was rolled up in a tight ball, her teeth clenched tight, lips drawn back, hissing with each breath.

Adrian unlatched the equipment tray's top and took out the surgical scissors. And cut away her singlet. All the way up one side. Swung her over. Cut the other, ankle to collar, shifting her around so as to maintain one continuous line. He pulled away the two segments, let them drift off. And reached for the pitcher.

The goop was beyond complex, even minus all the supposedly required ingredients he couldn't find in the ship's pharmacy. Fresh tar from a bubbling pit. Ground bone from a male wolf's skull.

Nix on the bone.

Mostly it came down to ingredients available from the galley – honey, brandy, mustard seed, concentrated lemon juice, black and red pepper, garlic, and traces of numerous other condiments.

Thankfully the skipper was an epicure and came from a region where no meal was complete without spices.

The result was a treacly substance with a fragrance Adrian found impossible to define. Pleasant and awful and pungent, all at once.

He was trying to keep his hands steady enough to hold the pouch's nipple to the pitcher connection point when Leighton giggled.

For a moment, he thought his ears were playing tricks. Then he glanced over and saw her eyes were open, her limbs somewhat relaxed. 'You can't be laughing.'

'Sorry.'

Enough of the goop escaped to make his eyes water. 'Go on, then. I could use a joke.'

Her voice was hoarse from the strain of what just passed. Her skin was covered by a sheen of perspiration. 'Since you've got me naked here, I guess it's time for you to know my first name.'

This time it was his turn to tense. 'Don't. I'm not, you know, trained. I need . . . Distance. I have to focus on . . .'

She gave him what Adrian could only describe as a bottomless look. 'Do it.'

Bonding with Mars proved very difficult. As was maintaining a strict focus on the spell.

Then Leighton entered another spasm, and all those trivial things like her utterly naked, utterly stunning beauty and their closeness, everything not absolutely necessary, just went away. There simply wasn't room for anything but helping her.

If he could.

Just the same, the act of bonding remained marginally fractured, a new experience, one he hated. When he was certain it was fully there to call upon, Adrian began the fourth spell. One he had entitled the *energy spell*.

He repeated the words and motions used during the preparatory stage, taking one of the drinking pouches and filling it partially with the yellow-brown goop. As he did, a stream of tiny sparks followed along, light and beautiful and fizzing. He wanted to have her see, take it as hope this might actually work, but when he looked down . . .

Leighton uncurled, but not from any degree of comfort. Instead, the spasm took hold of her extensor muscles, pulling her out straight, further and further, until she curved in the opposite direction. Toes gripped, back arched, arms rigidly akimbo.

He pressed the tube between two fingers, pushed out a trace, held his fingers to her nose. 'Breathe in. That's good. More.'

There was no change to her rigid stance, nor to the shrieking gasps. But her eyes partially opened. Watching him. Desperate. Unable to speak.

'I'm turning you slightly.' A gentle prod was all it took, shifting until her right side was directed upwards. 'Here we go.'

The fourth spell's ancient intention was to release clogged energy. For numerous cultures down through human history, this was seen to have been the root cause for numerous ailments. Adrian had doubted its merit, given modern medicine's focus on identifiable, measurable components of the body. But he had learned it anyway, for the simple joy of finding another spell that resonated.

One hand held the pouch, the other gently squeezed the aperture. He began tracing the first lines. Starting at the base of her skull, down both sides of her spine. Painting the goop over one buttock, all the way down the back of her leg, finishing on the heel. He reached back to the lower spine and started the second branch.

He tilted her again, so he looked down on her face and front. 'Can you relax any? I'm just hoping you might . . .'

Her eyes were fully open now. Clenched teeth and tight, hissing breaths, but the tea-kettle shrieks had stopped. 'Maybe a little.'

Actually, he thought she unwound rather a lot. Enough for him to feel a jolt of very real hope. Enough to say, 'Outstanding.'

He restarted the chant and the tracing. Right temple this time, along the jaw, neck, down her left side and then her right, streaking her with the mustard-garlic-honey concoction, ribs, hips, thighs, shins, all the way down her feet, ending on the big toe that was now fully extended. Not actually relaxed. But still.

The chant had become so intense he could almost hear a drum-beat, what a medicine man might have used as a backdrop, the wordless force of others joining to the healer with the power of sound. For the first time in his life, Adrian felt a kinship to all the earthly healers that had come before.

Leighton was breathing easier now. Eyes calmer, the pain a tight glint, nothing more. She watched him with a tense calm as he started the routine's final stage. This time he touched points along the center of her body, starting with just below her navel, then up in a steady final chant, same words, even more intense as he touched the soft point at the base of her throat, then her forehead, and finally . . .

He smeared the goop liberally on his left palm, then held his hands about two feet apart, maybe ten inches above the top of her head. Adrian heard two versions of the final chant, the words always the same, a request for the body's own natural *chi* to restart a healthy flow. His voice sounded calm, steady. And yet, the power seemed thunderous. He did not shout, and yet his own body now resonated with the force as . . .

He *slammed* his hands together.

The force liberally sprinkled her face and neck and chest with the goop.

He stepped back. The work was over. Leaving him drained. And something else.

There in front of him lay this beautiful woman. The ability to focus beyond that, see her as a woman in need, was so very hard. He cleared his throat, asked, 'Feeling better?'

'Much. But it still hurts.'

'We'll probably need to do this again. Several times.'

Her body was coated with a sheet of perspiration. 'I need a shower. Is that OK?'

'Absolutely.' He forced himself to turn away. Breaking the other spell. 'I'll see which of the recovering female patients is up to helping you.'

THIRTEEN

The treatment left him exhausted and ashamed in equal measure. Especially as it was not the healing but rather the image of Leighton's body that carried Adrian to sleep.

Two hours later he rose, showered, ate and did the rounds. He found Leighton and his other six most serious cases resting well.

The sight of her only made his shame burn hotter.

Next time he would insist on a female crew member serving as attendant. Watching over them, witnessing the act, keeping him grounded. He should have thought of that the first time. But going forward, he and Leighton would not be alone again.

Much as he might have liked it otherwise.

Adrian slipped away to the galley for his first hot meal in forever. The main dining area was empty, hardly a surprise given the small number of active crew. Soon Adrian found himself lost in recollections of the only love he had ever known.

Emma Rouse was a wonderful lady, six years older than Adrian, very caring and utterly complete in herself. She had accepted his upbringing as part of what had made him special, and gradually winnowed him away from the chains gripping his heart. She insisted he was capable of a love not poisoned by drugs or fury or all the personal traits that had rendered his parents utterly unsuited to raising a child. Emma had listened to his memories, cried with him, held him until his heart began the process of knitting itself back together.

Emma had also been the one to challenge him with the impossible quest. Move beyond the past. Enter the present with an open heart. Learn to trust and to give without the burdens of all that had come before. Adrian never felt like he had been able to do as she wanted. But she loved him for trying.

All the while, Adrian had assumed she shared his dream. Travel to Mars. Become a wizard.

And Emma did. But she had never intended to come with him.

Two weeks after the treaty was signed restoring transport and trade with Mars, the pod crew application portal reopened. This was, for Adrian, a cause for major celebration.

For Emma, it was time to reveal her intentions.

She was never leaving Phoenix.

She had no desire to go anywhere else, much less to Mars. She was a woman of the Arizona desert, born to live and flower and die right there. She would love him long after his own dream carried him far, far away.

The crushing prospect of losing his first true love almost cost him everything. Adrian struggled endlessly with the impossible dilemma. Stay and lose his dream. Go and lose everything else.

They fought. For the first time ever. They fought so much Adrian found himself slipping back into the nightmare habits of his childhood.

Emma recognized this as well. Finally she told him it was over.

She held him a final time, loved him with all the warm beauty that was hers to give. Then pushed him away.

Adrian sat in the crew's empty mess hall and felt anew the gentle force that she had used that final hour together. Loving him with the finality of farewell. Because that was only how he might hold on to his dream. And Emma would have it no other way.

Three months later, the Gamma virus struck. Adrian was one of the first to go down.

He was also one of the fortunates, at least so far as the Gamma onslaught was concerned. He recovered, the Phoenix lockdown started, and he worked in a hotel that now served as a secondary hospital.

He repeatedly tried to contact Emma. See if she needed anything. Asked friends within the ambulance service to check on her.

Nothing.

When it was over, he looked for her himself. And asked. And searched. And found the truth.

The one and only love of his life was no more.

In the months that followed, Adrian's circular emotions resumed a straight-line intent. He would go. He would do all he could to become a wizard. A good one.

It was his fate to remain alone. The words became a mantra that carried him through the mourning and on to his destination. A life beyond the one he had lost.

FOURTEEN

Adrian made another round, moving in an almost mechanical fashion, still weighed down by the memories, the loss, the choices he'd made and been forced into accepting. Afterwards he retreated to the exec chambers he had claimed as temporarily his own.

It seemed like he had scarcely lain down when Adrian was drawn from sleep by an idea.

He rose, washed, and tried to dismiss the concept as utterly outlandish, completely against everything he had read and studied. Just the same . . .

While he dressed and started the next rounds, he argued with himself. Tried repeatedly to push it away. Was still in the throes of doubt when he entered the sickroom.

Leighton greeted him with, 'Check this out.'

Adrian watched as she rose to a seated position. Wincing, but still. 'Wow.'

She nodded solemnly in return. 'My thoughts exactly.'

'Do you want another treatment?'

'Can it wait?'

'Absolutely. We're in totally uncharted territory.'

'I'd like to see how long this lasts.'

'Probably an excellent idea. So long as you alert me the instant anything goes sideways.'

'Don't worry, I will.' Her voice carried the gravity of where she had almost gone. 'That was beyond scary.'

Adrian settled against the center table. Debating whether he should speak. Struggling with . . . Everything.

'What's wrong?'

'I've had what's probably a bad idea.'

'Bad as the idea you had regarding my treatment?'

He liked that about her, this ability to parse away the unnecessary and go straight to the heart. He shifted over and eased himself onto the bunk beside her. Closing the distance. He almost whispered, 'You know what I said about the spell I used with you, how it impacts the body's energy.'

'So?'

'I've been wondering if maybe I could use it on all the patients showing more extreme risks. You're the only one with muscle spasms. At least so far. But there are some major issues we're treating with antivirals. Eyes, ears, taste . . .'

Leighton added, 'Speech, heart, one with lung congestion. Throats, three of those.'

'And maybe the antivirals are enough,' he said. 'At least, they've worked so far.'

'What's the potential downside?'

'My fear is that the spell might actually energize the sickness and make things worse. Add to the negative aspects. Take the patient to a total dead end. Literally. Blindness. Complete loss of hearing, taste, speech. Heart stops. Terrible risks.'

Leighton was quiet, then, 'We know so little about the Gamma. Its original state has been well defined. But this thing mutates at frightening speed. The fact we've all gone down, after being vaccinated and thoroughly checked out, this is a perfect example of how fast it morphs.' She gave that a beat. Thinking. Then, 'You want my advice.'

'Absolutely. Desperately.'

'Ask the skipper to join us. Run your idea by him,' Leighton said. 'It's his crew. This should be his decision.'

But Captain Otieno only allowed Adrian time for a few sentences before cutting him off. 'Where are you now?'

Leighton responded, her voice very weak but clear. 'Sickbay, Skipper.'

'Stay right there.'

Adrian saw Leighton exchange a concerned look with the crew member who had served as Adrian's first patient. The young man's name was Van Hues, and during the last watch he'd recovered enough to volunteer as Adrian's aide. Clearly both Leighton and Van Hues thought the captain was angry over this idea of experimenting on his staff.

But when Otieno arrived, he first demanded to hear about how Leighton was faring. The ship's medic tersely described the before and after impact of Adrian's work. Otieno turned to Adrian and said, 'I've heard enough. You are offering this to volunteers only, correct?'

'Of course, Captain.'

'Leighton's improvement is sufficient evidence for the moment. We can go into more detail once we've put this in motion.'

The medic asked, 'So you approve?'

'I think it's an excellent idea. Very forward-looking. The sign of a good officer is the ability to parse away unnecessary doubts and apply what works to new potential problems.' He extended one finger, poised it before Adrian's eyes like a punishment rod. 'That said, you were wrong to take such a step without my approval. Next time you come up with an untested concept, you pass it by me first. Understood?'

'Yes, Skipper. Sorry, sir.'

'Proceed.'

By this point, all the sickbay crew knew more or less what was about to happen. Just the same, Adrian stood in the entry, Captain Otieno to his left, and explained in detail the spell he had used on Leighton. He began by describing the concept of a personal *chi*, or energy flow. The potential benefits that might, just might, come from correcting and strengthening their *chi*. Then, 'The risk is, heightening your energy could actually feed the secondary illness you're facing.'

Otieno said, 'As you've heard, this process has already helped Leighton. Quite a lot.'

'Her issue was specifically nerve-related,' Adrian replied.

'You said it yourself. The spell does not actually name the nervous system.'

Adrian liked this back-and-forth between him and the skipper. Laying it out in a dialogue that granted the patients time to think things through. 'When the spell was designed, nerves were not yet identified.'

'How much do we know about the role of bodily energy in the Gamma virus's secondary afflictions?'

'Not a lot, from what I've read,' Adrian agreed. 'I don't even know if it's been considered.'

'Only in passing,' Leighton confirmed.

'Yet we do know that some people are impacted much worse than others with these secondary attacks, yes? And thus far, there is no better explanation for why some are stricken.' Otieno ended the dialogue by addressing the crew. 'I for one think this has merit. But I also acknowledge the risk. You are invited to volunteer.'

One of the crew asked, 'Question, Skipper.'

'Fire away.'

'If you were lying here . . .'

Otieno nodded. 'I would do this. Immediately. Without hesitation.'

All of the patients requested the treatment. Their volunteering carried a tight urgency, their fear genuine. Adrian said, 'I think I have enough solution for everyone. I'll be right back.'

But when he started down the corridor, Otieno halted him with, 'Point me to an empty pallet. I'm going down hard.'

FIFTEEN

Four months later, Adrian had a second-row seat for their landing maneuvers.

The ship kept Earth's time, as that was its home base. A multi-faceted digital clock dominated the left-hand wall, showing dates and times for both planets, along with time-since-departure, time-to-arrival, and other numbers Adrian couldn't be bothered to learn during his first visit to the bridge. He was too overwhelmed by the planet dominating their front portals. The ship's spin had been halted, the shields drawn back, the stars and the planet and two tiny moons hung in artistic majesty.

Mars was *right there*.

Since Adrian's arrival three hours earlier, there had been an almost continual stream of chatter over the ship's comm-link. Captain Otieno had kept the connection on the open channel, so the entire crew could listen in. Adrian counted six different voices calling in from Mars.

Mars!

He understood what was transpiring because Otieno had explained. Being a totally closed city, the capital Marsopolis was fanatic when it came to any risk of imported viruses. Which was why news of a ship whose crew had suffered from a Gamma outbreak had put the government's representatives into a major-league freak.

Four of the planet's representatives sounded irritated to the point of barking. The other two remained very professional, almost bored. Otieno responded to all six with the same terse calm.

The exchanges between Leighton and the planet's medical bureaucracy, however, carried substantial heat. Adrian suspected Captain Otieno's steady gaze was why Leighton wasn't shouting invectives.

Just the same, the medic's responses carried a great deal more irritation than her captain. Clearly the planetary doctors were looking for someone to blame. They questioned whether the ship had left Earth without all the necessary blood tests, vaccines, boosters and so forth. Leighton responded with enough bite to silence them, at least after she sent down copies of her own meticulous records, and

Otieno backed her up. Adrian watched the other bridge personnel as much as Leighton; they took the medic's acidic comments as rare entertainment.

A good deal of the skipper's semi-polite quarrels took place in what to Adrian sounded like official jargon. But Adrian was fairly certain he followed the major points. Over a meal taken in their seats, Otieno explained it anyway.

'They do not want us to land. They want the pods, or rather the contents. They also sought to refuse permission to offload our cold-sleep passengers.'

A junior comms officer said, 'They couldn't have thought you'd ever agree to that.'

The senior navigator offered, 'What Mars wants and what Mars gets has been two different tales since the very first landing.'

Otieno said, 'Anyone care to tell me why I didn't threaten?'

A junior navigator replied, 'You didn't need to. They knew your unspoken ultimatum was there from the outset. They need the mining equipment, agricultural supplies and medicine in the pods. Either they hold to treaty regs or they get nothing.'

'That's certainly correct,' Otieno said. 'But it's not what I was looking for.'

Naxos, the senior comms officer, held a second role, that of weapons chief. He had served two tours in the Canadian military before opting to space. On a freighter between planets, his secondary role held little importance. What it mainly stood for was the need for a battle-ready officer in the face of mutiny. Naxos offered, 'You've said it many times, Skipper. Mars is looking for an excuse to revolt again. We can't light the powder keg.'

'That is a valid point. And a vital one.'

For the first time, Adrian felt drawn into the bridge's conversation. 'Sir . . .'

'Go ahead, Adrian.' The skipper had continued using Adrian's first name since emerging from sickbay.

'Soon as we land, the ship's crew is going into quarantine. There has to be a standard period—'

'Forty days,' Leighton confirmed. Her chair was positioned on the upper tier, beside Naxos, across the bridge from where he sat.

Adrian knew all eyes were on him now. 'It seems to me, you were doing your best not to burn bridges. Making sure they didn't make our time in quarantine any worse than it is already going to be.'

Otieno's gaze narrowed briefly, perhaps the skipper's version of a smile, Adrian couldn't be sure. 'Correct.'

Leighton rose from her chair. 'Skipper, permission to clear up.'

'Carry on.'

'Adrian, come give me a hand.'

Van Hues helped. He continued to serve as Adrian's aide, only now with the skipper's endorsement. Leighton waited while they handed their loads to the galley staff, then told Van Hues, 'You're dismissed.' When the young man departed, she said, 'Adrian, I want a word.'

'Shouldn't we get back in case Mars wants you—'

'Adrian, I want a word *now.*'

The galley crew smirked their sympathetic farewell as Adrian followed her into the central corridor. Leighton wasn't able to stomp her way down the hall, but she gave it her best. Her expression was enough to have the two crew they passed cram up tight to the side walls. One of them even winced at Adrian in pity, which he thought was a class move.

She halted by the sickbay portal, coded in the electronic lock, said, 'Inside.'

She closed the comm-link, ditto to the door lock. The quiet sigh of the portal sealing sounded to Adrian like a coffin lid. He had no idea what he'd done to make Leighton so angry. Her face was almost parchment white from some internal strain, like she'd spent hours tamping down on a tempest he had not noticed until that very moment. He wiped sweaty palms on the sides of his tunic, ready to leap at his first opportunity to apologize.

'You're avoiding me. Don't even think about denying.' When he remained silent, she demanded, 'Tell me why.'

'Leighton—'

'My name is Chris. Say it.'

'No. I can't.'

She took a step, forcing him back. 'You mean you won't.'

Adrian felt a huge and undeniable pressure to say, 'I've worked hard as I can to keep things right between us.'

Another step toward him. 'Define right.'

He backed up until he was jammed tight against the central workstation. He knew the words were a nonsense jumble. But it was as clear a confession as he could manage just then. 'You know what I mean. Me helping you heal. Keeping this straight. Correct.

I can't do that and speak, you know, even think your name. It's not your name, it's . . .'

She stopped him by taking a two-handed hold of his face, pulling him down and kissing him. Hard.

Adrian felt this huge invisible dam break apart, flooding him with a dangerous, threatening torrent. Carrying away all reason.

He clenched her, arms tight with everything he'd struggled to hold back.

Her own embrace was just as fierce.

An endless time later, she leaned back, not far, remaining so close he felt her breath on his face. This time she whispered, 'Say my name.'

Adrian had no idea how long they'd been absent. But the bridge personnel seemed unconcerned when he followed Chris – *Chris!* – onto the flight deck. He floated back to his assigned place, the chair normally occupied by the chief engineer. Adrian turned his chair so as to keep Chris – *Chris!* – from his line of sight. He stared at the red planet. Tried to stabilize his state of mind. Keep from smiling. Stop his heart from zinging. All that and more.

The bridge dominated the cockpit's bow like the topping on a squat ice-cream cone with a round flat base. The bridge's upper boundary wall held an array of mystifying electronics and chairs, or stations. This was the domain of Senior Comms Officer Naxos, whose remit also handled all visual and longer-distance surveillance. One giant step down, and the second tier was split into threes. Engineering to the left, the captain's station on a slightly raised dais at the center, maneuvering and pods controls. Since all engineering personnel remained sequestered aft, Adrian had been assigned one of the empty stations to the skipper's left.

The front row was referred to as the flight deck. The ship's executive officer now served as pilot. Harrow was tall and slightly overweight, a rarity among the ship's crew. He had remained hostile even while Adrian was saving his life. Beady eyes tracked Adrian's every movement, as if hoping for a reason to have the man sent back to his pod. They had only spoken a few times, and never since Harrow had risen from his sickbed.

Ever since Adrian and Chris returned to the bridge, Harrow had been shooting him tight glances. Taking aim.

The comms officer said, 'Skipper, Mars has granted permission to land.'

'Do we have a destination?'

'Aye, captain. LZ-Q.'

'Thank you, Comms. Patch me through to Engineering.'

A momentary pause, then the gruff senior engineer said, 'Chief here, Skipper. How goes it up top?'

'Back in full form and ready to decouple.'

'Roger that. See you on the other side of quarantine.'

'Don't drink Mars dry before we get there, Chief.'

'I'll do my best to save you one final glass.'

'Bridge out.' He turned to Harrow. 'Exec, go for decoupling.'

A final venomous look Adrian's way, then, 'Aye, sir. Decoupling in three, two, one.'

There was a slight nudge, a gentle shift, then, 'Cockpit decoupled, Skipper.'

'Take us down.'

There was another nudge, this one constant, as the cockpit's mini-ion drive was ignited. Their descent was only noticeable when Adrian looked away from the front portals, then back. Mars's atmosphere just one twenty-fifth of Earth's and extended a mere hundred kilometers above the surface. Which allowed Harrow to accelerate until the planet began noticeably growing in size. Dominating their view-ports.

Mars.

Adrian needed to consciously force himself to breathe.

'Eight minutes to braking maneuvers,' Harrow said.

'Proceed.'

Harrow cut the ion drive, bringing their mini spaceship into freefall. Adrian still detested the absence of gravity but had readied himself with the bonding process. The pilot made a graceful one-eighty spin and re-ignited the drive. The resulting G-force became noticeably stronger as Adrian watched the mother ship, his home for the past seven months, gradually shrink in size.

He realized Otieno was watching him. The skipper asked, 'Sorry to see it go?'

On one level, it seemed an odd question, given the strain and exhaustion he had experienced. Just the same, Adrian found himself responding, 'A little, sir. I've learned so much.'

'And done so much good.' This from Van Hues, his first patient, now monitoring their ion drive.

'You're a good shipmate,' Otieno said. 'I want you to consider signing on. Becoming a member of our crew.'

Adrian knew it was Harrow who softly snorted. The only objection their executive officer could safely make to his superior's invitation. Just the same, the sense of threat tainted how the rest of the crew watched and waited. 'Captain, I'm honored.'

'Think about it,' Otieno said.

Adrian respected the man enough to respond fully. And honestly. Even with Chris seated on the upper row almost directly behind the skipper. Where he could not help but see the new spark to her gaze. 'I've spent my entire life taking aim at Mars.'

'I realize that. Two things you need to keep in mind. First, the Mars government has become increasingly hostile to practitioners of magic. There's a very real chance you won't be granted a license.'

Adrian decided not to respond with the truth. Which was, nothing and no one would keep him from doing magic. 'I've read what rumors make it to Earth.'

'They're not rumors. Point two. You've done an excellent job of practicing your magic during transit. When it mattered. Clearly standing on Mars is not the crucial element to your abilities.'

Adrian remained silent. But what he thought was, he was desperate to see what standing on the Martian surface did to those very same abilities. Not to mention the spells he had yet to attempt.

Harrow chose that moment to announce, 'Landfall in five hours and counting.'

Otieno told Adrian, 'You have forty days in quarantine plus the remaining free time on Mars before we start the return journey. Think about it.'

'Aye, sir. I certainly will.'

Otieno rose from his chair. 'Come with me. Leighton, you too.'

As Adrian stood and followed the captain, Harrow glanced back. Shot him a final look of pure poison.

SIXTEEN

They took the glass chute. The ship's momentum, pushing now against Mars's gravity, gave them a more definable up-and-down perspective. Even so, Adrian used the handrail to keep him stable during what was now a descent.

Soon as the door slid shut, Otieno said, 'Perhaps now is the time to inform you that you're officially listed in the ship's log as Sub-Lieutenant Capstan.'

'Yes, sir.' They had already covered that ground. Twice. Making landfall as a crew member was necessary, as no pod crew were allowed in the cockpit. Adrian had the impression the skipper was waiting for something. What that might be, he had no idea.

Chris said, 'Skipper, I don't think Adrian gets it.'

'Ah. Let me make myself clear. You are to be awarded an ensign officer's pay and benefits.'

Adrian managed, 'Sir?'

Chris was grinning now. 'From the outset of this voyage. Through quarantine.'

'Plus a hazard-duty bonus.' The captain did not actually smile. But he came very close. 'Doc, do you think perhaps he understands me now?'

'Aye, sir. I believe it's gotten through.'

The loading bay served as coordination point for all goods and equipment entering the quasi-independent spaceship known as the cockpit. Their ion drive took up most of the circular base, with the smaller central airlock only used when the cockpit was bound to the mother ship. The loading bay and primary airlock sat atop the cockpit's ion drive.

The circular room was filled with a mountain of gear. Crewmen flitted in and out, adding to the piles. A senior technician stood to one side, making notes on her pad. More crew fashioned the gear into tight units linked by carry-straps. Canvas sacks, carry-alls, metal canisters, electronic equipment, and water. A *lot* of water.

The skipper gave Adrian a moment to take it in, then said, 'Rules governing our transit upon landing are very strict. Crew are permitted one carry-all, ten kilos Earth standard, everything searched and listed. Contraband was a real problem in the early days. No longer.'

Chris added, 'But we're entering quarantine. The first ship's crew to do so since the revolt.'

'This hopefully grants us some leeway,' Otieno continued. 'How much is open to question. You heard our conversations with ground control.'

'Your arguments,' Adrian corrected.

'We did not raise our voices,' the skipper replied. 'Nor did I threaten to keep all imported goods on board, pending our and the cold-sleep immigrants' release. I did not argue when the landing authorities raised their concerns. Which will hopefully result in eliminating any conflict with the guards monitoring our transfer to quarantine.'

Adrian asked, 'Why am I here?'

'I suppose you've heard the rumors regarding the state of the quarantine barracks.'

'A prison.'

Chris said, 'One that hasn't been used in four years, perhaps longer.'

Otieno went on, 'The place is most certainly grim. I had a friend who was quarantined there two years before the revolt. There's every chance the conditions have become . . .'

'Terrible,' Chris said.

'The water may well be tainted. And we have no idea how long the Mars authorities will take, responding to any requests, no matter how urgent.' Otieno pointed at the pile of goods. 'Is there some way you can mask this, make it invisible, so that we can transport it unseen?'

'I'm sorry, sir. No. I can't. I've never come across any kind of spell that might work here.' He started to explain the seven spells where he had felt any sort of bonding, then decided that could definitely wait.

'Ah, well.' Otieno started for the chute. 'We will throw ourselves on their good graces and hope for the best.'

Which was when the idea struck. 'Skipper, there is one thing I could try.'

SEVENTEEN

Otieno listened to what Adrian proposed, then brought them back to the bridge. Adrian liked how the captain involved all his crew in the decision and whatever came next. What Adrian proposed did not magically impact any one specific crew member. In that respect, it was not like his healing work. Instead, the *outcome* impacted *all* of them.

The crew's response was as shocking as it was unexpected.

He was still running through the concept a second time, building on the initial design, working it out for himself as well as the others, when . . .

Virtually everyone on duty except Harrow and the skipper volunteered to serve as Adrian's trial subject. Loudly.

Otieno offered one of his patented captain-like smiles. A brief tightening of the lines around his eyes and mouth, a glint to his dark gaze, nothing more. When the bridge went quiet, he asked Adrian, 'Anything else I need to consider before making my decision?'

'No, sir. Well, yes, there is one thing. If there's a drone, or even a distant observer, anything we attempt with the guards will be a waste of time.'

The chief navigator was also third in line for command, a sharp-edged woman named Meishi. 'There's bound to be a carry-all with drivers for the guards.'

Otieno nodded agreement. 'Adrian?'

'Sir, if this works, I can apply the same spell to them.'

'It's doubtful they'll waste a drone on crew transiting from the LZ to quarantine,' Otieno said. 'Just the same. Number two, you will be responsible for drone scouting once we've landed. Radar and visual.'

'If this works,' Harrow replied sourly. 'Aye, sir.'

'Comms officer, if a drone is spotted, the last possible moment you will blast the area with a jamming signal.'

'Roger, Captain.'

Otieno continued, 'So we're absolutely clear. You want one of

my crew to volunteer. So you can try and make them so completely
and utterly wasted—'

'Actually, sir, that's not a proper medical term,' Chris offered.

'Noted. You try.'

'Higher than Deimos works for me.'

'This will be a revision of the same spell I used to ease the
patients in Gamma-induced crisis,' Adrian explained. 'I call it a
soothing spell.'

'Which is definitely what it did for me,' Van Hues confirmed.

'In order to see whether it will work under these conditions,'
Adrian continued, 'I need to perform this spell with two walls
between us. The walls need to be clear, so I can maintain a line of
sight. Just like I would, doing this from within my space suit.'

'Makes perfect sense.' The captain looked at his medic. 'Doc,
you're the logical choice to witness this first-hand.'

'Sorry, Skipper,' Chris replied. 'I need to remain on standby just
in case.'

Meishi, the navigations officer and third-in-command said, 'With
respect, Skipper, I feel my seniority places me in top position for
this particular duty.'

Naxos, the senior comms officer replied, 'If you're after using
amateurs, I'm sure Commander Meishi will do just fine. I, sir, on
the other hand—'

Adrian said, 'Captain, if I may, I'd like to propose Van Hues.'

'Explain.'

'Soon as he recovered, Van Hues began serving as my aide.
Round the clock. We could very well have lost someone without
his assistance.'

'Van Hues, are you willing to volunteer?'

'Skipper, this is a duty I was made for.'

'Very well. Carry on.'

EIGHTEEN

There was a certain irony, Adrian reflected, on how he had spent years working toward this moment. Landing on Mars. Preparing his first post-landfall spell.

So he could render his targets completely and utterly stoned.

Thankfully, this was a rendering of the same initial spell he had used to treat so many of the ship's crew. Only this time the outcome was all about rendering the watchers unable to, well, watch. Or at least not care what they saw.

Chris suggested they work through the initial preparations alone. Which Adrian thought was probably a good idea. As they entered the sickbay, Adrian said, 'I hope your pharmacy holds drugs that will form . . .' He went quiet when Chris locked the door and silenced the comm-link. Not to mention the look she gave him.

Chris said, 'Come here.'

It was close to the hardest thing he had ever done, planting a hand between them and saying, 'Chris, no. I can't.' He hated the hurt look that came to her gaze. Just hated it. 'My heart is already zinging. Another kiss and I lose my focus. Which could very well mean I can't bond.'

'That's the word I was thinking of,' she replied. 'Bonding.'

'Not the way I meant. I have to bond with Mars—'

'What do you think is going to happen when we enter quarantine? You plan on spending forty days choosing between me and magic?'

'I'm doing my best not to think about, you know, all that. At all. I need to focus.'

'I'll give you focus. Take a look around this place. An empty sickbay. Because of you. Working against the impossible. Overcoming distance and stress and exhaustion.' When he did not respond, she demanded, 'Are you always such a worry-wart?'

'I have no idea. This is totally new terrain for me.'

'Well then.' She brushed his arm aside and closed the distance. 'Follow my lead.'

*   *   *

Adrian needed forever to bond.

With Mars.

It wasn't this more recent kiss. Or the dark womanly depths to her gaze. Or how Chris smiled before switching the comm-link back on. Or the promise of together-time in quarantine.

It was all of that. And more.

Forty-nine people were relying on him to get this right.

Finally, after several semi-failed attempts, he managed to clear his head and make that all-important connection to the red planet. He lifted the pitcher holding four fingers of water, started casting the spell, gave her the nod, then followed Chris into the pharmacy.

The plexiglass shelves and cabinets held a library of boxes and syringes and bottles, most labeled with names that meant nothing to him. Chris shut the door behind him, ensured his comm-link was on and said, 'Tell me exactly what we're after.'

'A concoction that will induce euphoria.'

'That's too broad a term. Distill that down for me.'

During the weeks that he had served on constant duty, Adrian had learned that a reforging of the bond with Mars was required before every new spell. Once that bond was renewed, intoning the spell's first few words formed a totally secure link. He could stop, speak with patients, change rooms, deal with a different crisis, then pick up where he had left off. He could even say, 'I heard from Van Hues that you're a fully fledged doctor.'

'Georgetown start to finish. Undergrad, med school, masters in interplanetary studies. All so I could waltz my way through my very own pharmacy, playing gopher to a greenie wizard.'

Adrian started to apologize for not asking that before now. But Chris touched her lips, then pointed to the ceiling. Adrian replied, 'Greenie is right.'

She shot him another of those deep and utterly feminine looks. But all she said was, 'Define euphoria.'

'They have to stay totally alert. Not getting sleepy on the job. Or so blitzed they lose total interest.'

'That's what you don't want. Now tell me what's your ideal result.'

'These guards need to become so juiced and happy they'll agree to anything the skipper suggests. Totally off-the-charts willing to go along with our carrying everything we like. Feeling so good and pliant nothing else matters.'

He watched as she started opening panels and fingering various items. She thought out loud as she selected . . .

'A strong hypnotic will make a good start. Here we go. Benzodiazepine. How much do we need?'

'No idea. Remember, they're not drinking this. I'm trying to send the force—'

'Over distance and through walls. Right. So a lot. Let's call it twenty times the normal dose.' She shook out the capsules, slipped them into the pitcher's double-lock, waited while Adrian chanted and swirled, then, 'And now for anti-depressants. Let's see, here are three excellent products. Paroxetine, mirtazapine, escitalopram. Can't have too much of a good thing, right?'

'You're the doc.'

'And that's the right answer.' Another addition to the pitcher and the spell, then, 'What would you call a healthy dose of codeine?'

'You're enjoying this.'

'Can't I be a total professional and still have a little fun?' She waited through his procedure, then continued, 'Now then. What we have so far could send our guys to sleepyland. So we need a kicker. This is perfect. Epinephrine.' She unwrapped four syringes, squirted them into the pitcher. 'And last but not least, here we go. Methylin. Sure-fire guarantee our fellows stay alert through this particular watch.'

She watched him complete the spell, then said, 'Sickbay to Captain.'

'Otieno here.'

'Sir, we are ready for our volunteer.'

Adrian followed her back into the sickbay's front chamber and said, 'The skipper made a good point.'

'Did he?'

'You really would make the ideal first subject.'

'Not on your life.'

'We desperately need a clear idea of what takes place. You're a trained professional . . .' He watched her angrily slap the comm switch. 'What?'

'Let's review this for one brief second. Say you give me a euphoric high. Which means I lose all inhibitions, correct?'

'No, I guess, OK, maybe . . .'

'Is that a glimmer of realization I hear in your stammer?' Her face was beet red. 'Good. I'm so glad we cleared that up.'

They decided to use the operating theater.

'Just in case, you know, things go horribly wrong,' Chris said.

Van Hues scattered an anxious gaze around the room. 'You're a real confidence builder.'

'If you like, I can ask Adrian to hold off a minute, let me introduce you to my collection of surgical knives.'

'Adrian, tell her to stop.'

'What stop. You volunteered.'

'To get toasted, yes. To have you play mad doctor, definitely not.'

Adrian liked how Chris pushed the young man to lighten up, loosen his grip on control. 'If it would make you feel more comfortable, maybe we should ask her to go through the trial with you.'

Chris shot him a hard look, but it was the young man who said, 'No way. What if the doc gets happy and goes after me with the bone saw?'

'Saws,' Chris said. Still glaring at Adrian. 'Plural.'

Adrian said, 'Enough with the saws. Van Hues, what's your first name?'

'Lars.'

'OK, Lars. Here's the thing. We're placing you in the surgical ward because it's as close as we can get to me shooting this spell through two space suits or into their transports. Clear walls between me here in the sickbay and you standing there.'

'Right. Sure. That makes sense.'

'We need answers to some key questions. Does it work. If so, for how long. And equally important, can I pinpoint just one person? I can't end up spraying the skipper and have him go wandering off into the desert.'

The comm-link pinged. 'I absolutely concur with that very crucial point.'

'There won't be much distance between the captain and our guards. I need a rifle-shot approach. Which is why the good doctor is about as far from you as the skipper will be from the guards.'

A silence, then, 'No saws?'

'Awww . . .'

'Stop it, Leighton.' It was Adrian's turn to go tough. 'Enough with the surgical jokes.'

Lars added, 'Doc, you have a terrible, wicked, twisted, terrifying, not-funny sense of humor.'

'Oh come on, Lars. It's a teenie bit funny.'

Adrian decided it was time to proceed. He warned the bridge crew as much as Lars, 'I'm going to be holding the pouch inside my suit, shooting the spell across this much distance, maybe more. Taking aim at guards inside *their* suits. Not to mention drivers in vehicles even further away. There's every chance this will fail. In which case, according to the skipper, we'll be on the Mars quarantine version of bread and water for forty days.'

Lars straightened. 'This is for real. I get it.'

'Ready?'

'Go for it.'

Adrian shifted behind the sickbay's central station. Decided to restart the spell. Then, 'Chris, ready on the timer.'

'Smoke 'em if you've got 'em.'

'Sick, sick, sick,' Lars replied.

'Sickbay to bridge.'

'Otieno here.'

'Skipper, I think we're ready.'

'Proceed. And keep the comm-link open.'

'Aye, sir.' Deep breath. 'OK, taking aim.'

NINETEEN

Adrian focused tightly on Lars. Doing his best to ignore the grinning Chris three feet to the crewman's left.

Almost everything he did was mental. The only external element was a simple flick of three fingers, using the hand not holding the pouch.

And . . .

Otieno said, 'Report.'

'Sir, I can't tell that it has worked at all . . .' He stopped when Chris leaned in closely. 'Doc, any change?'

'His eyes have dilated. Lars, say if you feel something.'

The young man offered a robotic, 'If you feel something.'

Chris laughed out loud. Lars gave no sign he heard.

Otieno said, 'Doc?'

'Skipper, it appears our trial subject is well and truly baked.'

Laughter spilled over the intercom. 'Bring him to the bridge.'

It was like herding a very agreeable cat. Blinking lights, changing scenery, passing crew – all held equal interest. All that and more would have veered Lars off course, had Adrian not stood to one side and Chris to the other. Soft course alterations, a couple of words, the same tone they'd use with a young child. Step up. Enter the elevator. No, don't touch the buttons. Here we go, step forward.

They were met with resounding cheers.

Lars responded with a gentle smile. He stared at the starlit expanse with a blank intensity.

Otieno demanded, 'Van Hues, can you hear me?'

He nodded. 'Hi.'

'How are you feeling?'

Each word required a forever amount of concentration. 'Feeling. Feeling is good.'

The skipper asked Chris, 'You were standing beside him?'

'Almost as close to him as I am now, Skipper.'

'You don't feel anything?'

She grinned at the young man. 'A little jealous, maybe.'

'Any visible results of this . . .'

'Treatment works for me,' Chris replied. 'His pulse rate is accelerated. Eyes remain dilated. No more than you'd expect for a young man . . .'

Naxos offered, 'Who is stoned right out of his tiny mind.'

Meishi added, 'Such a waste of a perfectly good high.'

Otieno asked, 'Number two, what's our count?'

'Landfall in two hours, twenty-six minutes, Captain.'

'Very well. Comm-link open to all quarters. Attention, this is your captain. All nonessential crew are ordered to the loading bay. Suit up, strap yourselves into everything you can possibly carry, and prepare for our departure.' He looked at the young man still fascinated by the starlight. 'Lars, can you take your assigned station?'

'Aw. I'm happy here.'

Chris gripped the young man's elbow. 'Good, Lars. I'm glad. But we need you to take a seat.'

'Sitting is good.'

It was like shaping a pliable doll into the station. When Chris finally had him strapped in, she straightened and reported, 'Skipper, it appears we're as ready for landfall as we're going to get.'

TWENTY

Twenty minutes later, there were just five plus Adrian on the bridge. Landing pilot and backup, senior comms officer, Lars, and Otieno. Meishi had been tasked with prepping the landing party, ensuring all essential equipment was packed. Plus their remaining food and all the water they could carry. Chris was back in the sickbay, preparing a triple load. Everything she and two crew could manage.

Adrian was assigned to watch their test subject and report, 'Skipper, Lars is coming around.'

Otieno shifted his chair ten degrees. 'That true, Lieutenant?'

Lars was sitting straight now, his gaze clear but worried. 'Sir, did I do anything monumentally stupid?'

The senior comms officer replied, 'Nothing more than usual.'

'Any more of that, Naxos, and you will find yourself removed from the next trial run.'

'Sorry, sir. Comment totally retracted, sir.'

The captain asked Van Hues, 'How do you feel?'

'Fine, sir.'

'Really?'

'I feel great. Like I just had the finest siesta of my life.'

Naxos muttered, 'I have got to get me some of that.'

Van Hues's forehead creased with concentration. 'Only, I don't remember much of anything. I was in the sickbay. Adrian started working his magic. Now I'm here. Truly, Skipper, I acted OK?'

'You did fine.' To Adrian, 'How long was he gone?'

'Twenty-four minutes.'

'Van Hues, do you feel up to helping prep for departure?'

'Aye, sir.'

'Head down to the loading bay, suit up, have Doc use you for carrying medical items.' He waited until Lars was in the chute to tell Adrian, 'Well done.'

'Thank you, sir.'

'The question is, can we make it to the quarantine zone in twenty-four minutes.' Otieno shifted aim. 'Number two, have you identified the Q?'

'I think so, sir,' Harrow replied. 'We have a circular heat signature that's faint but clear.'

'Put it on a bow monitor.'

Instantly the large view-screen showed a dark terrain with a dozen or so human figures clustered together, two rectangular blobs that Adrian assumed were vehicles, and then a circular orange mass in the screen's left-hand corner.

Naxos asked the question Adrian had been pondering, 'Why is it so dim?'

Harrow fretted, 'If the Q's heat pumps aren't fully functioning, we're finished.'

Otieno frowned, shook his head. 'Comm-link, bridge to medic.'

'Leighton here, Skipper.'

'When was the last official report of a ship carrying transmutable disease?'

'Let me check.' A pause, then, 'The records I have available show two Earth years before the revolt. But I'd need to access full cloud data to make a thorough search.'

'Thank you, Doc. This will do.'

But as he started to cut the connection, Chris added, 'Captain, I was about to contact you.'

'Regarding?'

'We need to assume Adrian will have trouble with Mars's gravity. I suggest assigning Van Hues duty as Adrian's backup.'

'Very well, Doc. Make it so. Bridge out.' To the crew on duty, 'There's every likelihood the Q hasn't been used since that last official outbreak.'

'Say they haven't,' Harrow agreed. 'This means more than six years' worth of storms.'

Naxos said, 'The Q could be covered by a full meter of crud.'

'So let's assume for the moment heat will not be an issue,' Otieno said. 'How far from the LZ to our habitat?'

A pause, then Harrow replied, 'I make it four hundred and fifty meters from the LZ beacon to the Q's boundary.'

'Too far,' Otieno said. 'Number two, shift our approach so that we land off the mark.'

'Ground control will scream bloody murder.'

'Let them. How much of the distance can you cut off without threatening our welcome committee?'

Harrow pointed to the two squarish blobs. 'A hundred and fifty meters. Any more and we crush their ride home.'

'Make it so.'

'Aye, sir.'

'What's our timing?'

'Landfall in a minute thirty-six.'

'Bridge to Meishi. How are we faring?'

'We're locked and loaded, Skipper. Waiting for your signal.'

'Very good. Captain to all crew. Prepare for landfall. Otieno out. Number two, take us down.'

'Roger, sir.' A longish pause, then, 'Landing in three, two, ship is down.'

'Naxos, any sign of drones?'

'Sky is clear, Skipper.'

'Maintain surveillance via your handheld.'

'Roger, sir.'

Otieno rose to his feet. 'Excellent job, everyone. Number two, seal the bridge. All personnel to the loading bay. On the double.'

TWENTY-ONE

Adrian was the last and the slowest to suit up. Chris and Lars then strapped on Adrian's pack, ensuring the bulky object did not block the movements of his arms. By the time they had it secure, Otieno and his two executive officers had almost finished checking each crew member's loads.

Harrow stepped in front of Adrian. Sour as always. Refusing to meet Adrian's gaze as he gripped the two shoulder straps and jerked Adrian so hard he lost contact with the floor. Which caused the second-in-command to snort in derision before moving on.

Then Harrow realized the captain was watching. There was a silent exchange, the skipper thoughtfully concerned, the pilot ashamed and angry both. Otieno stepped forward, asked loudly enough for all to hear, 'What is our gentleman wizard carrying?'

Chris replied, 'Emergency surgical kit, Skipper. Including two oxygen mini-tanks and a respirator.'

'Weight?'

'Hundred and thirty kilos, Earthside. Here, about forty.'

'Compact and heavy. Good choices. Wouldn't you agree, number two?' He paused for emphasis, then told Adrian, 'This should be enough to stabilize your footsteps. But your pack's inertia will be according to mass. Which means stopping or changing direction will be a challenge. Slow and steady is best.'

'Aye, sir.'

'Where is your joy juice?'

Adrian lifted his left hand. Keeping the pouch in position was one reason why it took so long to suit up. 'Taped to my palm, sir.'

'Good. Doc, you're with me. Adrian, you and Van Hues follow three steps back. Naxos, how are the skies?'

'Clear of drones, Skipper.'

'Everybody paired and know their position? Number two, you and Meishi are last to depart.' They had already covered this twice before, but Adrian found a distinct comfort in Otieno's calm repetition. 'Every second counts, people. Two at a time through the lock. Once you're outside, keep a careful eye on your partner, make sure they're stable. Move fast, move steady, stay safe, no talking. We have twenty-four minutes to cross three hundred yards and cycle through the Q airlock. Who are the next six in line after Adrian and Van Hues? All right. You're assigned duty inside the QZ. Cycle through, unstrap, dump your gear, don't unsuit. Your job is to clear the airlock fast as you can. Everyone else, unstrap in turn and shift your gear through the airlock, then stand by to help the next pair offload. Speed is everything. Questions? All right. Doc, on me. Good luck, everyone. Let's move out.'

Adrian had two choices. He could gawk at his surroundings and lose himself in the wonder of being here. On the surface of Mars.

Or he could stay upright, keep moving forward. And do his job. Hopefully.

He walked.

His pack was heavy, but not overly so. Once the Gamma crisis started easing, Adrian had followed Otieno's stern advice and put in daily gym time. The cockpit had a full complex of equipment designed to maintain bone density, muscle mass, lung and heart, the works. With the surgical kit strapped to his back as anchorage, Adrian was glad he'd put in the effort.

Three guards wore suits of burnished orange with shields adorning their shoulders. They stood clustered ten paces from the airlock. Otieno offered a wave and approached at an easy amble.

Time to get to work.

Adrian started the revised soothing spell, then his boot caught on a rock hidden beneath the Martian dust. A slight tilt as he tried to correct his balance and . . .

If Van Hues had not been there, he would have gone down hard. Boom. Fine end to all their planning.

As it was, Van Hues held him upright and kept him moving forward.

Adrian started over, focused now, relying on Van Hues to maintain balance.

Otieno did his best to keep the trio of guards fully occupied. 'Allow me to introduce our chief medical officer, Doctor Leighton. She's ready to answer any queries your team might have regarding the health of my crew.'

The lead guard kept trying to step around Leighton, which Adrian assumed meant the next fully loaded pair had come through the airlock. Adrian nudged Van Hues with his elbow. Thankfully Lars understood, and shifted Adrian further to one side, so that he could aim around Otieno and Chris.

The guard pointed and asked, 'What are those two carrying . . .?'

Which was when Adrian finally got it right.

He popped his right wrist and flicked his fingers, just as he had through the two glass walls at Lars. Adrian mostly took aim with his eyes and his mind.

The lead guard never finished his thought.

Otieno filled the abrupt silence with, 'We are carrying the requisite personal items, as is standard for entering quarantine.'

'All of the ship's crew are fully recovered,' Chris added. Glancing back, watching as Adrian took aim at the next two guards now on approach. 'Their bloodwork has come through virus free. Everyone is fine.'

The first guard intoned, 'Fine.'

Adrian took aim at the transport vehicles lined up behind the first guards. Eyes on the drivers' stations. Then back to the next line of guards.

Otieno said, 'We can proceed?'

'Proceed.'

As they passed the silent guards, Adrian shot a glance behind him. It was a good thing the cockpit's airlock was designed large enough to admit a fully loaded forklift. The ship's crew emerged so burdened they looked like packing cases with helmets and legs. Sherpas in space suits.

Adrian took aim at the next three guards. Then the ones after them. Aiming far across the Martian surface now, then adding a second booster on close approach. His comm-link echoed to multiple puffing breaths as the crew hoofed their way forward.

Their destination was nothing more than a circular hump in the Martian surface, a large round hill blanketed by dust. The only sign they were headed in the right direction was the airlock, a tall metal door lined with dimly glowing lights.

Otieno and Chris helped the first six unstrap their gear and cram into the airlock together. As they cycled through, the captain demanded, 'Time?'

Naxos huffed, 'Twenty-one minutes.'

Otieno aimed a gloved finger at Adrian's face-plate, then pointed to the ground five paces removed from the airlock. Adrian unstrapped with Lars's help, then took up position and . . .

Gaped.

The sense of arrival almost overwhelmed him. The stark beauty, the contrast of Mars and sky, the parade of crew performing a low-gravity ballet across the red-grey surface, the sun at fifteen degrees above the horizon, the pale wash of stars directly overhead . . .

Lars stopped helping to unstrap the next pair. He stepped in close. Gripped Adrian's shoulder, shook it gently, then pointed.

The three guards closest to the landed ship were now slowly turning, straightening, heading toward the last crew members. Moving somewhat unsteadily. But taking aim.

Adrian had no idea what distance did to his spell. Or if distance mattered at all. He took two further steps to his left, making a clear path between himself and the three targets. And cast the spell again.

The trio stopped in their tracks.

Someone along the line huffed a soft, 'Appreciate it.'

Adrian sketched a wave, then began recasting toward each group of guards in turn. And the vehicles. Working his way back toward where he stood. Then starting over.

Otieno kept urging the last arrivals forward. Every time the airlock flashed green, crew members worked in tandem, shoving in the last of their gear. Next came the crew themselves, herding them forward, cramming as many as possible inside. Otieno stepped over beside Adrian, scouting the terrain, watching the crew gradually make their ways inside, showing through example the threat was not over simply because the guards drifted about in their happy carefree buzz. Adrian understood. The guards would have a dedicated radio link, and their watchers would not be hearing what they expected.

The sun was a pristine golden globe, the shadows a series of rose-hued etchings that carved gentle lines over the dusty landscape. The scene was, in a word, ethereal.

Then it was his turn. He shared the airlock with Lars and Otieno and Chris and Naxos and Meishi, so tight they all puffed in tandem. When the internal portal opened they spilled out, and Adrian fell atop a pile of gear and lay there. Now that the task was completed, he did not have the strength to rise.

TWENTY-TWO

The Q, as the crew called it, was a cage. A bad one. Old, smelly, large, hollow, filled with furniture ready to give out at any moment. The air was so dry it felt acidic, burning his throat with every breath. The dust coating every surface made it worse. Martian, silicate, nearly impossible to clean up because they had no water to hold it down.

Water was a constant concern. What came out of the taps tasted vile and smelled worse. Even with the containers they had brought and their two purifiers on constant duty, supplying forty-nine crew with sufficient drinking water left very little for personal hygiene and even less for managing the dust.

The high domed ceiling held numerous light strips, but less than a third worked, and those shone dully. Naxos was their resident in-house do-it-all electrician. He explained they probably were meant to recharge naturally via solar panels embedded in the roof. Only these were now encrusted with years of dust.

Multiple glass panels were placed throughout the dome, and more formed tall strips around the walls. These too were blocked by the same solid crust, adding mightily to the Q's claustrophobic atmosphere.

The sleeping chambers were surprisingly large, no doubt intended to hold families. But the lighting was worse here, the furniture in dreadful shape. Most of the crew elected to sleep on the floor. Which made enduring the dust harder still. So they turned four sleeping chambers into dorms and did their best to make them dust free. About half the crew were partnered up, and the intention was for them to gradually clear out private chambers they could eventually share. But for the moment, in these initial hard watches, all that had to wait.

Late on day two, while they were still settling in, making a run at cleaning up the galley and eating area, fixing what would become their first hot meal, Captain Otieno suffered a relapse. Long-Gamma slammed the skipper hard.

Which left his number two in command.

Harrow.

Him with the poisonous attitude toward Adrian. And now with the power to take aim. Which Harrow did. Within minutes of assuming command.

The very instant Adrian emerged from what was now Otieno's sickroom, calming solution still in his hand, there he was.

Harrow stepped in close enough for Adrian to see the hatred and the pleasure in his gaze. 'I never fell for whatever foul magic you used on my crew.' He shot a glance at Chris helping the chef and his mates in the galley. 'Some of them, anyway.'

Most of the crew were there in the central room. Playing chess. Cleaning up. Testing the furniture, storing everything that could not handle further use in a former sleeping chamber. Passing out cups of purified water. Anything but look in Adrian's direction. Adrian knew the public shaming was intentional. Only he didn't feel ashamed. Nor did he find any need to respond.

'You are hereby restricted to your quarters until further notice.' Harrow asked the horrified Meishi, 'Where has he been assigned?'

'The medic has requested she share separate quarters—'

'Out of the question. And you will refer to me as sir or skipper. Is that clear?'

'Aye, sir.'

Harrow raised his voice. 'This charlatan's influence on my crew ends now.' He pointed to the lone sleeping chamber beside the latrines. 'Seal yourself in.'

Adrian lifted the pouch. 'What about the skipper—'

'Give me that. From now on, the *medic* will handle the *medic*'s duties.' Harrow tossed the pouch into their rubbish chamber. 'Now get out of my sight.'

Adrian's room was huge, extending from the chemical latrines to the bone-dry shower room. With the door sealed, odors were thick enough to coat his skin.

The chamber was lined with eight bunks. The central space was long enough for him to take five paces, which was good, because as soon as he entered he knew what he wanted to do. And the fifth spell in his arsenal required a *lot* of motion.

There were risks. Big ones. As in, get this wrong and the exterior walls might vanish. And his air. With his space suit piled in with all the others, he put his chances at survival at nil.

After a fitful sleep period, Adrian spent the first full day doing trial runs.

But first he gave several hours to what he classed as secondary spells. He bonded with Mars, then worked several spells with which he'd experienced no sense of bonding. The result was nil. No matter how carefully he bonded with the Mars power source, he was unable to access any spell other than those where he had experienced that special link on Earth.

Just the same, he found an odd sense of purpose in his isolated hours. For one thing, Adrian was coming to terms with what it meant to be a wizard on Mars. Throughout the voyage he had suspected the seven spells he'd linked with back on Earth would prove the only ones that were his to claim. Perhaps with time and the help of other wizards, this might change. For now, these seven spells formed his magical boundaries.

Beyond that, Adrian experienced his first real sense of privacy – nowhere to go, nothing to do, no urgent patient crises – since entering the cockpit. This granted him space to split apart the two huge issues he currently faced.

Mars.

And Chris.

He didn't need far-seeing abilities to know the lady was not after some short-term fling.

What was more, he grew convinced Chris and Otieno had discussed his future crew status before she put on the moves. He had come to know the skipper at least a little. Enough to be certain Otieno would first check with the head of the department where Adrian had served before making any such offer.

Which meant . . .

Actually, it meant a lot.

Despite how Adrian might feel about returning off-planet, Chris deserved his careful consideration.

It helped clarify things to practice bonding.

Not that he came to any decisions. Not even close. Adrian realized early on that he needed to get out, see Mars, become involved in the local wizards' daily existence. The years of yearning and taking aim deserved nothing less.

Of course there was always the other possibility. That he was fooling himself. A lonely guy building a romance from Martian dust and a couple of kisses.

Adrian spent hours bonding with the red planet. Connecting at the *chi* level, stepping back, watching it fade. There was no way he could describe the sensation. But he wanted to. Desperately. He longed for the chance to share this with Chris. The lady who wanted him to leave it all and fly away.

Maybe.

Van Hues brought his meals, then returned for the trays. Saying nothing. Which Adrian took as strict orders from Harrow.

Soon as the door closed and his paltry meal was consumed, he was back at it.

Bonding.

The bed finally pushed Adrian into action. Work the next of those spells with which he had bonded. Take the risk.

Even at thirty-eight percent of Earth's gravity, the bare mattress defined awful. Lumpy. And the smell.

Adrian shifted the chamber's paltry furniture to one side. He tied a singlet over his nose and mouth against the dust he was bound to raise. He bonded. And began.

This particular spell had been a curiosity since the moment of discovery. The Sanskrit and Aramaic and Sumerian renditions were almost identical, right down to a name that went on for pages. Adrian would have ignored it entirely, except for how his entire being resonated with each glance. Concentrating, memorizing, practicing; all caused the page to spark. At least in his mind. But still.

His new name for this fifth spell was a single word.

Rewind.

As in, shift his physical surroundings to a previous era. Note to wizard: the spell did not work on people. Or any living breathing entity. Inanimate objects only.

Until their arrival in the Q cage, Adrian had never expected to have any use for the spell.

Adrian took his time, spending over an hour on this first casting. Pausing repeatedly to reinforce the boundaries. Walls, floor, ceiling. Focusing tightly on creating a force that would not, could not, extend further.

Or so he desperately hoped.

The final elements, what Adrian considered the punctuation marks, were all about timing. Which had brought out its own share of nightmare worries.

How far back should he aim? And dated to which calendar? None of the early authors had probably ever thought their work might one day be performed on Mars.

Finally, in the long smelly hours spent trying to rest, Adrian decided it was time to ask a question of his own. Come what may.

Why not be the one to decide?

So much of his other spells had come down to this point. Rewriting the unwritten.

The basic issue regarding his use of this spell was simple. Adrian was not after half-measures.

Otieno's mates, the crew who had spent their own forty days here, had described the Q zone as a cage, a prison. And that was *before* the revolt.

Why simply cast his way back to a marginally cleaner and less lumpy version of where he was now?

So at this point, when he punctuated the spell with the timing, Adrian did not say a date.

Instead, he spelled it out as best and clearly as he could. Take the room back to when it was fresh and new.

While he was still in the process of defining precisely what he meant . . .

The storm erupted.

The room's dust rose all at once. A dry fog so thick he feared the cloth wrapping would do no good and he would choke to death.

Only the dust did not touch him.

Instead, Adrian became surrounded with a swirling greyish-reddish wall. He stood in the eye of a tornadic force, thundering in intensity, the sound a rumble or humming, so low he felt it in his chest while hearing nothing at all.

The sensation was incredible. He stripped off the cloth so he could shout the final words, screaming them at a volume to compete with the storm.

Lightning flickered and danced in the surrounding mass. As if timed to his final words.

He was actually sorry when the spell was cast.

Adrian lowered his arms. The dust storm vanished. Revealing . . .

The same room. Except everything was new. Pristine. The walls were painted a fresh creamy yellow. The sort of color that might be chosen for a favorite child.

A gaily painted chest stood snug beneath yellow shelves, all filled with children's toys and stuffed animals.

The bunks held fresh mattresses, on which were stacked bed linens and towels.

Adrian had no idea how long he stood there, surrounded by success. Finally the door sighed open.

But it was not Van Hues with his next meal. Instead, Meishi stepped inside. And gaped.

Adrian said, 'I tried a spell. It worked.'

'So I see.' Meishi gave the refashioned chamber a long look, then said, 'The skipper is worse. And Harrow has gone down. I'm in charge now. And you are welcome to join us.'

TWENTY-THREE

Adrian accepted a cup of water, then a mug of tea, and stood in the galley watching as Chris prepared him a ready meal. Then she sat across from him while he ate. The other crew left them alone, as close to intimacy as they could manage under the circumstances. She waited until he finished eating, then asked, 'Will you show me?'

He led her to the room that had served as his prison. Several of the crew stood around the doorway. They shifted back and allowed Chris to enter. Adrian took his time, describing the restructured spell's timeline, speaking loud enough for his words to carry. When he went quiet, she thanked him and asked if he'd like another tea. His only water for the past three days had come with his meals. Adrian felt as if he might never be fully sated ever again.

She prepared a mug for herself, sweetened his with condensed milk, gave it to him, then said quietly, 'I missed you.'

He reached for her hand. Standing there, the two of them leaning against the galley counter, faces turned from the crew filling the ready-room and studying his recent handiwork.

Chris opened a drawer and drew out his pouch of calming fluid. 'I retrieved it soon as Harrow wasn't looking.'

'Thanks.'

She set it on the counter between them. 'Deny Harrow treatment. It's what he deserves.'

'Is that part of the medic's code? Refuse treatment to anyone we don't like?' When she remained silent, he went on, 'We do all we can. For everyone. Equally.'

Chris took a long time responding. She finished her own mug, released Adrian's hand, shifted to the cleaning rack, busied herself and avoided meeting his gaze. 'My first trip, I served as aide to a wonderful medic. She was a lovely person inside and out. A great doctor. I had this ensign, he would not leave me alone. And when I made it clear I wasn't interested, he became overtly hostile. Bitter. Looking for a way to sabotage my career.' She was silent, then, 'I finally confronted my boss, demanded to know why she did not get

this ensign off my back. The chief medic replied that she'd take it
to the captain if I insisted. But I needed to be very certain this was
what I wanted. Because whatever I did this first trip, it would carry
forward. Which I knew, of course, was the reason I hadn't done
anything before then.'

'What did you do?'

'Found a quiet moment. Confronted him. Calmly. Kept my
temper.' She almost smiled. 'Not easy.'

'Did it work?'

'Not really. He claimed it was all in my mind, a total fabrication.
But while we were talking, my superior happened by. Gave him a
look. Didn't speak, just glared a warning and left. The ensign kept
his distance after that.'

'Still, it must have made for a tough voyage.'

'It could have been worse,' Chris replied. 'A couple of watches
after I confronted the ensign, my boss told me something that's
carried me through a lot. She said that for an attractive crew member,
there would always be a Harrow. She used the ensign's name, of
course. But you know what I mean.'

'That's hard.'

'That's life on board a deep-space vessel.' Another quiet moment,
then, 'What she meant was, I had to find a way to protect myself
from the Harrows. Because there would always be at least one
troublemaker on board.'

He took his time inspecting her. 'I feel like I have a name now
for how you act. The tough-as-nails face you show everyone.'

'I'm a ship's officer. I have to carry myself as one.' She wiped
her eyes with an impatient gesture. 'Even when it hurts. Even when
it makes me the loneliest person on the ship.'

Adrian decided to confront Harrow first. Get the worst over with.

Soon as the door opened, the ship's officer snapped, 'Get out of
here. Whatever you're offering, I don't want it.'

'That's certainly your choice. There are almost no recorded fatal-
ities from long-Gamma.' Adrian stepped inside, closed the door.
Glad for the conversation he'd just had with Chris. 'But there are
hazards.'

Harrow showed him an angry, hostile gaze. 'Hazards.'

'Long-Gamma wears you out, weakens the system, risks a number
of secondary—'

'How do I know you won't twist me? Force me to . . .'

'Make peace,' Adrian supplied. 'Suddenly discover I'm a great guy. Your very best friend.'

Harrow smoldered.

'It's a valid question.' Adrian settled on the narrow bench extending from the side wall. Pretended at an ease he didn't feel. 'You probably heard I spent years studying magic and spells back on Earth. The original records date from times when journeys between nations were far deadlier than our voyage to Mars. Communication was extremely limited. And yet these records include spells that are amazingly similar, using more or less the same ingredients, words, hand-signs, the works. I found this count-less times. This parallel structure was a primary way I separated what was real from the fakes. And there were a lot of those. Fakes.'

'Why don't you go tell Chris your little stories. She's more interested than—'

'The only reason I could come up with for this similarity was magic once existed on Earth. This power I gain from Mars, thou-sands of years ago it existed on our planet. Then something happened. The force drained away, or became cut off, something. My guess is, Earthbound wizards called upon the power for dark purposes. Evil. Deadly. Poisonous. And so the force simply stopped.' Adrian stared at the rear wall, returning to musings that had carried him through the years. 'Maybe someday we'll arrive at other worlds and discover the *potential* for magic is present everywhere. The raw force, if you will. Long as we elect to use it in a positive manner. Maybe there is some kind of regeneration that takes place through the proper use of this energy.' He shrugged. 'Maybe we'll never know.'

Harrow didn't want to ask. But the smoldering anger could not completely hide his interest. 'Does this have a point?'

'Life is precious. That much even you and I can agree on. But there are other ways than murder to taint magical energy.' Adrian leaned forward. 'Perhaps a more insidious way to misuse the power is by twisting an individual's free will. One of mankind's greatest gifts is each person's right to choose their own life's course. Which emotions will dominate their hours. How they elect to spend the time they have. Every breath counts, don't you agree? Who they choose to love. How they endure disappointments. How they recover—'

'Get out.'

'I can't help but wonder if your suspicions and accusations actually come from what you'd do if you had the power—'

'*GET OUT!*'

Adrian rose to his feet, waited for Harrow's coughing fit to ease. 'I'll check back in a couple of hours, see if you've changed your mind about accepting treatment.'

TWENTY-FOUR

A drian finished giving the skipper his dose, then returned to Harrow's quarters. The executive officer was angry, silent, sullen, but also in pain. Enough so that when Adrian asked if he wanted a treatment, Harrow fumed but nodded.

When he came out, almost all the crew were there in what passed for a ready-room. There was really nowhere else to go. Adrian felt all the eyes track him as he walked over to where Meishi stood with Chris. The new acting exec asked, 'Are you hungry?'

'More thirsty than anything.'

'I'll get it,' Chris offered, and headed for the galley.

Meishi pointed to the central table. 'Come join me.'

Even in low Mars gravity, most of the chairs wouldn't have accepted a person's weight. Almost all had been consigned to the rubbish heaps which now filled three chambers. He seated himself on the bench across from Meishi, thanked Chris for the tea, and watched as the crew gathered around them.

Meishi said, 'There are all kinds of reasons why a person journeys into deep space.'

She kept her voice low. Even so, the room was quiet. Intent. The crew still filing past Adrian's former chamber did so in absolute silence. Not just listening. Adrian sensed the acting exec spoke for all of them. And they wanted him to know it.

'Becoming a ship's officer requires years of work. And sacrifice. You put in the hours, you jump through the hoops, you compete when you must. You choose your specialty and you become the very best at whatever that may be.' She gave it a beat, then added, 'What the system doesn't measure is whether this officer is a whole person. You understand what I'm saying?'

Adrian sipped from his mug. Chris had added so much condensed milk it went down like liquid dessert.

'Someone you can willingly entrust with a ship,' Meishi went on. 'Or the lives of a crew. Or know that – in a difficult situation – the officer will choose sacrifice over personal ambition. That is the hardest dilemma of all. Because sometimes you can't predict what will be revealed in a crisis. Personal or otherwise.'

Adrian remained silent.

Meishi continued, 'Andrew Harrow is an excellent ship's officer in every way. Except the one which matters most.'

Adrian gave that the space it deserved. Finished his tea. Pushed the mug to the center of the table. Spoke to all the gathered crew. 'You want me to revamp the entire Q.'

'Can you do that?'

'Yes. I can.'

'You're so certain?'

'The question isn't about redoing the interior,' he replied. 'The two issues are, first, can I do this and not wind up erasing all the supplies we brought with us.'

Meishi was with him now. 'And secondly, can you keep the QZ intact.'

'Clear away the crud,' Adrian confirmed. 'Free up the solar panels and the windows. And not wind up fracturing the dome itself.'

'But we're not just talking about bad lighting and claustrophobic conditions,' Meishi said.

'It's our air supply,' Chris said. 'The air purifiers are driven by the same panels. Which means they're running at thirty percent. I have two crew with early signs of Mars throat.'

'We need to get rid of the dust, both inside and out,' Meishi said. 'We can't spend even a few more hours in these conditions. Much less thirty-seven days.'

Adrian nodded. 'I need to get outside.'

TWENTY-FIVE

A s Meishi put it, they were saved by the storm.

A major blow had struck while Adrian was in lockdown. Mars's storms could last hours, or days, sometimes much longer. This storm was gradually easing as he enjoyed his final mug of tea. The Q's cover of dust and crud was so thick, their dwelling was almost soundproofed. Adrian only noticed the rumble when Meishi mentioned it.

This granted them a very tight window.

The guards who had sort-of watched over their transfer to Q were long gone. In their place was a drone. One was enough. A boring duty, according to Naxos, probably assigned to a cop on punishment detail. Their senior communications officer spent his time on Mars with his cousins, two families involved in mining. Naxos liked Mars, loved the life his family had built here, hated the government. Being a ship's officer meant Naxos could say out loud what most locals were afraid to even whisper.

'Some poor cop probably ran afoul of the bosses.' Naxos prepped the handheld device as he talked, readying for the moment they stepped outside. 'Shot off his mouth in the bar where beat cops gather. Either that or he tried to arrest the wrong kid. He's not demoted. He's not kicked off the force.'

'Or she,' Chris corrected, helping Adrian to suit up.

Naxos grinned. 'Nah, something this stupid, it has to be a cop of the male persuasion.'

'You got me there,' Chris replied.

'So now he's stuck in some windowless box, twelve on, twelve off. Flying a drone in little circles overhead. Watching nothing, because that's exactly what there is to see. Learning to keep his mouth shut and his head down.' Naxos pointed to the airlock. 'But the storm means he can't fly his little toy. Not even a stir-crazy idiot would fly a drone in a Mars dust storm. That would be a firing offense.'

Four of them were suited up – Adrian, Lars, Naxos and Chris. Naxos because he was by far the best at scouting Martian terrain.

Lars because Adrian couldn't possibly accomplish what he needed and be safely back inside before the watchers returned.

Chris came because she insisted.

For the sake of timing and speed, all four of them crammed into the airlock together. The instant they cycled through, Adrian got to work. Naxos remained by the airlock, scouting the sky and his handheld. Gesturing with his free hand, urging them to hurry.

Which was very hard indeed, because the vista was spectacular. A low-slung veil captured the sunlight and sparkled like fairy dust. Going was difficult, as the wind remained strong enough to push him off balance. But Lars kept him steady and Chris backed them up. Literally. She pushed them both from behind. Her gloved hands pressed hard, accelerating the pace to as near a jog as Adrian could manage.

He clutched the rusted leg from a ruined chair as a wand. Drawing the designs required by the rewind spell in the sand. Mentally chanting the preliminary boundary spell as they drove him forward.

They were slightly past the midway point when Naxos murmured, 'Incoming. Six klicks and closing.'

They ran.

To be outside while quarantined broke so many regs it was unthinkable anyone would even try. This from Meishi. Any crew member so stupid or desperate would be stripped of flight status, isolated for the remainder of their forty days, then imprisoned.

They ran harder still.

Adrian's spell became a jouncing jumble of thought-words. The makeshift wand scratched a broken string of incomplete symbols.

'Hurry.' Naxos did not need volume. 'Closing fast.'

That did it. Lars and Chris actually lifted him off his feet and bolted. Thankfully they carried Adrian at a tilt, helmet first, which meant he could keep his wand in the dirt. Sort of. He stuttered over the spell's final remnants.

Naxos stood by the open airlock, waving both arms like a circus clown. He reached forward, gripped Adrian by the hand no longer holding his wand, and *threw* him into the airlock.

When the door sighed shut, Adrian realized the three of them were laughing.

The inner portal opened and they tumbled out. The helmets came off, revealing three sweating, grinning faces. And Adrian.

Lars said, 'Let's not ever do that again.'

Chris said, 'I thought that was fun.'

'Like I said,' Lars replied. 'The doc has a twisted, sick, warped sense of humor.'

Chris asked, 'Did they spot us?'

'Doubtful,' Naxos replied. 'The wind gusted.'

'I felt it,' Lars said.

'It was definitely strong enough to push their poor drone into a serious tilt,' Naxos said. He leaned over and pretended to inspect Adrian. 'You OK there, sport? You look a little green.'

Chris showed mock concern. 'Do you want to go back outside and do it again?'

Lars said, 'If he does, he's doing it alone.'

Friends.

TWENTY-SIX

A drian couldn't be certain the preliminary spell was in order. With the jouncing run over the last thirty paces, he'd count it fortunate if he got it half right.

Even so, at gut level Adrian thought he had done enough.

Chris retrieved two soft-tip pens from her surgical pack, supposedly used to outline patterns before knifing a patient's skin. Together they moved through the Q, drawing stars on every item they had brought with them. Everything they wanted to keep intact once the spell was over and done.

Meishi stepped from one doorway to the next, watching and listening as Adrian told Chris, 'I'm still trying to figure out what is and isn't crucial in my spell-casting. I skipped over major portions when I did the one chamber. Even more while we were outside. But what I'm thinking, and this is coming from a total beginner—'

'Skip the windup,' Chris said.

'We're with you,' Meishi agreed. 'Give us what we need to know.'

'I think it's going to work,' Adrian said. 'The spell will fix the Q and get us into proper quarters.'

'I like the sound of that word,' Meishi said. 'Proper.'

'But I can't be certain,' Adrian persisted. 'There's still a chance we'll have the quarters in place, but the walls will be gone. And the roof. And all the Q's support structure. Like air. And the water tank.'

'That is not a prospect I want to even consider,' Meishi said.

Chris asked, 'What's the likelihood of that happening?'

'No idea. None.'

The medic asked Meishi, 'What would you say is the punishment for doing away with the Q?'

'Given the state of this place, they should pin medals on our guy.' She wasn't smiling. 'Just the same, I doubt they'd be pleased.'

'Still, we don't have much choice,' Chris said.

'Another few days and half our crew could be down for the count,' Meishi agreed.

'Mars throat is a terrible illness and very difficult to treat,' Chris said. 'Impossible in our current circumstances. I won't stand by and watch our healthy crew become stricken by a coughing, hacking, fever-ridden, life-threatening ailment.'

'We need a haven,' Meishi agreed.

'We could complain to the authorities,' Adrian said. 'Demand better treatment.'

'Tried that,' Meishi replied. 'So did Harrow.'

'And?'

'They said they'd be back to us directly. I asked what that word meant timewise. Directly. They cut the connection.' She told Adrian, 'The decision's been made. We take the risk because the alternative is unacceptable.'

Meishi ordered the entire crew to suit up.

Including Otieno, whose only response to being assisted by Naxos and Chris was a silent humor.

Unlike Harrow, whose feeble struggles meant four crew were required. He blasted warning in every direction, especially when he realized no one cared what he thought.

They formed a tight cluster in the central chamber. Harrow and Otieno were laid out on the middle table. Being positioned beside the skipper meant Harrow was held to a fuming silence. Which was beyond good, Adrian reflected. The last thing he needed was to blow the spell because of interruptions from an executive officer who *wanted* him to fail.

Or maybe Harrow stayed silent and perfectly still because he realized how important this was. Changing this wretched Q, doing away with the dust and damage that threatened their safe passage through quarantine.

Adrian had worried about casting such a complex spell while surrounded by an audience. But in the end it didn't matter. He stood on the table next to the one holding the skipper and Harrow. He bonded with Mars, then turned in a slow circle. He swept his hand through the Sanskrit curlicues, redrawing the outer circle. This time he was careful to inscribe the design as precisely as possible. That done, he continued the protective shielding around every item now marked with stars. Then the crew.

Then he shifted to the crux, the change, the rewind.

The resulting tempest was massive. The silent force caused his suit to shudder so violently it fractured his vision.

The earth shook; the entire dome vibrated. The dust rose and encircled and became laced with ribbons of force.

None of this impacted Adrian's concentration, not even when the crew started yelling.

Adrian's only response to the chorus of terror was to shout the final segments. He *screamed* the words.

When he finished, they stood in a chamber transformed.

The light was brilliant. The overheads all worked. The floor of polished Martian stone positively shone.

The crew could not get out of their suits fast enough.

They shouted and hooted and laughed. For the first time, no one was there to help Adrian unsuit. His ungainly struggles were simply another cause for hilarity. Nor did he care. Not really. Even the skipper chuckled. But not Harrow. The ship's executive officer glared at everything, including Adrian, with an expression of bitter regret. Or defeat. Something so potent Adrian looked away so as to maintain the moment's joy.

Adrian watched as over a dozen naked crew forcibly stuffed themselves into a shower room meant to hold six. So many bodies, Adrian doubted some even managed to get wet.

The skipper gestured to Adrian, said over the clamor, 'Help me up.'

Chris hurried over and took Otieno's other side. Together they eased him off the table and through the jostling, jolly crew. When they were inside the sparkling clean cabin and the captain was unsuited, Otieno told Adrian, 'You've done well.'

'Thank you, Captain.' Otieno's fragile state was revealed in how he needed to be lowered in stages. Once he was prone, Adrian asked, 'Can I give you another dose?'

'In a minute.' To Chris, 'Have Naxos and Meishi join us. On the double.'

'We're here, Skipper.' The senior navigator and comms officer stepped inside.

The captain addressed Naxos. 'What's the latest you've heard from your family?'

'They haven't been in touch since landfall, Skipper.'

Otieno rubbed his face with an unsteady hand. 'You told me that earlier, didn't you.'

The senior comms officer offered Chris an uneasy glance. 'I don't recall, sir. Aye, perhaps.'

'Their silence tells you what?'

'Things have only gotten worse since my last visit.'

Meishi asked, 'What does that mean, worse?'

'Later,' Otieno said, still watching Naxos. 'How do you expect the government to react here?'

'Depends on who's talking, Skipper. But if the ones in power are the group my family opposes, I expect they'll come down hard.'

Meishi asked, 'Were we wrong to have Adrian correct things?'

'No,' Chris replied. Hard and definite. 'You said it yourself. We couldn't risk the crew going down with Mars throat. Or worse.'

'The state of this place was unbearable, sure enough,' Naxos agreed.

The captain closed his eyes. Breathed twice. Then, 'You need to set up a round-the-clock surveillance. Air, ground, comms.'

'Aye, Skipper,' Meishi replied. 'But what exactly are we looking for?'

'I have no idea.' He opened his eyes. 'Adrian, I may not be able to protect you.'

Chris demanded, 'Protect him from *what*?'

Otieno might as well not have heard. 'Remember, you are a ship's officer. However bad your situation might become, they cannot hold you—'

'What are you talking about!'

'We will be lifting off soon as the pods are refilled and Engineering confirms the ship is ready. At which point they will be forced to release you—'

Chris shouted, '*No!*'

Otieno closed his eyes. 'I suggest you prepare yourselves. We may not have much time.'

TWENTY-SEVEN

In the end, they had six hours.

Long enough for Adrian to enjoy a meal, a shower, a rest. An intimate hour with Chris.

Otieno's warning left them both moving beyond the tentative barriers that otherwise might have separated them. There wasn't time for hesitation. Only the now.

Even in the height of passion, the spell-casting left him feeling as if his muscles had been partially disconnected from his brain. He was not tired so much as floating. When he confessed as much, Chris not only understood but willingly adapted. Taking control, guiding him, sharing her strength as well as everything else.

Afterwards they lay in languid ease, limbs intertwined, breathing together. Adrian found himself thinking back to his last dreamtime journey before departing Earth. The altered word. Finally.

Chris must have sensed his mind roaming beyond the room's confines, for she murmured, 'Mars to Adrian.'

'I was thinking about leaving Earth. How far I've come.'

'We're not talking about the physical distance.' When he remained silent, she said, 'Tell me one thing about your life before now.'

He loved how that sounded. A former existence, and a new one, so totally alien from everything before, he could not even define it. In that very same instant, he knew what he wanted to say. Or rather, share. Because this was not about telling. It was not some story he offered. He was opening himself in a new way. Wanting her to know, even when it hurt to dredge up the past.

He began, 'About six months after Phoenix left the Gamma lockdown, my mother passed away. I'd lost touch. A month after I turned eleven, I was made a ward of the court. That gave me the chance to build walls she couldn't penetrate, and that's how things remained.'

Chris released him. Rose to a seated position, planted her back on the wall. Looking down at him. 'How old were you then? I mean, when your mother passed.'

'Twenty-three.' He reached up. 'Come back down.'

'Once you're done with the telling.'

'I miss you *now*.'

She planted a hand on his chest, keeping him prone. 'Don't you dare try and close that door.'

He liked that too. How she saw what he half-wanted to do. Adrian took hold of her hand, keeping it positioned over his heart. 'I didn't even know she'd remarried and outlived her new husband. A lawyer contacted me and said I needed to come back for the reading of the will.'

'Back where?'

'Palm Springs.' He couldn't relive that experience and look at her. So he focused on the ceiling above the bunk. Freshly painted, lights turned down to a pleasant glow, shadows soft and welcoming, door shut against the building tumult, a quiet moment, a warm haven. All evidence of the man he was now becoming. Which included this intimacy with a woman as beautiful as a Martian dawn.

She said softly, 'Tell me.'

'There are two worlds inside that desert realm,' he said, remembering. 'The interstate runs arrow-straight along the valley. One side is green, beautiful, rich. The other, where I'm from, was the exact opposite. And I'm not talking about what you see.'

When he went quiet again, she made do by pressing on his chest. Pushing out the words, as forcibly as when he'd been standing in the pod. 'My mother made it out. She and her husband had moved to one of the middle-class neighborhoods in Palm Springs. The house she'd left me was nice enough. A bank account, a life-insurance policy she'd shared with her new husband, a guy I never met. I signed all the documents, put the house up for sale, closed her accounts, and started back. Didn't even stop for a meal, rest, nothing. By that point it was closing in on sunset, I figured I'd drive all night, be back in time for work. Put the whole deal in my rearview mirror.'

This time, when he went quiet, she pressed again. Gentle. A lover's touch. All it took.

'It was almost like I was drawn across the valley. I crossed over the highway, entered the town where I'd been raised. First time I'd been back since the courts took me away. Twelve and a half years. A lifetime. I parked across the street from our former home. The place was beyond awful. I mean, so much worse than I remembered. The three houses, ours and the ones to either side, had windows covered with plywood sheets. Gang ink was sprayed over the walls.

All the streetlights were busted. When it grew dark, people started filtering out. And there it was.'

She whispered, 'Who you could have been.'

Having Chris understand made his eyes burn. 'I sat there and listened to them scream this drugged-out laughter. Only that's not what I heard.'

'It was you,' Chris said. 'The person you didn't become.'

'All because of some stupid dream,' Adrian said.

'It wasn't stupid.'

'It hurts me, how close I came to never knowing this place. This time. Or you.'

When he couldn't keep talking, Chris slipped back into his embrace. Offering her own healing magic to his swollen heart. Sharing the near loss, the wounds he hoped might become healed. Someday.

TWENTY-EIGHT

Meishi came for them soon after. Scratching on the door, a noise Adrian scarcely noticed, but Chris was better turned to nuances between female crew. She rose, opened the portal far enough to accept two mugs, then came back and announced, 'Naxos says they're coming.'

Adrian had a hundred questions about what was about to happen. More. But just then he couldn't be bothered. The simple fact was, nothing he gained in terms of new intel would alter the coming events. One glance at Chris's expression was enough to know Otieno had been right to warn them. The die was cast. Had been since he revised their quarantine dome.

He showered and dressed in a fresh singlet. He accepted a pair of thermal socks from Lars, who simply said they might come in handy during the Martian nights. He seated himself at the central table and accepted a ready meal from Meishi's own hand. The crew who met his gaze did so with the solemnity of people saying farewell. He actually had no idea what to say and was grateful when Chris slipped onto the bench next to him, her hair still damp from the shower. He was tempted to lean over, lick the droplets from her neck. She must have seen something in his expression, because she met his gaze with the hard-edged humorous warning that only a beautiful woman could manage.

Naxos was seated opposite them. His side of the table held a portable scouting device and a handheld communications system. Meishi seated herself next to the comms officer and asked, 'How many, and how long?'

He held up one finger, listening to something on his earpiece. 'There's a lot of traffic. But all I've spotted coming our way is just the one Rolligon. Two senior officers, a couple more serving as driver and backup.'

'What variety?'

'Hard to say. They talk like cops, is all I can tell you for certain.'

She tapped her fingers on the table, thinking, then decided, 'We should meet them outside. I don't want to give them any reason to appropriate our gear.' She asked Adrian, 'You mind suiting up?'

'Not at all.'

'I'm coming,' Chris declared.

The vehicle was a reddish metal cube supported by six massive deep-track tires. Each wheel operated like independent arms, which created an ungainly sort of loping gait, yet the body remained stable. It was long as a bus, but taller and squarer. A large gold shield was stamped on its side, just ahead of the airlock. Adrian could see two people through the front window, both in uniform.

Soon as the Rolligon halted, the side airlock opened and two individuals stepped out. One was so tall he had to stoop to exit the vehicle's exterior portal, the other was squat and solid as the Rolligon. Their suits both had shields imprinted on their right shoulders. The taller individual had gold filigree above and below the shield. He demanded, 'Who's the officer in charge?'

'That would be me. Commander Meishi. And you are . . .?'

'Riggins. Senior investigator with our Ministry of the Interior. And that is Agent Gupta, Inspectorate of Magic.'

Meishi said, 'I am unfamiliar with any such inspectorate.'

'A new component of our government. One long overdue.' Riggins had a monitor built into the suit's left sleeve. He checked the screen, demanded, 'Where is Captain . . . Otieno?'

'The skipper is indisposed.'

'Which means what, exactly?'

Meishi watched as the squat agent began patrolling around the dome, halting now and then, inspecting. She gestured to Naxos, who started tracking him. 'What exactly does your new inspectorate do?'

'Exactly what you are witnessing as we speak. We inspect. We maintain order. We ensure the use of magic remains within the licensed boundaries.' He halted her next question with, 'Who is your medical officer?'

'I am. Leighton.'

'That word. Indisposed. Explain.'

Despite her suit, Adrian could see her rising irritation. 'Captain Otieno suffers from symptoms common to some post-Gamma patients.'

The tall man took a half-step back. 'You still have infected crew?'

'I take it your responsibilities in whatever it is you do doesn't include one *iota* of medical training.'

Meishi said, 'Doc—'

'Which is extremely odd, wouldn't you agree? Sending a pair of unqualified officers from some bogus-sounding agency to a quarantine zone.'

Meishi stepped between them. 'What the doctor intends to say—'

The inspector snapped, 'I and my associate are both highly trained.'

'So you say.'

Meishi commanded, 'Medic, answer the inspector's question. That is an order.'

'Post-Gamma symptoms have never, not once, been tied to a recurrence of the virus.'

The two of them, the towering Mars inspector and the doctor, traded glares until Meishi said, 'Our medic does raise a valid question. Why isn't there a trained medical officer with you?'

'We are here to investigate the improper use of magic.'

But Chris was not done. 'I assume you refer to our making alterations to your *wretched* quarantine zone, which we found in such *terrible* state it *endangered* the health—'

'Leighton. Enough.'

Riggins demanded, 'Where is your wizard?'

Only now it was Meishi whose ire was raised. 'I assume you refer to our *crew member*. The individual responsible for repairs that you people should have done in advance of our arrival.'

'Hardly possible, since we only learned of your infestation hours before you landed.'

'Infestation,' Chris said. 'That's another naïve and idiotic term if ever I heard one.'

Meishi added, 'Perhaps I should also point out it only required our *crew member* less than an hour to make the changes we have been requesting. For days.'

Another glare, then, 'Where is your wizard?'

Adrian decided it was time to step forward. 'That would be me.'

'Your name?'

'Adrian Capstan.'

Another check of his monitor, then, 'You are not licensed to practice magic.'

Chris declared, 'This is *Lieutenant* Capstan's first landing on Mars.'

The squat officer returned to stand beside Riggins. He watched the taller officer scroll through his monitor. Then, 'You don't show any prior record for this wizard?'

'Nothing. But we won't know for certain until we have his prints.' He waved to the drivers. In response, the Rolligon's rear wall rose up. The wall's lone window was cross-hatched with thick wire-mesh bars. 'Capstan, or whatever your name is, you are hereby arrested for the unlawful use of magic.'

Gupta noticed something on the horizon, and tensed. 'Boss.'

Riggins tracked his associate's gaze. 'Oh no.'

The approaching vehicle was several times larger than the inspector's Rolligon. Everything about it shone in pristine splendor. The upper deck was dominated by a huge copper dome which sparkled in the sunlight. Not a speck of dust tarnished its massive body. And it was *fast*.

The crawler halted directly behind the officer's vehicle, effectively blocking access to the rear cage. Instantly the side airlock opened, revealing a pair of individuals in suits as pristine as the vehicle. 'Just in time! Good day to everyone. And isn't it just splendid weather!'

The second voice belonged to a woman whose tone was as dry as Chris was angry. 'This is Mars. No weather.'

'Well of course there is. Hello, hello, hello. Here we are, all suited up and ready to proceed. How splendid!'

'You have no business here, Roth.'

'On the contrary! I have been *ordered* here by none other than the Justice Minister himself!'

'The Justice Ministry has no jurisdiction—'

'Oh, let's not mar this beautiful day with a quarrel over such trivialities.' The face-plate revealed a well-fleshed gentleman with a huge smile. 'And who do we have here?'

'Commander Meishi and three ship's officers. And you are?'

'Forgive my lack of manners! Jurgen Roth, attorney at law and duly sworn officer of the Mars courts. And this is Senior Agent Clara Sousa with the Ministry of Justice.' He beamed at the angry officer. 'And how is my favorite policeman doing this fine day?'

'Senior investigator, as you well know.'

'Well, of course you are.' He aimed his smile at the squat man. 'And your associate is . . .'

When the two men remained silent, Jurgen's associate offered, 'Gupta. Magic Inspectorate.'

'How very curious. No doubt this officer of our newest government department is here to grant your wizard official thanks for doing such a fine job of repairs.' He pretended to search the surroundings. 'But where, pray tell, is your medical officer?'

'An excellent question,' Chris said.

Riggins snapped, 'I am here to arrest a criminal.'

'What an astonishment! Arrest someone who took care of matters that should have been seen to before our new guests arrived!'

'Another outstanding point,' Chris said.

Riggins gestured to Adrian. 'Gupta, arrest him.'

'Point of order, Officer Riggins.' Jurgen Roth's smile did not waver as Sousa stepped between Gupta and Adrian. 'I regret to inform you that your arrest warrant has been rescinded.'

'That's not possible.'

'Countermanded by the Justice Minister! Check your log, sir. See if it is not so.'

'I don't . . .' Riggins lifted his arm, inspected the monitor, and went silent.

'What is more, this entire crew are hereby declared guests of Mister Lambert himself. I assume you have now received that notification as well? How splendid!'

Gupta stepped around to where he could peer at the screen. Both men slumped in unison. Riggins protested, 'They are all quarantined.'

'Actually, inspector or officer, or whatever your title is these days, they are not.' He beamed at Meishi. 'As of this very moment, Commander, Miles Lambert has accepted personal responsibility for your safekeeping.'

Chris started, 'Who is—'

But it was Naxos who stepped forward and said, 'On behalf of myself and all the crew, sir, we thank you most sincerely.'

'Kind of you, sir. Very kind.' He said to Riggins, 'Of course this means you and your most capable associate are hereby free to pursue the *real* criminals. Which must be a relief to two people of your profound abilities. There are, after all, so *many* dangerous elements running amok these days!' He did his best to clap his suited hands. 'Now then! Which of you is the wizard?'

'I am, sir. Adrian Capstan.'

'Splendid! Come along, won't you. We must be off.'

When the attorney turned and started toward the massive vehicle, Chris demanded, 'Wait, what . . .'

She was halted by two actions that came almost simultaneously. Naxos gripped her arm, and the lawyer's associate stepped in so close that their face-plates touched. Sousa told Chris, 'This is your get-out-of-jail card. Use it while you still can.'

'But . . .'

'The wizard comes with us.' Sousa started toward their crawler. 'You. Capstan. Let's move.'

TWENTY-NINE

There were worse ways to take his first ride over the Martian landscape, Adrian reflected, than inside a limo the size of a house.

OK, a small house. But still.

'Can I ask where you're taking me?'

'You can ask anything you like, young man! Anything at all!' Jurgen Roth was an actor by nature. His jovial manner struck Adrian as not so much false as a useful tool. Roth did not try to lie through his smile. He simply expected to get his way and saw no need to add muscle to his requests. 'We have a rather urgent matter to take care of. Soon as that is completed, you may join your friends. How does that sound?'

'Thank you for releasing me and the crew.'

'My pleasure, may I call you Adrian? The joy that brought me, you cannot imagine. Twisting the tail of that sanctimonious, over-blown policeman and his bully of an accomplice. I am in your debt!'

His associate, Clara Sousa, was a knife-edged woman who only pretended at ease. Her eyes matched her short-cropped hair, dark and holding the tight coppery glint of someone trained to take aim and never miss. 'They'll make you pay for that.'

'They will most certainly try! That's what they're best at, no?' Roth was dressed in a rich man's version of a singlet, with tapered lines that almost masked his ample pouch. He bounced in his chair like a happy child. 'I can't tell you how much I enjoy doing battle with the likes of those two.'

They were seated in the Rolligon's dome, a palatial lounge on wheels. Adrian felt as if he was on the upper deck of a desert yacht, designed and constructed with no concern whatsoever for cost. Far below his globular perch, six massive tires spun up clouds of dust as they jounced and jostled across the uneven terrain. But up here, all was stable, utterly smooth, glorious.

Jurgen Roth said, 'You mentioned a question?'

He selected one from dozens. 'Who is Mister Lambert?'

'Miles Lambert, young man, is a living legend. He started as a prospector and hit gold, both literally and figuratively.'

'Lambert was the first miner to utilize wizards,' the woman said.

'Indeed so. Until then, there was an unending debate over whether this force or power that some claimed to possess was anything more than the Mars version of a parlor trick. But Miles saw potential here. He harnessed the force, he hunted, he succeeded, and in the process he made himself one of the richest men on two planets.'

'Miles Lambert is also ambitious,' Sousa added. 'He invested his wealth, and now he's one of the planet's most powerful people. With enemies to match.'

Adrian asked, 'What does he want with me?'

'A worthy question. May I interrupt the flow with one of my own?' When Adrian nodded, he went on, 'You just arrived in that plague-ridden ship, correct? How often have you visited Mars before?'

'This is my first trip.'

'Under this name, of course. But you know very well what I mean. When were you here, and what name did you use?'

'I've never been to Mars before.'

Jurgen showed a momentary irritation. 'Come, come, young man. An erstwhile wizard simply doesn't plonk himself down on Mars and fashion the sort of magic you've accomplished.'

'Word is out regarding your renovating the quarantine zone. Those who know talk about nothing else,' Sousa confirmed. 'Sooner or later the truth is going to emerge. Who you were before, and why did you run?'

'Look around you,' Jurgen said. 'You have been plucked from the direst of possible fates. Those two officers intended to imprison you, and do their best to ensure you remained in captivity until they had wrung from you every secret you did not even know you possessed.'

'One of the most powerful men on the planet is now your official patron,' Sousa said. 'All we ask in return is the truth.'

Adrian found it easier to talk while watching the landscape. Empty, endless, a greyish-pink world holding silence and danger and mystery. A suitable vista for relating how he came to be where he was now. Seated in pristine luxury, traveling across the arid plain.

He told them about the dreams. What it meant in those hard early years. How it came over and over, anchoring him to the promise of a better life. One that felt real now. Watching wind-carved cliffs rising to either side of their valley plain. Great wheels spinning dust clouds behind them. Racing toward a future he could not name.

When he was done, the silence was amplified by the wheels' soft hum.

Finally Jurgen asked, 'Have you ever heard the like?'

'Never,' Sousa replied. 'That is . . .'

'What?'

'There have been rumors,' she replied. 'I assumed it was little more than idle gossip.'

'About this one?'

'Not exactly.' She hesitated, then said, 'You know Odell?'

Jurgen frowned. 'The name only. She's part of your circle, no?'

'It's not *my* anything. Odell has often spoken about using her far-seeing abilities to search for potential wizards on Earth. But with the need for secrecy, I've never actually heard if she's succeeded in bringing anyone to Mars.'

'So you believe this outlandish tale of his?'

'Look at what we're dealing with,' she replied. 'A ship's crew became the prime minister's latest tool to use against Earth. They were caged in a quarantine zone designed to have them begging for help. Instead, the officer monitoring their cage reports that the dome suddenly emerged from a major storm utterly pristine. Good as new.' When Jurgen remained silent, she pressed, 'You obviously believe him, else we wouldn't be racing to the port, intent on doing the impossible.'

'I believe he is a wizard,' Jurgen replied. 'But this? A stranger to Mars is guided by interplanetary dreams, and spends his young life preparing?'

Clara leaned forward. 'Adrian, can I take your fingerprints?'

'Of course.'

'Fingerprints can be altered,' Jurgen pointed out. 'As you know full well.'

'Blood, then. A DNA sample. That OK with you, Adrian?'

'Sure.'

Clara settled back. 'Does that sound like a man with something to hide?'

'Everything I hear both confounds and mystifies.' Jurgen ran both hands through his salt-and-pepper hair. 'Then again, such a mystery as this may be precisely what we need just now.'

Clara went back to scouting the terrain. 'There you go.'

'Something to jostle the status quo. Poke the government, force them off their complacent little perch.'

Adrian started to ask what they meant, when the cliffs to his left faded and lowered and joined the plain, revealing . . .

'What is *that*?'

'Takes your breath away, doesn't it?' Clara agreed.

Adrian stood by the glass now, drawn to his feet by the sight.

Skeletal remains of a pod jutted skywards, a stark and silent ruin. The behemoth stood at a cadaver's angle, rising to a tangled mass of girders that stabbed the sky.

He had read about the revolt that had almost halted his dreams, the fierce battle that risked demolishing mankind's only successful planetary colony. How Mars's government until that point had been dominated by appointees shipped over from Earth, temporary assignments, and driven by paramount goals. Supply the rare-earth minerals that Earth desperately needed. Keep the profits for the regimes on Earth. Maintain a strict monopoly on trade. Everything shipped to Mars was charged onerous customs duties, and these revenues remained Earthside as well.

The revolt changed all that.

The problems did not simply vanish, however. The destroyed pod stood as a monument to the struggle that was still ongoing, the rage simmering just beneath the surface.

Adrian remained by the glass, tracking the pod, until Sousa announced, 'Heads up. We've arrived.'

The Mars landscape held some similarities to the empty desert reaches around Phoenix. Cliffs and hills were carved here by wind and time. Not water. Shapes were drawn in drastic edgy lines that defied logic. Storms over thousands of years had etched their way deep into defiles that went nowhere. Plains and valleys were covered by a shale that reflected sunlight with artistic precision.

The destroyed pod was still visible over the ridge, separating it from the planet's main spaceport. Those jagged steel girders rose like fingers of warning, pointing toward an uncertain future.

Their Rolligon halted well away from the main landing site, granting Adrian a chance to see the structure in its entirety.

MarsPort was not an inviting place. The vast structure was

nowhere near as bad as Q. But even from this distance, Adrian could see it was headed in the same direction.

The MarsPort had formed the only poster he'd carried from one foster home to the next. Only those photographs had shone with artistic brilliance. The facility was divided into five domes, holding customs and ore awaiting shipment, incoming goods and arriving immigrants. These encircled a central structure designed as an alien lighthouse. It rose tall and fairy-like, with lights that ran up the curving edges, spinning in smooth beauty, climbing to a brilliant beacon atop the highest point. Its base formed two cradles, steel arms ready to accept the pods and MarsPort's new arrivals. Making them not just welcome, but offering the assurance that here, on Mars, man had made a home.

No longer.

One central cradle was empty, the other held a pod. But the entire facility appeared void of life and activity. Numerous crawlers stood silent and motionless by massive airlocks. Less than half of the central structure's lights still functioned. They flickered with feeble defiance to the passage of storms and time.

Adrian again found himself grateful for the Gamma virus and how it meant his ship had not landed here. He stared through the limo's bubble top and remembered the long, lonely nights lying in his childhood bed, staring at the shadowy poster, lost in the dream of landing in MarsPort. Finally.

He asked softly, not really expecting an answer, 'What happened?'

Jurgen took that as a reason to rise and stand beside him. 'We suspect the central structure's plasteel was not up to grade. During the revolt, we were struck by five of the biggest storms on record. Even then we might have returned it to its former beauty. We would have. Except those cretins who took power *wanted* to showcase a ruin.'

Sousa warned, 'Take great care, Jurgen. Even here.'

'Cretins I said and cretins I meant.'

'Keep it up, Counselor, I'll be duty bound to report you.'

'Cretins.'

Adrian stated the obvious, 'You want me to restore this.'

'Can you?'

'I have no idea.' But what he felt was a thrill so intense his body actually vibrated. Shimmering like water touched by an unexpected wind. He stared at the near-wreck of a structure and felt the draw, the *potential*, of returning it to the state that had carried him through so many hard hours. 'Possibly.'

'Will you try?' When Adrian remained silent, Roth pressed, 'We will pay you, young man. And pay handsomely.'

'Why now?' Adrian remained by the glass, studying them in the reflection, two faces imprinted upon the Martian landscape. When Roth looked at the woman and did not respond, he pressed, 'There has to be a reason for this haste—'

'We have at great cost and effort used this one brief moment to completely clear out the port,' Roth said. 'The newly unloaded pod remains empty because the ore it is scheduled to take back has not arrived. Payments have been made, schedules changed. All the goods imported from Earth have cleared customs and been carted away. One shift has departed, the next has not arrived; why should it since there is nothing—'

'That's not what I'm asking and you know it.'

Roth continued to watch the woman from Justice, as if seeking her help. Sousa said, 'Now would be the time to make your demands.'

'Answers,' Adrian replied. 'I need to understand.'

'Very well.' Roth stepped in closer. 'I give you my word. Everything you wish to know, everything that is in my power to explain, Clara and I will do so.'

'But not now,' Sousa said. 'We can't.'

'The cretins in power will do everything they can to keep MarsPort exactly as you see it,' Roth said. His words accelerated now, pressing hard. 'This structure was designed and built and financed by Miles Lambert, who then leased it to the government. Miles is also the current regime's most powerful opponent. To those cretins, a demolished spaceport in this wretched state is precisely the warning they want to show Earth.'

'Once they know what we're trying to do,' Sousa said, 'this window of opportunity closes.'

'The lackeys we just bested are currently shrieking their news back to the very same officials who would like nothing more than to see you buried in a very deep hole,' Roth said.

Adrian nodded to his own reflection. This was what he had been after all along, though he had not actually put it into words.

Allies.

'Then I should get started. How close can I get to the center?'

Sousa rose from her chair. 'Define close.'

'The other two times I've done this spell, I stood right in the middle of what I was trying to accomplish.'

Now that it was happening, Jurgen showed a fretful face. 'Truly, you've only just arrived on Mars? Never been here before?'

'He's already answered that,' Clara shot back. 'Adrian, do you need to be alone?'

'I don't understand.'

'Timing,' she said. 'Seconds. Can we drive you there?'

'Absolutely, I guess.'

'Definitely, maybe,' Clara grinned for the first time. 'Works for me.'

THIRTY

The driver took a tunnel used for transporting ore to the pods. They emerged into the Mars light between the empty cradle and the central pillar. Up close the damage and wear was all too evident. The plaza was rimmed by miniature structures meant to mirror the lighthouse. But most were reduced to states only slightly better than the destroyed pod.

Adrian was suited up and standing by the airlock when they halted. He had no idea whether being inside one structure, while trying to cast another version of his rewind spell over a second larger space, even mattered. But it seemed best to mimic what had already been proven to work.

In the end, they all came because he asked. The driver's name was Franklin, a silent dark-skinned man with the easy falseness of a born killer. He stood slightly removed from them, scouting the terrain via a handheld device similar to what Naxos had used. Roth demanded, 'Anything?'

'All clear, boss.'

'We're down to final seconds,' Clara warned.

Adrian took a breath, bonded with the planet upon which he stood, and began.

There were several differences this time. The storm resulting from his rewind spell was massive. The lightning was more pronounced, an almost continuous force that threaded through the tempest like it was lacing the dust together. The three people, Roth and Clara and Franklin, shouted their fear or astonishment, whatever. Louder and louder they yelled, or so it seemed to Adrian. Far more continuous than the ship's crew, who had all previously been aided through the dread Gamma illness by his hand.

Then it no longer mattered. None of it. Not the storm, the bursts of electric flame, their fear, nothing.

Adrian became so enmeshed with the force that he couldn't even hear his own words. Perhaps he stopped speaking aloud. He had no idea.

He felt as if he was being split in two. One minor segment

remained standing there at the lighthouse's base, waving his arms and completing the spell.

The other rose up. Higher and higher, until he was poised above the storm, atop the pillar, looking down at the maelstrom now covering all five domes. And something more. The lightning came from him. He was the focal point. At least, this disembodied portion of himself. The encircling wall of dust and debris, the explosive streaks of power, all originated here. From him. In him.

Then it was over.

He stood where he had been standing. The others turned and gaped at a structure transformed. Silent. Awestruck.

He wanted to join them. See the spaceport as he had envisioned. Back in the hard days and nights when the central beacon drove him to focus on a life beyond the immediate.

But just then he did not have the strength to remain upright.

'Adrian?'

He collapsed to the ground. He had one glimpse of the beautiful miniature sculptures forming a Martian desert garden. Then he was gone.

THIRTY-ONE

Adrian was alone in the vehicle's dome. The lawyer and the Justice agent were downstairs, leaning into the driver's cabin, the three of them laughing and chattering about something he could not be bothered to hear. Adrian had not actually requested a few minutes alone. But they had offered it anyway, sensing his need during this gradual resumption of normal functions. They had stripped off his suit, Roth and Clara and the driver, Franklin. Adrian had only been partially aware of events as the three of them maneuvered his sorry carcass up the staircase and into the dome. Settling him into the chair, and leaving him there. Happy to be alone.

The sun was a dim glowing bulb, just shy of what Adrian assumed was the western horizon. It lit up his work like a carefully placed spotlight.

The seven domes of MarsPort shone a burnished copper. Lights of large transport vehicles, segmented like insects back on Earth, drifted across the darkening landscape. And over it all shone a fairy-like structure. The lights embedded within the steel lighthouse spiraled as they raced up, a beacon that was both utterly alien and yet beautifully human. It was, Adrian decided, an almost ideal way to welcome immigrants to mankind's outpost on Mars.

He was filled with a lassitude so potent he felt poured into his chair. He watched as Clara emerged from the staircase, holding a two-handled mug with a sealed top and drinking tube. It looked like something an invalid might have used Earthside. 'How are you doing, sport?'

He liked the sound of her voice, the easy familiarity, the happiness in her gaze. 'Coming around.'

'That's what we like to hear.' She handed him the mug. 'This might help.'

Adrian took a tentative sip, and actually groaned with pleasure. 'What *is* this?'

'You really are a newbie. Slow down, that's strong stuff. Too much at once and it's liable to blow the top of your head off.'

'This stuff is amazing!'

The hard lines to Clara's face were not erased. But the edges were softened, as was the sniper's glint to her gaze, revealing a softer element. One that found genuine humor in watching Adrian pull on the drinking tube. 'Take one more sip. OK, now you need to wait a while. It's not going anywhere, and you should pace yourself.' She nodded approval when he settled the cup in his lap. Reluctantly. 'Sometimes after a hard gig, I think maybe that first hit is the finest, sweetest moment on Mars.'

'What is it?'

'Wizard's brew. Don't ask me what it contains.' She started for the stairs. 'Every recipe is different, all of them secret. Remember now. A dozen breaths between each swallow.'

'Clara, wait.' When she turned around, he hefted the mug. 'Does this mean you're a wizard?'

She studied him a long moment, then said, 'Answers to some questions carry a lot of red flags. You understand?'

'Not really, no.'

'Say I was to answer yes. Say the news got out. I'd lose my job, my professional standing, my chance to work with Miles. Understand now?'

'I won't say anything. It's just . . .'

'What?'

'I've never met another mage before.'

Her sniper's intent was back full force. 'And you haven't met one now. Got it?' She started down the stairs.

He took another exquisite sip and resumed his inspection of the world beyond the dome. They were parked in a place so ideal, Adrian wondered if perhaps it had been designed for this particular purpose. So this huge luxury vehicle could tuck itself away, sheltered from any stray windstorm, and enjoy the view. The miniature cave stood on a rise perhaps five kilometers from the spaceport. Adrian couldn't properly gauge distances on this planet, but he thought that was about right. The bowl-shaped shelter stood about a third of the way up a ridge directly opposite MarsPort. From this vantage point, the sheer enormity of what he had accomplished was on full display.

Then Franklin called from the driver's cubby, '*Incoming!*'

A few moments passed, then Adrian noticed the low-flying insect that inserted itself into the otherwise pristine sunset. But in his magically exhausted and totally zoned-out state, he was tempted to accept it as part of the moment.

The black dot wobbled slightly, caught in some sunset wind. Then it straightened and kept coming.

Down below, Jurgen asked nervously, 'Are you certain? It looks like just another . . .'

Then the drone grew a tail.

'*Brace! Brace!*'

A missile shot across the distance. Impossibly fast. And suddenly their shelter became a trap.

Adrian played the gawping tourist. Staring at the rocket, immobile, until . . .

The missile struck.

The impact made no sound. But the atmosphere surrounding their vehicle seemed to go *sproing*. The air shimmered. The explosive flash spread like some poisonous and dying bloom, until there was nothing else in front of the vehicle, only fire.

The explosion faded . . .

The rocks fell. The entire cliff face spilled on top of their vehicle. Or rather, it would have, except for the shield. Stones and boulders struck the shield like a billion desert raindrops, the circles radiating out, then . . .

Nothing.

Sousa shouted, 'Get us *out* of here!'

'On it.' Their driver, Franklin, nudged the rock pile, again, a third time, gently shoving his way forward, pushing the rubble over the cliff's edge.

But the trail they had followed to climb up was no more. Which meant . . .

'Hang on.'

Adrian thought they were going to topple over. But Franklin was a pro. He slithered and danced the massive vehicle down the ridge's nearly vertical slope. Faster and faster and faster, the shadow-surface racing toward them. At the very last moment he tilted slightly, so the three right tires met the surface.

When they were stable and racing across the surface, Sousa shouted, 'Adrian! A little help here!'

Adrian was still far from being fully connected to his limbs and brain. Even so, Clara's shrill plea jolted him from the chair. He managed the circular staircase because he had to, and entered the driver's cubby.

The bulbous front windscreen showed them racing full-bore across the Martian plain. Their multiple headlights sliced through gathering shadows, revealing an uneven surface blurred by their speed. Franklin was seated in the right-hand chair, Jurgen beside him, Clara leaning over the co-pilot. There was something in the way Clara stood, one shoulder slouched over like she'd taken a punch to her ribs, that fully reconnected Adrian to the moment and the danger.

Franklin hunched down, his entire body clenched, then he announced, 'Two more are inbound.'

Jurgen had entirely lost his joviality. The lawyer was quiet, focused, calm in a manner that only heightened the threat. He searched the two monitor screens and said, 'I can't see a thing.'

'They're there.' Franklin pushed the massive vehicle faster still.

Clara demanded, 'How far out?'

'I make it ten and a half klicks. Closing fast.'

Jurgen asked, 'Clara, can you shield us again?'

'An indirect strike, maybe. But I'm an hour from full recharge. More.' She glanced over. 'Adrian, can you . . .?'

'I have no weapons spell. None.'

'Here they are.' Jurgen then pointed to a different spot on the central monitor. 'A third drone is inbound.'

'We're in trouble,' Clara said. To Adrian, 'Suit up, fast as you can—'

Jurgen said, 'Missile away.'

Clara hunched her shoulders, lifted one arm in a gesture that resembled a broken wing. Creased her features in desperate concentration.

'Ten seconds.'

There was no time to think. Adrian's response was visceral, far below the level of logic or thought. It came from somewhere much deeper, a reaction of his lizard brain to incoming death.

He gripped Clara's outstretched hand and cast the sixth spell.

When he had first come across this particular brand of magic, and then bonded with it so powerfully, his reaction had been incredulity. Was someone telling a joke three thousand years in the making?

His name for this sixth spell was one word.

Joining.

At the time, nothing about this had made any sense. So much so that when he had experienced the bone-deep resonance, Adrian had been tempted to ignore it anyway. What possible purpose could it offer? Join with another wizard? And do what? Why even bother? Especially since he could stand at a distance, cast the far-seeing spell, and remain internally intact. Because the one warning this spell's introduction had made mightily clear was . . .

It worked both ways.

As in, the other spell-caster could peer inside him.

After spending a lifetime hiding his secret aims? Pu-lease.

But this was crunch time. Life or death. And if he kept to his solitary role, remained a lone spell-caster, they would all be dead in . . .

'Five seconds.'

He shouted the spell. Screamed. A rapid-fire incandescent flame of words.

Time stopped.

At least that was how it appeared. Suddenly Adrian had the temporal space to understand how Clara's magic required a much longer period between spells. Which meant they would soon be just more Martian rubble when the next missiles struck.

Except for one thing.

Adrian now had all her powers there at his behest. So long as she allowed him to reach inside . . .

Sousa welcomed him.

He had no idea if she was actually conscious of this act. But it seemed to him that she was opening an internal portal, allowing him to see . . .

Her arsenal.

There were four spells at her disposal. All but one were accurate close in. Rifle-shot spells intended to be used, aimed at one specific target, then afterwards the wizard needed to wait and recharge.

The fourth was different. In Clara's act of opening up, revealing, sharing, Adrian felt as if she too was pointing this one out.

Storms.

There was no actual pause or space between their joining and Adrian's application of her fourth spell. He simply kept shouting.

He watched with the others as a giant fist of dust and debris rose up and *slammed* into the missile.

The fist unfurled and became a solid grey sheet, a wall that halted the drone and second missile simultaneously. Adrian knew because the debris curtain became briefly illuminated by two harsh flares.

Adrian found himself guided by what Jurgen and Franklin viewed in the central monitor. Two further drones. Missiles.

Thwarted.

Another drone, more missiles, all of them enveloped and consumed.

The merger with Clara's magical arsenal was so intense, the energy drain so swift, Adrian felt himself drawn toward an empty void. It would have been such a simple act to release the hold on himself and drift away. Falling into the nothingness of no-self.

Instead, he let go of Clara's hand.

He thought Jurgen's voice sounded incredibly weak, shaky. 'All clear.'

This time, the darkness's assault was almost violent.

THIRTY-TWO

When Adrian drew the world back into focus, he lay on a bunk in the vehicle's main chamber. Four sleeping alcoves lined one side, overlooking an oval table with eight swivel chairs similar to those upstairs, and beyond that was a fully equipped kitchenette. Plus a bar, crystal glasses, drinks cabinet, and what appeared to be an entertainment center. Sousa sat at the table's head. Jurgen bent over something on the stove. A huge window dominated the vehicle's rear. But there was nothing to see. Black night, reflections. He could tell they were moving from the soft jounces and the hum of tires.

He heard Sousa say, 'Leave the bags in there a while longer.'

'You've had ten teabags steeping in this tiny little pot for an hour.'

'Six bags, ten minutes.'

'This brew is already so strong it will dissolve the spoon.'

Clara was evidently feeling the same lassitude that blanketed Adrian, for her head was back against the seat, her arms and legs limp. 'OK, pour in the honey and condensed milk. Now the cinnamon and nutmeg and lemon.'

'Yuck.'

'You don't have to drink it. You just make it. Are you sure there isn't any absinthe?'

'This is a crawler. On Mars. No absinthe.'

'Correction. This is a crawler with a bar. And all the spices of a decent restaurant. OK, then pour in the bourbon. Not too much. That's good. Bring it here.'

Sousa made a genuine effort and straightened in her chair.

'You need my help?'

'No.' She took the pot, held it close to her face, shut her eyes, and whispered. Then, 'A mug, if you please.'

Adrian ungummed his mouth and said, 'Make that two.'

Roth winked in his direction, clearly enjoying himself, and asked Clara, 'Did you just cast a spell over my teapot?'

'A little something my grandmother taught me. No, Jurgen. Don't you dare taste, it'll turn you into a frog.'

'Wizards have all the fun.' He helped Adrian shift over to a chair by the table. 'Isn't that right, young man.'

'I haven't been one long enough to know.'

If anything, the brew's impact was even stronger. Adrian had to fight against the urge to drain his mug and ask for more. He followed Clara's example and sipped, breathed, breathed, breathed, sipped.

Clara said, 'I suppose now's the time to speak the words. What on earth was that?'

'I call it a spell of joining.' Another sip. 'Did you, I'm not sure how to ask this. Feel anything?'

'You mean, like somebody stepped inside my private space. Yes, sport. I felt it.'

'What I meant was, it felt as if you let me in.'

Clara hid in her mug, then, 'Panic.'

Adrian nodded. 'Panic sure works for me.'

Jurgen cleared his throat. 'As someone who is immensely fond of his own skin—'

'And his own voice,' Clara said.

'Don't be rude. Thank you, Adrian. I am in your debt.'

Through the driver's open doorway, Franklin called back, 'That makes two of us.'

Clara said, more softly than the others, 'Three.'

Franklin must have called ahead, because when they pulled through the tunnel airlock and entered the largest interior space Adrian had ever seen, Chris was there. Smiling. Ready to embrace him the instant the portal opened.

Finally she released him and told the others, 'That's the biggest car I've ever seen.'

'It's a Mars-sized car. Hello, young lady. I am Jurgen Roth. We met briefly. This is Clara Sousa, and the gentleman locking down our oversized limo is Grady Franklin.'

'Hi. I'm Chris.'

'Doctor Leighton,' Adrian corrected.

'Chris Leighton. My stars.' Jurgen was at his charming best. 'All of Marsopolis talks of the good doctor who descends from the heavens, heals everyone within reach, then leaves us all bereft when she returns to her far-flung home.'

'Oh, please,' Clara said.

Chris asked, 'Did Adrian really work his magic on the spaceport?'

'Word is already out,' Clara said. 'Is that good or bad?'

'It's inevitable, is what it is.' Jurgen told Chris, 'I have just witnessed a transformation that dwarfs even our limo.'

'Your man did good,' Clara agreed.

'Outstanding.' She pulled on Adrian's hand. 'You'll have to excuse me. I'm due on shift and I want to show him around.'

They took what to Adrian looked like a golf cart with bulbous wheels. They needed to, because the Lambert compound was as big as a fair-sized town back on Earth. That was actually how many inhabitants of Marsopolis referred to the place. Lambertville.

Some said it with envy, even hostility. Others with respect. A few spoke the word in aspirational tones, as in, someday they might themselves become rich enough to own their own domes. Plural. Three of them. The main Lambert residence was off-limits unless or until Adrian was invited in. The vast structure where they started included its very own hydroponics farm, maintenance, reclamation and storage. The third dome held offices, staff housing and guest quarters. So many it could easily absorb all forty-nine of the ship's crew.

He learned all this as Chris spun through the domes and connecting tunnels at a breathless pace. He would have called it reckless, except for how everyone he saw drove even faster. Chris showed the excitement of a young child as she related how their quarantine restrictions were a thing of the past. Anyone with a shred of medical training knew the post-infection Gamma transmission risk was zero. Nada. Yet another Justice memorandum had restored their freedom. Temporary IDs had been issued to each crew, thanks to Miles Lambert himself, and they were now free to roam the city.

Chris related how Naxos had described it as a bold, in-your-face defiance of the current regime. Something only a man as powerful as Miles Lambert could pull off. He was now personally invested in their well-being, thanks to the man of the hour. None other than Adrian Capstan.

The breathless tour ended in the staff dome's main lounge area, a haven large as a city park, replete with blooming flowers, stunted trees, cobblestone boulevards, fountains and birds. The feathered immigrants flitted about, singing, chirping, filling the air with a music Adrian feared he might never hear again.

Chris ignored a number of crewmates who grinned as she kissed him hard, handed him a packet with ID and credit-ring and keypass for his quarters. Her parting words were as hurried as her driving. How she had hoped for a longish private hour instead of a quick ta-da tour, rushed instructions on how to find their apartment, and off. But she always served as visiting doctor upon landfall. As soon as her name appeared on the list of crew released from Q, she had been assigned a regular shift at the city's main hospital. For which she was now late. 'I'm so sorry.'

'It's OK, Chris. I understand. I'm happy you're involved here.'

'Which I can only assume means you're happy I have to run. I'm not sure how I feel about that. Maybe we should discuss happy after my shift.'

He eased himself off the passenger seat. Even standing still proved taxing. 'I wouldn't mind a rest and a meal. I've had a hard shift myself.'

Her response was to rush around and hug him again. 'You should hear what people are saying about you and MarsPort.'

He decided news about what happened after could wait. 'Careful with the merchandise. I'm in a fragile state.'

'I'll give you fragile.' She embraced him harder still. 'I'll be back soon as I can.'

Another kiss, and she was off.

THIRTY-THREE

After Chris left, he decided to shower first, then rest, then eat. The order was determined mostly by Sousa and her wizard's brew. The drink's energy still zinged, and apparently cut off any real interest in food.

Adrian's guest quarters were, in a word, palatial. Large bedchamber, kitchenette, dining space for two, grand bath. The floors and many walls were tiled in polished rose-gray Martian stone. All in a city where rent for even the most minuscule of live-in closets was astronomical.

Bad joke.

A teckie whose life Adrian had helped save during the Phoenix lockdown had accessed several supposedly private Mars-based chatrooms. The teckie had assumed it was Adrian's means of escape during the Gamma crisis. Which was at least partly true. Adrian had spent hours trolling through their discussions, offering a few comments of his own, but mostly reading and yearning.

Rent, housing, water, medicines, food. The five crisis points for most families.

He knew nothing about the current political situation because that was precisely what he read. Nothing. No comments, no quips, nada.

Rents were so high, young single staffers complained over how hard it was to fully unfold a bed and sleep with their door closed.

Yet here he was, guest of the man a number of these discussions had referred to as a legend. A living myth. Miles Lambert had not been seen for years. Yet his imprint remained firmly fixed on the planet's pulse. Being hired by the Lambert group in even the most menial positions, moving into the Lambert staff quarters, was a major cause for celebration. And envy. And genuine hostility. Friendships and burgeoning love affairs had often been ended over someone, as was often put, going Lambert. The amount of rage expressed at times baffled him. How relationships and families became fractured over somebody taking a new job.

Why it mattered so, what the real reasons behind such poisonous responses were, no one said.

And here he was, stretching out on an oversized double bed, in private quarters larger than his studio flat back in Phoenix.

He drifted. He knew he was asleep, but remained comfortably cocooned in a safe, quiet space. He almost surfaced several times, then drifted back into dreams of rose-colored sunsets and planetary sculptures that writhed and danced like they were alive.

Just as he started to rise into full wakefulness, Adrian had a new kind of dream.

It was similar to those about Mars, in that he was both fully aware and engaged. In almost every other aspect, however, it was markedly different. Jarringly so.

He was not transported. Instead, he was simply *there*. Standing in the Arizona high desert, on a path leading from Sedona into the painted hills. He could almost smell the aromas of creosote and desert sage and heat, but suspected this was a play of memory, for Adrian had spent many hours hiking these reaches. The sky was a pale blue wash, a desert color that came the hour before sunrise and again for fleeting moments at dusk.

Adrian was utterly confounded by the image. He had no idea what it meant, or why he was here. Back where he had spent the better part of his entire life struggling to escape.

He remained standing there, waiting for some message, answer, concept. Something. But finally he felt himself journeying back to the comfort of a luxurious chamber, where he opened his eyes and found himself standing by the bed. Panting breaths that sawed in his ears. Like he had run the race of his lifetime. Rushing back to where he belonged. Fleeing Earth and whatever this strange dream might mean.

The food hall was large enough to hold several hundred people. Some were eating in noisy, boisterous groups. There were also a number of families, and others working their way through a solitary meal with tablets or spreadsheets for company. It was a busy place, and Adrian sensed a good energy. Focused and intent, but calm. He thought most of these people were happy to be here.

The set-up reminded him of a mid-level restaurant back stateside, but magnified. Booths lined the walls, longer tables filled the central space, and cloth-backed partitions and focused lighting offered a clear sense of separation.

Two very distinct branches dominated the rear wall. One side was a fresh-food market, people shopping and then going home to cook. He saw packages of tofu and the Mars versions of veggie meat substitutes. Slanted shelves offered a considerable variety of produce.

Adrian opted for the second line. The aromas were exquisite, but all he faced were a series of automated screens. The prices meant nothing. The selection process reminded him of dining in Oriental restaurants, where pictures showed what unfamiliar dishes looked like.

Clara Sousa stepped up beside him. 'Hungry?'

'Starving. How do . . .'

'Let me. What are you in the mood for? The syn-steaks here are pretty good.'

'Great.'

'Salad, greens . . .'

'Yes and yes.' He watched her operate the controls, then added tea and a chocolaty dessert. All she took for herself was coffee. When Clara started to press her thumb-ring to the blinking Pay dot, he said, 'I should pay.'

'Forget it. We're on the company dime here.'

He followed her to the long line of delivery slots, watched her touch the thumb-ring a second time, and accepted the tray when it appeared. He followed her back into the main hall. 'I thought you worked for the Ministry of Justice.'

'I wear several hats.' As she started to slip into the booth opposite, her pocket chimed. She pulled out a comm-link, checked the screen, said, 'I have to scoot. Shouldn't be long. Listen, we need . . .' Her phone chimed a second time. 'Don't go anywhere. Soon as you're done, we need to do a thing. It's urgent. Stay here. I'll be back . . .'

She was gone.

The food was excellent. Adrian took his time, savoring his first real meal on Mars. Not in Q, not prepared and transported a hundred and forty million miles, not tasting of the plastic packaging. Real Mars food. Grown, harvested, cooked. The steak was especially good.

A few of the crew stopped by, asking how he was, saying they'd heard good things about his MarsPort work, general chit-chat. No one stayed very long. These people were accustomed to granting shipmates privacy, even in cramped and crowded confines. Adrian was polite, friendly, but not welcoming. He had a lot to think about.

The solitude was important. Necessary. He went back over that last waking dream. The vivid nature was something that before he had only experienced when drawn here. To Marsopolis. And always with a final one-word message, a confirmation of its importance. A promise of things to come.

His concern was clear enough. He worried if the dream was a message intended to bind him, take him back, show what was yet to unfold. It was a definite possibility. Which would have been enormously troubling, except for how that particular concept did not feel right. There was no harmony at gut level. No sense of being left with a need to prepare. Or do something to make it happen. Nothing like that.

He liked having a chance to dwell on this. Take his time. He did not expect to come upon an answer. It was enough to open himself to possible—

'May I join you?' Chris did not wait for a reply. 'How do you like the food?'

'It's almost as great as my room.' He pushed his tray to one side and reached across the table for her hand. 'I think I'll stay here a while.'

'Given how they're talking about you and what you did to MarsPort, I imagine you'd be welcome here for years.'

'Who is they?'

She waved her free hand. 'Everybody.' She offered an impish smile. 'Maybe you should give me a tour of your quarters.'

'I thought you had duty.'

'Nobody's sick today. Can you imagine? This huge great city, big hospital full of empty beds. All the staff just sitting around playing checkers. I got bored and left.'

'Liar.'

'I begged. They moaned. I left anyway. End of story.'

He loved watching her like this. Just another couple enjoying a little downtime. Being public with their affection. 'Clara says I need to do something with her.'

'And Clara is . . .'

'One of the two people who took me to MarsPort. Clara Sousa, Ministry of Justice. She says it's urgent.'

'Tell her you're sick. I'll write you a note.'

'I don't think . . . Here she comes now.'

He started to pull his hand away, but Chris held fast. Turning so as to meet the approaching woman head-on.

Clara arrived at one pace off running, her strides adapted to the low gravity, more of a sliding-and-gripping-and-slide. She took careful note of their clasped hands and Chris's expression, then said, 'We need to be going.' When they remained planted in the booth, she said, 'Adrian, we're running late.'

'I'd like Chris to come. If she wants.'

'I do. Very much. Where are we going?'

Clara started to respond, the sharp negative there in her stance, gaze, the works. But she checked herself, which took some effort. 'There is a group of senior wizards known as the Circle. They want to meet Adrian.'

'OK.'

'This isn't the official council. That one was disbanded for taking part in the revolt. This group is . . . different. Older.'

Adrian asked, 'Are you saying Chris can't come?'

She studied them both, then, 'To tell the truth, I have absolutely no idea.'

Adrian released her hand and slipped from the booth. 'So let's go.'

THIRTY-FOUR

C lara drove them in a buggy identical to the one Chris had used for her too-brief tour. Sousa's driving was astonishingly bad. So awful, in fact, Adrian would have insisted on walking. Only he had no idea where they were going.

Twice uniformed officers stepped into the vehicular-traffic lanes and flagged Sousa, ordering her to stop. Clara responded by holding up her badge and accelerating. Adrian found a distinct comfort in knowing he was not the only one who considered Clara borderline suicidal.

Chris, on the other hand, appeared utterly unfazed.

He had fleeting impressions of a city laid out beneath a series of arena-sized bubbles. The periphery, back where they emerged from the main Lambertville connecting tunnel, was mostly low-strung structures, not well kept, warehouses and hydroponics and manufacturing. But he couldn't be certain of anything. The buildings and pedestrians and other vehicles formed blurry pastels to either side.

Chris exclaimed, 'Isn't this fun?'

Adrian decided to wait until they had stopped to inform her that he was walking back.

They zinged through another tunnel and entered a realm of broad thoroughfares and grandiose buildings. Clara accelerated even further, then took a squealing right turn and zipped down a narrow lane.

She stopped in front of a shop with crowded glass windows and the gilded title, Curios and Curiosities. 'Your acting commander, Meishi, is about to be arrested.'

Chris flashed from joyful to outraged. 'On what charges?'

'Doesn't matter. They've gone after her because she's the officer in charge and they can't get their hands on Adrian.' She tucked the vehicle tight into an alcove, almost but not quite clearing the lane. 'Soon as we're done, Adrian needs to hold up in his quarters until Jurgen can get this sorted out.'

Chris asked, 'Who?'

'The attorney who freed you from the QZ.' She waited impatiently as Adrian unkinked and managed to stand upright. 'Inside.'

The shop was lined with glass-fronted shelves, all of which were crammed with junk. Or so it appeared to Adrian. Antique ornamental tables and ornately carved chairs and free-standing cabinets made the place feel very cramped. Ladders on rollers were connected to both side walls, rising to more shelves holding books and scrolls. Adrian could have spent numerous happy days in this place.

'Straight on,' Clara said. 'Keep moving.'

'Just a moment there.' An older woman was perched on the left-hand ladder. One of the cabinets was open while she dusted. She slipped off reading glasses and let them dangle from a chain around her neck. 'They're expecting just two.'

'This is Doctor Leighton.'

'Who?'

'The ship's medic.'

'Ah.' The woman nodded to the man behind the counter and went back to dusting. 'All right. Let them in.'

The man was short and middle-aged and very alert. He kept one hand hidden beneath the counter. 'Two means two.'

'And I'm telling you it's OK.'

'You should check.'

'I've heard about the good doctor. And you shouldn't keep them waiting. Now let our guests through.'

He lifted his hand, closed a drawer in the counter, then touched something beneath the counter's leading edge. A rear door clicked open. 'It's on your head if they don't like this.'

'You're being tiresome.' She offered Chris a smile as they passed her perch. 'And you are most welcome, Doctor Leighton. It's a pleasure to meet you.'

Behind the shop opened a patio surrounded by high stone walls. Far overhead shone the city's central dome, a translucent structure illuminated by the sun's pale wash. The patio walls were decked out in trellises that held climbing plants, several of which Adrian recognized from Phoenix. Star jasmine, clematis taiga, climbing hydrangea. All of them well adapted to dry climates where water was scarce. Their fragrances formed a sweet welcome.

The courtyard was tiled in the familiar pale stone and inlaid with an octagonal star. The eight tips held symbols Adrian did not recognize.

He knew a tight thrill, standing in a space probably designed for Mars magic.

The people seated on benches lining both side walls were all ages, races, and both sexes. To Adrian's right was a very tall man, a giraffe in human form, whose limbs extended almost halfway across the central design. He asked, 'Is this the one?'

Adrian expected Sousa to reply. But it was a woman at the rear of the courtyard, almost hidden beneath the trellises and their shadows, who replied, 'Indeed so.'

'I thought he'd be older.' The tall man glared at Adrian. 'Or smarter. Something. He looks far too normal to have pulled off what they're claiming.'

One of the other men said, 'Don't be impertinent.'

A slender woman who appeared to be still in her teens said, 'Impertinent is Jacob's middle name.'

A man seated to the teen's left shared the young woman's caramel skin. 'If Jacob couldn't be impertinent he wouldn't be anything at all.'

The teen said, 'Jacob would deflate like a weary balloon. Left with nothing but a vacuum surrounded by floppy skin.'

'I'd like to see that,' the man said. 'Jacob finally reduced to a silent blob that can't be impertinent—'

'We need to be certain,' Jacob snapped. 'Now more than ever.'

The teen said, 'After what he accomplished at MarsPort? What's worse than impertinent? Imbecilic?'

The man seated next to her said, 'Politeness requires us to stop at impertinent.'

'Enough,' the woman at the back of the courtyard rolled her wheelchair forward a trace. 'Come here, young man. My eyes are almost as bad as my limbs, and they are very bad indeed.'

Adrian crossed the octagonal inset. He disliked towering over the woman, so he squatted down, lowering himself to where he could meet her darkly glittering gaze. 'You're the one who called me.'

Her eyes tightened into a smile. 'I did indeed.'

'Thank you for that. So much.'

Her limbs were knotted and twisted by windswept years. She studied him a long moment, sharing his pleasure. 'You're a handsome one. How old are you?'

'Twenty-eight, by Earth years.'

'Which means you first heard me . . .'

'I was nine. It was a terrible time. Your dreams were a gift. And so important.'

She traced unsteady fingers along the edge of her mouth, wiping away the damp. 'Tell me how you came to arrive here so well prepared.'

'That's the right word to describe my life on Earth.' The look she gave him was so intense he could have wept with the aching joy of being here. Kneeling beside her chair. Sharing this moment. 'Prepare. It's what I did to survive. I studied. And I hoped for the chance.'

She pointed back behind him. 'Clara, your sponsor, informs us that you served as assistant to the ship's medic in a crisis, is that correct?'

Chris said, 'Adrian was the one who identified the crisis. Before it even arrived.'

'No names,' the tall man snapped.

The teen replied just as sharply, 'Jacob, enough with playing the impertinent one.'

The old woman gave no sign she'd even heard. 'You recognized the power even before landing on Mars?'

'As soon as we passed the moon's orbit,' Adrian replied. 'I thought maybe it happened because we had entered deep space.'

'That is certainly something to be studied. How many spells can you claim as your own?'

'Seven.'

'A goodly number. Tell me, lad. How did you recognize your claimed spells while still bound to Earth?'

He liked the term so much it hummed inside his bones. *Claimed spells.* 'I studied and researched and collected most of my life. Ancient spells and their original languages. Seven spells held a special sort of connection. Or energy. Something.' He hesitated, then added, 'I copied all the original source materials that I could find. At least, everything that seemed real to me. I have them in electronic form. They're yours, if you want them.'

'If we want,' the teen said. 'Ha.'

Another wipe of her mouth's edges. 'So. A young man, self-taught while still on Earth, journeys with seven spells in his arsenal. And he begins to use them while months away from his first landing on Mars. Interesting.'

'I have so many questions,' Adrian said.

'As do I, young man. And remember, I have been waiting for this moment as long as you. Actually, longer. Years longer.' When Adrian nodded, the old woman smiled. 'I see you understand what that means.'

'I think so. Yes.'

'So ask your first questions, young man. We can spare you a few moments. Not more. Not now.'

Choosing what to ask required no deliberation whatsoever. 'Did I choose the seven spells or did they choose me?'

'Does an artist choose their medium? An individual select their gifts?' She shook her head. 'Spells form a component of your birthright. That is all we know, at least in the present time. Perhaps someday we will have the resources and freedom to search deeper. Perhaps.'

'Is my magical ability restricted to these spells?'

'Yes and no. A gifted parent may share some fragment of ability with a gifted child. Bonds to new spells can occur with time and age and study. But your first spells remain your strongest.'

'Are there others? Like me, I mean. That you've called.'

'Hundreds called. Few arrived. You understand how I've managed to make this happen, yes?'

'Some specialized form of far-seeing is your primary gift.'

'More than that, young man. It is my life.' One tear emerged from the corner of her right eye. Its passage down her cheek so amplified her age and trials Adrian had to struggle not to weep. 'So. Your first questions asked and answered. Now everything else must wait. Time is not our friend.'

'Thank you,' Adrian said. He reached out and touched her fragile arm. 'So very, very much.'

She settled her hand on his. Allowed the moment to linger briefly. Then, 'Jacob, you may begin.'

THIRTY-FIVE

Jacob rose to full height, a towering figure close to eight feet tall. Everything about him was elongated – limbs, hands, jaw, forehead, even his ears. He pointed to the star's center and told Adrian, 'Stand there.'

They assembled in a circle, each standing upon one of the unfamiliar symbols. Adrian wondered if perhaps the participants had designed the symbol for their station, a means of claiming the spot as their very own. Or perhaps they had inherited the emblem from someone long ago. Or perhaps both. His accelerated heart and electrified mind shot impressions and thoughts at a heightened pace.

They made for a motley assortment, ages and shapes and races and attitudes, from mildly bored to Jacob's permanent scowl. No hint of formality, no haughty attitude of power, no ritual, candles, incense, wands. Nada. All the old-timey elements that had so taxed him. Before.

Jacob told him, 'Your task is to bond with the force that emanates naturally from this planet—'

'Obviously he knows all that,' the teen said.

The man now standing on the adjacent symbol added, 'Do get on with it, Jacob. Like Odell said, the clock is against us.'

Jacob grimaced. 'Who serves as our anchor?'

'That would be me.' Clara walked over to stand beside the old woman's chair.

'Everyone, bind. Ready?' He looked to the old woman, 'Odell, you may ask the question and cast—'

'Not me.' She pointed an arthritic hand toward Chris. 'Our new friend will cast the stones.'

All the Circle showed astonishment. Jacob said, 'Odell, no, she's not one of us. Or gifted. Or anything. I'm not even clear why she's here.'

'You don't need to be.' Odell motioned to Chris. 'Come here, young lady. Are you willing to serve a purpose?'

Chris almost whispered her response. 'I am.'

'Hold out both hands.'

The runes clicked musically as they spilled from Odell's worn leather sack.

'Walk over and stand beside Jacob. I will then ask a question. One so important it has brought us all here, even though the regime is doing its best to keep us apart.'

Jacob complained, 'Odell, how can you possibly think—'

'Even though the regime would like nothing better than to make us evaporate,' Odell continued. 'Poof. Gone. You understand why I am saying this? You need to see yourself as involved. Your energy, your own gifts, are focused upon healing. It is a potent force and you have honed it well. I want you to focus this power of yours, as intently as when you cut open a patient's chest and hold their heart in your hands. When I ask the question, you must send this force out with the stones.' She studied Chris, and must have found what she sought, because she nodded and said, 'All right, everyone. We begin.'

Adrian watched as Chris walked slowly over and halted where Jacob pointed upon the last empty symbol.

Jacob said, 'Everyone, link.'

The floor and its embedded symbols did not vanish. Just the same, Adrian could no longer see them. In their place rose a glowing mist, swirling like the dusty tempest he had raised. Only this vapor sparked and glittered, like a swarm of fireflies now swirled around him.

Gradually the participants joined with the mist, glowing like torches.

Jacob said, 'Ask the question.'

The old woman's voice rang clear and strong and as potent as when she had reached across deep space and invited Adrian to come and bind himself to Mars. And this gathering. And all the mysteries they represented.

She asked, 'Will this one survive?'

Chris gave a fractured cry.

Odell said, 'Focus, child. For all our sakes, focus.'

He could no longer see any of them. But he knew Chris was there. The bond included her now, so strongly he not only felt her distress. He *lived* it. The emotions and will and desperate intent to maintain her link to this event, her desperate drive to do as the old woman had said. She *focused*.

Odell must have sensed it as well, for she commanded, 'Now cast the stones.'

THIRTY-SIX

The old woman's question, would he survive, troubled Chris a great deal more than it did him. After all, he'd already lived through a number of missile strikes.

In fact, Adrian was excited. It clarified a great deal. He had entered into an arena on his new home planet where he had a role to play. His safety was not guaranteed. But he had allies, many of whom he might never know.

As the Circle gradually resumed being just a group of people, Adrian had a clearer sense of what was to happen next. The answers did not come with words. Nor was there any precise response, as in, do this and the little newly arrived squirt from Earth might live to mess up another day.

It was more like, the forces at their disposal could be marshalled in a particular way. If so, then the purpose that united them was amplified. Or allowed to remain and grow. Something.

Adrian had never seen himself as part of a greater picture. His life had been too focused on getting what he wanted. Which was basically to be standing here. In this circle. Surrounded by others who shared his ability to utilize magic.

The oddness of this group, their evident friction hidden beneath humor and mild exasperation, the old woman who had little time left, his newfound love for Chris. All of these elements were merely the human components of something much larger. These people were united by their desire to make things better. They served a greater purpose. Before, Adrian had no idea such things might ever exist for him. Now, though, as the bickering recommenced and the Circle divided and drifted away from their joining, he was left breathless by the simple gift of belonging.

The old woman beckoned, and a tearful Chris walked over. They spoke, or rather, Odell talked and Chris nodded in response.

'Hey there, big boy, come take a load off.' The young woman made a space between herself and the older gentleman and patted the bench. When Adrian seated himself, she asked, 'You OK there?'

'Better than OK. A lot better.'

'That's what we like to hear. Right, Pop?'

The gentleman said, 'I am Malik. And this child who dared to call Jonah impertinent yet refuses to grow up herself is Inyana.'

'What's the point of getting old and feeble?'

Malik replied, 'You would cause everyone around you a great deal less trouble.'

She sniffed. 'Hey, a little dose of trouble goes a long way, right, big guy?'

Her father said, 'That makes no sense whatsoever.'

'Sense is overrated, wouldn't you agree?'

Adrian said, 'I actually have no idea what you're talking about.'

'And that is the story of my life in a nutshell,' Malik said.

'Hey, get a load of this.' Inyana pointed to where Odell was handing Chris the small leather sack holding her runes. 'She's not actually giving her runes away, is she?'

Apparently she was, for Chris leaked more tears as she clasped the sack in both hands and held it to her heart.

'Well, I never,' Malik said.

Thankfully, Clara made the return journey driving like a sane person.

Chris held his hand, her own still damp from wiping her face. Adrian asked if they might make one detour and let him see the Wizards' Council building. In response, Clara turned off one thoroughfare onto the largest avenue of all. They traveled a few minutes beneath a sky of golden dome, then entered an empty traffic circle with a carefully tended garden at its heart. None of the surrounding structures was very tall. But all were grand, none more so than the one where they halted.

The Wizards' Hall was a monument to grandiose ideas. A dozen stairs rose to a pillared portico, with massive stone double doors and a podium waiting for some highly exalted pooh-bah to step forth and address the unwashed. Stamped upon the wall directly above the entryway was the emblem. The one from Adrian's dreams. All those nights. All those hard days. And now . . .

'You can go up if you like,' Clara said. 'But it's locked, and eyes are watching us.'

'I don't see anyone.' Chris's voice was an octave lower than normal. 'This is the first empty place I've seen in the entire city.'

'They're watching,' Clara said. 'Adrian?'

'We can leave.' He turned away. 'I'm all done here.'

They did not speak again until they entered Lambertville's main campus. Clara halted by the entryway to the public gardens and told Adrian, 'Don't leave Lambertville under any circumstances. Even here we won't be able to keep you safe for very long. There's every chance our opponents will come armed with whatever it takes to sweep you away. Do I need to go into detail?'

'Absolutely not,' he replied.

Chris demanded, 'Why are they so opposed to magic?'

'The regime is against anything that threatens their hold on power. More than that needs to wait. We're trying to set up a safe haven in one of the mining communities. There's a lot still to be put in place, but we hope to leave early tomorrow.'

Adrian said, 'I'll be ready.'

'We'll be ready,' Chris corrected. 'The two of us. And it's probably best if nobody argues with me just now.'

Clara merely nodded. She told Adrian, 'Miles wants to meet you. No idea when. I'll come get you when it's time.'

They bought meals from the electronic buffet and carried them back to Adrian's room. They ate in silence, then Chris came around and settled in his lap. Holding him in the manner of absent barriers. Gentle and loving and sad.

He decided there would not be a better time to make the same request she had made of him. 'Tell me something about who you are.'

She nuzzled his neck a moment longer, then settled against his chest. 'My early years couldn't be more different from yours. Happy home, great parents. One brother, nine years older – he treated me like his favorite niece. Growing up he called me the family mascot.'

Adrian lifted her and slipped out from under. The low gravity made Chris a fragrant warm bundle. He settled her in the chair and knelt beside her. Wanting to see her as he listened and absorbed.

'Long as I remember, my mom and brother volunteered at the city's main homeless shelter. My family supported it financially. Still does. They also financed the building of low-cost housing. Other stuff.'

'Where was that?'

'Annapolis. The most beautiful city on Earth. A great place to call home.'

Adrian started to say he'd like to see it someday. Then caught himself. 'What happened?'

'Around six, maybe even younger, I started begging to come with them. Serve the poor. The two of them always came back so *bonded*. Then Pop would show up from work, and it would be the three of them sharing something so powerful I could almost see it. I wanted that bond. They said I could join them when I was fourteen, the minimum age for volunteers.' She went silent, then, 'Thank goodness they made me wait.'

'Bad?'

She focused on him. 'You know, don't you.'

'Not the place. But the system.'

She quietly insisted, 'Tell me.'

Adrian didn't want to interrupt her flow but, looking into her eyes, he realized there was little risk of that. What she wanted was to *bond*. 'Mom's drug usage finally took hold. We lost our place and wound up in a family shelter. Which was when I was taken away and entered the system.'

'That's a terrible word. System.'

He nodded. 'Tell me what happened.'

'I couldn't handle it. All that sadness and anger and frustration and pain. I was *repelled*.' She looked away, captured by the memories. 'I felt so ashamed. So incredibly weak. I just wanted it to *stop*.'

'So you became a doctor. And went to space.'

'Sometimes I feel like I've spent my entire life running away from those memories, those people.'

'You know that's not true.'

'Do I?'

'Yes, Chris. You shouldn't lessen your own lifelong dream by thinking that.'

She heaved a long breath. 'My brother was livid when I told him. Going into space, working as a doctor and being part of a ship's crew. Leaving the family. It was the first real fight we ever had.'

'And your parents?'

'They were sad and silent. They still are. Sometimes I wonder if maybe they were glad to let my brother shout for them.'

'But you're doing what you wanted. Living your lifelong dream.'

This time, her nod dislodged a single tear. 'And so utterly alone.'

He rose and offered both his hands. 'Let's go to bed.'

THIRTY-SEVEN

Adrian discovered the apartment had a wall-console when it chimed and woke them up. He rolled over and read, 'Clara will be here in fifteen minutes.'

'No.' Chris snuggled deeper. 'Tough.'

'She's bringing coffee.'

She pulled the covers over her head and whimpered.

'Miles Lambert wants to meet us.'

The voice was muffled. 'Two hours.'

'Twenty minutes.'

'We're all booked up this morning.'

'We go straight from there to the Rolligon.'

She went quiet. Then sprang from the bed and entered the bathroom. 'The lady and I are having words about timing.'

They were ready when Clara appeared. It helped that they didn't have anything to pack. Her vehicle was parked in the broad corridor outside their doorway. She handed them both coffees and said, 'You drink, I'll drive.'

She took it easy enough for them to sip while traveling. As they entered the connecting tunnel, Adrian asked, 'What can you tell us about our host?'

'What you see is what you get.' She pulled up to a sealed portal and said, 'Be straight, be honest. Miles is already your ally. Treat him as such. If you don't have an answer, say so.'

Adrian had expected to enter the Mars version of a nouveau-riche palace. Gilded everything, imported items of questionable taste, chandeliers and waste.

He was disappointed, but in a very pleasant way.

Clara coded the entry, allowed the security camera to scan her right eye, then led them through an unadorned portico and into a smaller version of the public plaza. Same trees, blooming plants, birds. Broad empty spaces, a couple of tasteful sculptures, otherwise the place was almost austere.

Jurgen Roth was there to greet them. 'Miles, allow me to introduce my new friend and the good doctor.'

The old man was seated in a support chair, his legs covered by a blanket. Behind him, a wheelchair was folded and propped against a planter. But there was nothing frail about this man. He was alert, intent, and observed their approach with a laser focus. 'I understand you are responsible for saving the lives of my two dearest friends.'

'It's an honor to meet you, sir. Thank you for your hospitality.'

'Come sit.' He turned his attention to Chris. 'Doctor Leighton, our friends among the hospital's medical staff wish they could convince you to stay.'

'They do just fine without me, sir.'

'Call me Miles. Well, if you ever decide to cease your wandering among the planets, you have a place here.' He turned to where Jurgen stood beside his chair. 'Stop hovering and sit down.'

'Yes, your worshipfulness.' He plopped himself down. 'Right away, my lord.'

'You see what I put up with,' Miles told Adrian. 'Perhaps I spoke too hastily about the value of your deeds.'

'If I turned subservient, you'd boil me in oil,' Jurgen said.

'Only because it's what you deserve,' Miles replied. 'Why haven't you offered our guests tea and breakfast?'

'You just told me to sit. This is me, following orders.'

'I'll get it,' Clara said.

'No need,' Franklin announced, rolling in a trolley.

'Well, don't just sit there,' he told Jurgen. 'Make yourself useful.'

'Most certainly, your grace. I was just waiting for word from on high.'

As Franklin and Jurgen handed around plates and mugs, Miles asked Adrian, 'Clara has told me her version of how you reached inside her private space and saved them all. I'd like to hear how you saw this taking place.'

Adrian described the experience of utilizing his joining spell between bites of breakfast burritos. Sips of excellent green tea. Rough-hewn plates, linen napkins, Franklin seated to his left, listening intently as Miles drew him out with the briefest of questions.

The only interruption came when Chris demanded, 'Why am I only hearing about this attack now?'

'We've been a little busy,' he pointed out.

She sniffed her opinion of his flimsy excuse. 'The next time somebody shoots missiles at you, you tell me. Immediately. Without hours of silence and delay. Are we perfectly clear on this point?'

'Aye, ma'am.'

Miles clearly enjoyed the exchange. 'I always did appreciate a lady with salsa. My late wife was an Ecuadorian handful.' He waited while the dishes were cleared and mugs refilled, then asked, 'How are we on time?'

'We have a few minutes yet,' Clara replied.

He addressed Adrian. 'Let's start with a bit of ancient history. This city was founded here because the first major rare-earth mines were scattered all over these plains. You know how I got my start, yes?'

'You were the first miner to use magic.'

'My wife was the wizard. Always marry a woman smarter and more capable than yourself, young man. At least then you have an excuse for never winning an argument.'

'I hope you're paying attention,' Chris said.

'Viviana was the one who made the discovery, not me. Reaching out, searching, locating what we needed. First to survive, then to flourish.' A pause, then, 'In every way except the one that mattered most to her. Having children.'

Adrian sat and listened to the birds. A feathered orchestra, excellent tea, new friends, Chris. He could have remained here for days.

Jurgen said, 'The clock is ticking.'

'Indeed so. Where was I?'

'Boring us to death, as usual.'

Adrian said, 'Magic and mining.'

'Thank you, young man. Perhaps I should appoint you my new adviser and get rid of this nincompoop.'

'Your trusted and highly valuable nincompoop,' Jurgen said. 'Do get on with it.'

'My wife suffered from several ailments and was often unwell. In the midst of what became her final illness, she began having these impressions. Or dreams. Or something. Mind you, I shared none of my wife's gift. But when she told me of this new vision, I felt bonded to her in an entirely new way.'

'I've always wondered if something more could be passed between loved ones,' Clara said. 'There have been indications. My wizard's brew is a recipe and spell passed down through multiple generations. There should have been studies made.'

'Someday, if things ever settle,' Jurgen replied.

Chris offered, 'While we were involved with the Circle, Odell asked me to cast the runes. I felt . . .'

'Tell me,' Miles ordered.

'Exactly what you said. A bonding. Strong as anything I've ever experienced. And impressions. I need more time to sort them out.'

Clara added, 'Odell gave the doctor her runes.'

Jurgen said, 'There is never enough time to fathom the deeper meanings.'

Miles nodded, breathed, 'Back to the matter at hand.'

'Your wife's dream impressions,' Adrian said.

'She called it her final quest. Viviana said I should consider this bonding to be an assignment. I was to carry on in her absence.' He used both unsteady hands to lift his mug and drink. 'Viviana carried this final far-seeing to her last breath. I've worked ever since to try and find the answer. Tried and failed.'

'Other far-seers have found hints confirming the rightness,' Jurgen objected.

'So they claim,' Miles replied, cradling his mug. 'After they accept my coin.'

Clara said, 'Tell them what she saw.'

Miles nodded. 'Viviana's vision was of a new city. Grand, glorious, safe, and welcoming to magic. Designed and built with magic at the fore. Something neither Earth nor this regime would ever condone. And costing more than even I could afford. And something else. No domes.'

Chris asked, 'How is that possible?'

'An excellent question, for which I have no answer,' Miles replied. 'Now then. You will be traveling to a mining community I sponsor. There you will be among allies.'

'The family of your crew member, Naxos, are counted among the community's leaders,' Clara said. 'It's named after Miles's late wife. Vivianaville.'

'Just so. All of my wife's dream impressions were focused upon the region west of this new township. Why, I have no idea. Only that there is something vital about this location. What that might be, I cannot say.'

'The mines surrounding that community are not especially rich,' Jurgen said. 'Gold, half a dozen rare earths, but nothing that suggests a greater source than what we've already located elsewhere.'

'No, no, no, that's not it. We've had this discussion too often for you to insist on bringing that up again.'

Jurgen was unfazed. 'It's a primary reason why the regime leaves them alone and intact. The pickings are rather paltry. Vivianaville only exists because Miles supports it.'

Miles waved that aside. 'Young man, I would be grateful if you would attempt to use your abilities. See if you can find what has baffled everyone else.'

'Including dozens of miners and their mages,' Jurgen said.

'There are a multitude of wizards not employed by miners who also shelter there,' Clara said.

'Because Miles asked,' Jurgen said. 'Which means you should be safe, at least for a time.'

'The current regime drives more from Marsopolis every day,' Clara continued. 'Either they must prove themselves loyal to the regime or they are persecuted. Vivianaville has become a safe haven for mages being hunted.'

Jurgen snorted. 'Cretins.'

'Someday you're going to speak like that in the wrong place,' Clara said. 'Then it will be too late.'

'Cretins,' he repeated, but more softly.

Miles told Adrian, 'See if you can find what I and so many others have not. Tell this old man you have located the reason for his wife's final quest.'

THIRTY-EIGHT

They left Lambertville's warehouse dome in a relatively new transport vehicle. It reminded Adrian of a rock star's luxury bus back on Earth, only vastly larger. They traveled in a convoy of five massive vehicles, with their Rolligon tucked into the middle position.

The others were designed like long-distance trucks back on Earth, only with Mars-type adjustments. Cargo drivers shared a front cabin and cramped living quarters. Beyond the airlock ran a series of jointed carry-alls, capable of handling the rough terrain with ease.

Their own vehicle was smaller than the freight carriers, but only by comparison. The front cabin held space for two drivers and a dozen more passengers. This was followed by a large ready-room, two freshers, kitchenette, bunks, storage, and finally a sealed compartment that served as their larder.

They traveled north.

The sun rose into the pale wash that Adrian was coming to accept as a normal Martian dawn. Normal, as in, no storm. Their way ahead was so clear they might as well have been traveling an Earthbound highway, only this thoroughfare was an entire valley wide. Call it five kilometers, minimum. Tracks from previous transports crisscrossed and snaked in patterns that were almost artistic. Adrian assumed the designs had been carved by bored drivers seeking momentary release from the monotony.

Franklin drove. Clara served as his co-pilot. Directly behind them sat Naxos and Meishi. The commander had only that morning been released from jail. Adrian had not realized she and Naxos were an item until he watched them hold hands across the narrow aisle.

Malik and his daughter, Inyana, came next. The convoy was officially theirs. Malik was one of the most successful merchants allied to Miles Lambert, and the largest supplier of goods to Vivianaville. For once, his daughter remained quiet. If Adrian had needed any additional evidence that this was more than simply another journey, it was there in Inyana's worried silence.

Behind them, Jurgen Roth sat on his own, working through a

sheaf of documents piled on the empty seat next to him. Ditto on the expression of quiet concern.

Chris and Adrian shared the last row.

Four and a half hours after they set off, the valley narrowed as it skirted the western border of an ancient crater. Crawler tracks joined to form distinctly carved furrows in the rubble. Just beyond the crater, their route split. A steel marker rose like a sentinel, two stubby arms pointing east and west. The crawlers made a smooth turning west, away from the more heavily traveled route. The giant tires dug easily into the soft terrain. They made good time.

Two hours past the steel marker, previous travelers had flattened a semi-circular parking area on the boundary of a Grand Canyon-sized ravine. Adrian watched as the vehicles slowed and gathered and finally halted.

At a gesture from Jurgen, they rose and assembled at the ready-room's long table. Clara, Inyana and Malik began handing out meals and preparing tea. Jurgen said, 'In years gone by, this point marked the boundary-line of the capital city's control. Everything has changed now, I'm sorry to say. And not for the better. In case there are spies among the community up ahead—'

'Of course there are.' Clara handed him a mug and seated herself. 'Don't talk silly.'

'I simply find comfort in hoping for better days.'

'Maybe so. But right now you need to keep the fairy tales to yourself.'

'The lady's right.' Naxos gave Meishi a mug and meal-packet, stroked her face, and retook his seat. 'We're all pretty certain who the regime's spies are. But it serves us best to let them live. For now.'

Clara studied the comms officer. 'You're former military?'

He shrugged. 'I forget.'

Jurgen asked Meishi, 'How are you, Commander?'

'Shaken and bruised.' She looked severely aged, as if recovering from major surgery. She tapped her head. 'Not physically. Inside. Where it matters most. Or so it feels right now.'

'May I ask your first name?'

'Lei Lei. Call me Lilly. Makes for less verbal butchering.'

'A joke,' Naxos said.

'Tiny one.'

'Given how you were just released from custody, any attempt at levity is worthy of a medal.' Jurgen asked Naxos, 'And your first name is . . .?'

'Jean-Pierre.'

Meishi asked, 'Can someone tell me what is happening? I never even learned why I was being held.'

'To understand that, I must share a bit of our planet's recent history,' Jurgen replied. 'The revolt happened because Mars wanted to govern itself. Earth's monopoly refused. Their representative continued to act like our temporary king. We decided it was time to clarify the matter.'

'Interesting word,' Malik said. 'Clarity.'

'The revolt partly succeeded,' Jurgen went on. 'Earth recognized a Mars-based government. Only the wrong ones came to power.'

Naxos said, 'It was just your basic grab for the brass ring. The ones who manage things are living the good life. The rest are barely scraping by.'

'And terrified of being made to vanish,' Franklin said.

Clara added, 'Everyone in the capital who doesn't work for Miles is either loyal to the regime or running scared. We all know somebody who has gone missing.'

'Something else you should know,' Jurgen said. 'We're fairly certain the current regime has inserted paid spies among every ship's crew.'

Naxos shook his head. 'I was hoping against hope we'd arrive and discover that things have changed.'

'They have,' Franklin said. 'Only in the wrong direction.'

Naxos studied the driver. 'Have we met?'

Franklin smiled. 'I was wondering how long it would take you.'

'My brother pointed you out,' Naxos recalled. 'The one guy in MarsPort they said I could trust with my life.'

'Only you forgot.'

Naxos shrugged. 'A lot of time, a lot of miles.'

'Not much of an excuse.'

'All I've got to offer.'

'Then it will have to do.' Both men were smiling now. Franklin asked, 'Where did you serve?'

'Everywhere, it felt like. You?'

'I was a militia commander. Started as a driver, rose through the ranks.'

Clara said, 'A lot of us working with Miles used to be something else.'

Franklin nodded. 'Miles has a way of making us welcome. He kept us safe in the dark times, after the revolt and the wrong guys came to power.'

'Miles gives us hope for a better day ahead,' Clara said.

'Miles needed a driver with my skillset,' Franklin went on. 'Who am I to say no?'

'We fought Earth's monopoly so we could form a democracy,' Clara said. 'We got a dictatorship for our troubles.'

Chris asked, 'Why are the wizards in trouble?'

Clara said, 'When our elections were postponed the second time, the Wizards' Council made a formal protest. Suggested it was time for a second uprising.'

'Bad move,' Franklin said. 'Terrible.'

'The wizards assumed they were powerful enough to speak their mind,' Jurgen said. 'They were wrong.'

'The noose has been tightening ever since,' Clara said.

Franklin looked at Adrian. He was no longer smiling. 'Then you show up. Doing your magic tricks. Making fools of the bozos in power.'

'I prefer cretins,' Jurgen said. 'All power, no brains. Bozos suggest a group of clowns at work. Which these cretins are most certainly not.'

Franklin nodded. 'Point taken.'

Clara said, 'All the former council leaders have vanished. A lot of other wizards have fled the capital. They've flooded the mining communities. These outlying townships play a vital role in the planet's economy, and they know it. Some are loyal to the current regime. Most are fiercely independent, stubborn, and ready to fight. Wizards who remain in Marsopolis either take the regime's coin or they've gone underground.'

'Dime a dozen, wizards in the outlying districts,' Franklin said. 'You can hire one nowadays for the price of a decent meal.'

'Miles is working there too,' Jurgen said.

'We don't need to be discussing such things,' Clara said. 'Even here.'

'We're among friends. And these friends need to know.' To the others, 'Miles has set up an operation generating new IDs for former wizards. I say former because if they accept his help, they must agree to stop practicing magic.'

Adrian said, 'Things are very bad.'

'Oh no,' Franklin said. 'We left bad a long time ago.'

A day and a half later, they crested a final rise. Ahead was the mining community of Vivianaville. Adrian thought the township looked like a string of golden gemstones that had been tossed haphazardly on the ground and left for the storms to bury. The domes stretched in every direction, connected by tunnels that formed a Martian maze.

Inyana inserted herself into the aisle between Chris and Adrian. She squatted down and pointed through the front windscreen. 'Watch the crawler tracks. See how they gather at one point?'

'Yes.' The trail was clear enough, like a funnel had been drawn into the sand. 'The dome at two o'clock.'

'That's our warehouse and offices. Pop and I live there. If you need anything, you come.'

'I'll show him how to reach you,' Clara said.

They rose together and entered the rear space, a ready-room made tight by their gathering. They ate a final meal, drank more tea. Jurgen said, 'It's best to see this as the turning point. From here on, you need to be very careful.'

'Watch every step, every word,' Clara said.

'Be guarded,' Jurgen said. 'Stay alert.'

'I've worked inside mining clinics, including this one,' Chris said.

Clara tsked. 'You may think you know mining communities. But that was before, and this is now.'

Inyana asked, 'How long since your last landfall?'

'Twenty-six months, by Earth's clock. Give or take.'

Clara tsked a second time. 'Different era.'

'Things have changed, true enough,' Malik agreed.

Jurgen pointed down the length of the carry-all, through the front window. 'The dome at eleven o'clock, the one connected by just one longish tunnel. See that?'

'Yes.'

'It goes by the name Free-Dome, a play on why a lot of the miners came out here. Don't under any circumstances go there.'

'He won't,' Chris said. 'If he does, he won't survive the return.' To Adrian, 'Are we clear on that point?'

'Not really.'

Jurgen went on, 'Any stranger approaches you, any conversation that leans toward questioning or criticizing the regime, you run.'

'I know,' Adrian said. 'Spies.'

'No,' Clara said. 'Assassins.'

Adrian asked, 'The vision Miles told us about. The place Viviana saw that held special importance.'

'The million-dollar question,' Franklin said.

'Where was it?'

Inyana pointed west. 'Two days beyond that far ridge.'

Naxos said, 'The township was founded here because all the searching, all the miners, all the wizards couldn't find a reason to stay out there. Here the ground holds enough minerals they can make a living.'

'A paltry one,' Malik said. 'We're here because Miles supports us. There are much richer pickings elsewhere.'

'The miners do well enough,' Naxos said.

But Malik was firm. 'No miner in Vivianaville will strike it rich here. They survive, they take care of their families. They make a home.'

'Here we're safe,' Naxos agreed. 'We raise families among friends.'

Adrian asked, 'How many mining communities are there?'

'Seventeen,' Jurgen replied.

'There were eighteen,' Malik said. 'Before.'

Chris was aghast. 'The regime destroyed a mining community?'

'In all but name,' Naxos said. 'They were too loud in their opposition to the current regime. So the regime halted all supply trains.'

'Black marketeers operated for a while,' Inyana offered. 'Trying to keep the communities alive.'

'And a certain young lady almost got herself killed in the process,' Malik said, glaring at his daughter. 'The sleepless nights she caused me. The worry. The pain.'

'Daddy. Don't.' She reached for his hand. 'It's over. I'm here.'

Clara said, 'The regime is in the process of restarting it, since that region holds some of the richest veins we've found so far. Under tight control. Every miner vetted. Every wizard.'

'We don't operate there,' Inyana said. 'We never will.'

'Softly, softly,' Jurgen pressed. 'Time to move.'

THIRTY-NINE

Despite everything, Adrian couldn't help playing the happy tourist.

He and Chris were settled into an empty doctor's studio. The warren of medical-staff residences shared the same dome as Vivianaville's clinic. The clinic was one tunnel removed from what passed for the town's largest dome, Central. This held the best of everything, from diners to casino to government, such as it was.

The rougher trade, as Chris called it, the sort of places still referred to as honky-tonks in Arizona cowboy country, were clustered together in Free-Dome, six tunnels away. Their first free period together, Chris took him as far as Malik's warehouse dome. There she actually drew a line in the northern tunnel's floor. Here and no further.

He served a brief shift each day. Chris introduced him around, simply describing Adrian as a mage with medical experience. The nurses and lone doctor were wary, reserved. But they knew and trusted Chris. So they made no complaints as he mixed his wizard's soothing-spell brew and came when Chris called. Soon enough the others saw what he could do, and brought him when they thought his elixir could help calm, reduce pain, lower fevers, whatever. The rest of his time he helped unpack and stow the medical devices and drugs supplied by Malik. He found a distinct peace in fitting himself into the clinic's routine, quiet moments in the canteen, evenings with Chris. He knew it was temporary, and for the moment did not care. He stood at the eye of an unseen typhoon. Making himself useful. Staying close to Chris. Knowing it wouldn't last. Enjoying himself just the same.

Each day, someone was there waiting for him when he came off shift. Clara the first day, Franklin the next.

On the third day it was Inyana.

Inyana and her father were Pakistani in heritage and traders by nature, a profession their family had maintained for countless generations. The stallholders shouted complaints as they passed; terrible pricing, Inyana was worse than her father for starving them and their families. They warned Adrian time and again, smiling around the complaints, urging him to flee the Pakistani pirates before they stole the life from his body.

Inyana pointed Adrian toward a street-front café but, as she pulled back a chair she was snagged from behind by the nearest stallholder. The merchant woman who held her was four times Inyana's size. Maybe five. The woman cackled at Inyana's futile struggles, hugged her more fiercely still, then carried her over and dumped her in the chair.

A waiter smiled at Inyana's complaints, winked at Adrian, and set tulip glasses on the table. He poured tea from a battered metal pot, holding the container high over the table, while the fragrance of mint filled the air.

Adrian waited until Inyana's red complexion eased somewhat and her breath settled. He said, 'We need to talk about what happened in the Circle.'

She made a face. 'Why ruin an already wretched day?'

'Don't give me that.' He gestured to the smiling stallholder. 'You're the market's favorite scamp.'

'I admit a few of them aren't particularly stinky-awful.'

'That's why you came for me today, isn't it. So we could have this conversation.'

'It might have crossed my father's mind.' She sipped her tea. 'I put it down to indigestion.'

In the whirlwind that grew around Odell's questions and Chris casting the runes, Adrian had confronted several dire warnings, all of them incomplete.

Combat to come. Yet another uprising. Peril to all concerned with the Circle. A danger that risked eliminating magic on Mars.

Adrian had been left with the strong intuition these warnings had been meant to *amplify.*

The lone message the others had all received, after Chris cast the runes, had been brutally succinct.

Adrian was required to set a compass heading.

Everyone must take that course.

And not just members of the Circle.

Everyone involved in magic on Mars.

Inyana set down her tulip glass and cackled. 'You really put a knot in Jacob's bowels.'

'I didn't do anything,' Adrian pointed out. 'It was the runes.

Which Chris cast and Odell asked. I was as close to being a total bystander as humanly possible while still remaining in the courtyard.'

Inyana was unimpressed. 'Jacob said it was all your fault.'

Jacob had been so irritated he had risen to full height and did a human-grasshopper's version of jumping around the courtyard. Exclaiming to one and all how *insane* the message was. How could they *possibly* be expected to follow the hand of a so-called, reputed, suspect, apprentice wizard who had only just arrived from Earth?

And so on.

Adrian told the young woman, 'I have an idea.'

'The runes didn't say anything about ideas, sport.' Inyana waved to passers-by who shouted her name. 'I know because I was listening. What it said was, you point, we shoot.'

'The runes didn't say that either.'

'Close enough.'

'Do you want to hear or don't you?'

'Might as well.' Big sigh. 'Not like I've got anything else on today.'

So he told her.

The idea had woken him that morning. More of a vague notion at the time. One that had stayed with him through his shift. And gradually taken root.

A number of the details only coalesced into full form as he spoke. Most of them, really. When he finished, Inyana sat there in silence. Adrian took that as a good sign, the two of them surrounded by the market's noisy vibrancy, his idea enough to still the young woman's incredible energy.

Then she almost leapt from the chair. 'Time to bounce.'

He rose and waited while she handed bills to the waiter, who tried to refuse. Inyana then rushed over and kissed the huge stall-holder's cheek. When she returned, Adrian asked, 'Where are we going?'

'I need to tuck you back in your little box. Then I'm off to talk with my father, let him shoot holes in your idea.'

An hour and a half later, Adrian was preparing a meal when Chris came off shift. 'Isn't this nice. How did you know I was famished?'

'I didn't. But it seemed a good idea, in case they come for me.'

'Who?'

'Clara would be my guess.' He patted the back of her chair. 'Let's eat.'

She remained standing by the doorway, staring at him. When she spoke, Chris used what Adrian secretly called her command tone. Hard as a solid steel wall. 'Wherever you think you're going, I'm coming.'

'I was hoping you'd feel that way.'

'So, you're telling me, we don't need to have an argument about this.'

'No, Chris. I really, really want you to be with me. We need you there. At least, I think we do.'

'Long as we're clear.'

'Crystal.'

'In that case, I'm showering and changing. In case, you know, they come like you think.' She headed for the fresher. 'Five minutes.'

She was back in seven. Adrian pulled their plates from the warmer, stayed silent through the better part of their meal, then began. The longer he talked, the more slowly Chris ate. When he came to discussing the concept with Inyana, Chris set down her fork and asked, 'How long have you been working on this?'

'It came to me this morning. Grew into full form on our way to the clinic. It felt like there was this idea fog filling the corridor.'

'Idea fog.'

'I know it sounds silly.'

'No, Adrian. Silly is not the right word. Go on.'

'What changed everything was talking with Inyana.' He smiled at the memory. 'She's the market's absolute favorite woman-child. We were seated there, me talking, her silent for once, this clamor all around us, and I could actually feel my idea binding us together.'

Chris was silent for a long moment. 'And here I was, all ready to jump on you for holding back.'

'And you'd be right to do so.'

'Did this cloud thing happen to say anything about, you know . . .?'

'Our survival.' He shook his head. 'It was just the one concept. Nothing more.'

Her next comment was cut off by the door chime. Adrian rose, unlocked their portal and said to Clara, 'We're ready to go.'

FORTY

They gathered in Malik's office, a huge space containing two desks, flow charts, and an oval table large enough to seat twelve. The table's far end held stacks of manifests and bills of lading and customs documents. Through a glass wall, Adrian saw people scurrying about the main warehouse, shifting items onto pallets, unloading cargo Rolligons, laughing, shouting.

There were eight of them seated around the table. The two strangers were Jonah and Katarina. Within three minutes of seating himself, Adrian had Jonah pegged as somber, scowling, overweight, lumbering, cantankerous. Jonah's first words after dropping into his seat were, 'Nice of you to include representatives of the lost brigade.'

'Don't mind my brother,' Katarina told them. 'He was born nasty and has grown worse ever since.'

If Katarina had possessed a unicorn's spike and purple fur, she could not have been more different from her brother. She was tall, pale, ice-blue eyes, a Teutonic blonde with a muscular frame.

Katarina went on, 'If Jonah couldn't be pessimistic, he'd blow up and spew bile all over everybody.'

Inyana said what everybody was thinking. 'You two? Related? No way.'

'When I was younger, I thought some evil wizard had turned Jonah into a frog. One kiss and he'd become my brother the prince.'

'She slobbered all over me,' Jonah said. 'Still does. I hate it.'

Katarina shrugged. 'I keep hoping.'

The other six seated around the table were Clara, Malik, Inyana, Chris, Adrian and Franklin.

When Malik asked why Franklin was seated among the magically inclined, the driver gave an easy shrug and replied, 'Clara asked for a pinch hitter. I volunteered. Seemed like the right thing to do.'

Inyana said, 'I have no idea what that means. Pinch hitting?'

'Doesn't matter.'

'Back when the drones started their attack,' Adrian recalled, 'you identified them before Jurgen spotted them on the monitor.'

Clara said, 'Franklin is a far-seer.'

'I have this tiny smidgen of a gift,' Franklin conceded. 'And only when I am terrified.'

'Enough of a gift to have saved my skin,' Clara said. 'Several times.'

Lining the wall opposite the long window were Jurgen, Meishi and Naxos. Adrian had not asked for them to be included. But their presence added a significance. They treated this seriously. They served as more than observers. They wanted to be part of whatever came next.

Adrian wanted his uncertainty to be real for the others. He felt it was important to be entirely open. Let them know they were more than just participants. Their presence was not enough. They needed to be fully involved. Understand the goal. The potential outcome. And the risks.

He began, 'If you agree to go ahead, this will only be the second time I've tried this spell.'

Clara said, 'You need to understand, the first time Adrian made this spell, he saved my life. And Jurgen and Franklin.'

Jonah demanded, 'You think or you know?'

'He stopped three drones and four missiles.'

'Actually, there were seven missiles.' Franklin tapped the side of his head. 'Panic-stricken far-seeing at work.'

Adrian added, 'It was Clara's spell. Not mine. I just—'

'Made it work,' Clara said. 'More powerfully than I've ever managed on my own.'

Jurgen added from his seat by the side wall, 'This was after he did a complete renovation of the entire MarsPort.'

Jonah glanced at his sister and said grudgingly, 'We might've heard something about that.'

Katarina smiled and patted her brother's hand. Said to Adrian, 'So. This second go. What exactly does that mean?'

'If you agree, I want us to link in a form similar to the Circle.'

Jonah bolted upright. 'Wait! He's been here a week and he's met them?'

'Not just met,' Inyana said. 'He was why we gathered.'

Jonah's mouth mirrored his wide eyes. When he remained silent, Katarina demanded, 'You're part of the Circle?'

'What can I say,' Inyana replied, spreading out her arms. 'Famous, potent, world-changer, but Daddy dear still refers to me as his child. Can you imagine?'

Malik sighed.

Clara said, 'You understand, knowing who belongs to the Circle risks a great deal more than just our lives.'

Malik said, 'The future of magic on Mars is now in your hands.'

'When we met and cast the runes over our new friend, the warning was at the core of what we learned,' Malik said. 'You must never reveal what you are hearing.'

Katarina asked, 'You're a member of the Circle too?'

'And me,' Clara said. 'And Chris. Who was chosen by Odell herself.'

Katarina gripped her brother's hand. 'And now we're to become part of a new Circle? Why us?'

Malik lifted one hand a few inches from the table. 'I asked. You and your brother were the answer.'

Jonah said, 'There's a downside. I can smell it.'

'The spell is a binding, and a sharing,' Adrian replied. 'When I link with you, it's not just access to whatever spell you offer me. When you do this, I see basically everything.'

Clara said, 'When you grant him entry, he becomes aware. Secrets aren't secrets any more.'

Katarina gripped her brother's hand so tightly her knuckles turned white. Jonah opened his mouth, glanced down and remained silent.

Adrian went on, 'Chris will serve as the spokesperson. Or guide. She casts the runes. She asks the question. I'm hoping each of us will sense the right way to move forward. I'm also hoping when she names the task, I'll focus on that and nothing more. But I won't know for certain until we start.'

Inyana was grinning now. 'Because you obey the lady.'

'I try. Yes.'

She told Chris, 'I am liking your man more with every breath.'

'Sorry,' Chris replied. 'He's taken.'

Inyana shrugged. 'He's kind of old and crusty around the edges for my taste.'

Jonah said, 'One question. Or demand. Call it what you want.' When Katarina started in, he said, 'No, K. This has to happen. Now let go of my hand.' When she did so, he spoke to the table at large. 'K and I need to get paid. Times are beyond hard.'

Jurgen Roth responded from his place by the side wall. 'You will earn pre-crisis hunters' rates. And standard wizards' commission on everything we find. Or bonus pay if there's nothing of value.

Whatever you find, even if it's nothing at all, you'll be taken care of. You have the personal guarantee of Miles Lambert. If you want, I can put this in writing.'

'Jurgen,' Clara warned. 'No documents.'

'This is a hunter's contract. Nothing more.'

'No thank you,' Katarina said weakly. 'That won't be necessary.'

Jonah looked genuinely shocked. 'Really, K? *Really?*'

'Jonah, look around you. They're inviting us to become part of a *new Circle*. Do you really think they'd start by cheating us?'

He started to argue, but in the end he merely asked, 'Where do we sign?'

'You don't,' Jurgen replied. 'This is totally off the books. Never to be mentioned. Anywhere. This new Circle and the old both rely on your total silence.'

Adrian sensed that phase of the discussion was over. He asked, 'Your hunting magic. Tell me how it works. In as much detail as possible. Don't leave anything out.'

FORTY-ONE

Their conversation lasted another hour and forty-five minutes, including a quick meal taken at the table. Clara and Franklin and Jurgen and Malik all left at several points. Off to make things happen. Fast. Without any shred of delay.

Soon after, they went hunting for gold.

Chris was worried about not showing up at the clinic as promised, so Jurgen personally inserted himself. A few calls were enough, working through the miner who served as Vivianaville's erstwhile mayor, paving the way for Jurgen to then speak directly with the doctor and clinic head. Explaining that Chris was visiting the town at the behest of Miles Lambert, who had personally charged her with a second duty. One that had to take precedence. Because Miles made few requests of the community he supported. But this was one. And he, Jurgen Roth, personal representative of the old man, would like to go back and tell Miles that they had been most helpful . . .

Yada.

They traveled in the same miner's Rolligon that had brought them to Vivianaville. Personal property of the old man himself. Which apparently spent most of its time waiting. For this. The next attempt to solve his late wife's final riddle.

They rode with three ore carriers locked in place. Now the crawler was segmented, like a reddish-grey metal insect born to wander the planet's desert reaches. Fuel was supplied by the same ion-generation pack as the ships. Incredibly expensive. Rolligons were passed down, generation to generation, and were why most miners remained in debt all their lives long. It was in effect a mobile unit designed for living and working, as long as it took to fill up the ore carriers.

The empty carriers jounced and rattled as Franklin drove swiftly across the plain. Their destination was the heart of Viviana's vision. Just over a day's hard push from the town's domes. 'Miles sent the first miners out to where we're going,' Jurgen told them. 'They would have starved, except for how he offered them the same wages he's granting you.' Pointing at the unlikely siblings. 'They lasted, how long?'

'Nine months,' Naxos replied.

'A little longer than that,' Clara said.

Naxos shrugged. 'My family claims it seemed like an eternity. Stuck inside crawlers that don't come close to this one for comfort'. Kids going stir-crazy. Storms. A full season of blistering cold. Nothing to show for the effort of the hunt.'

Adrian asked, 'They didn't find anything?'

'Nothing they could mine.'

Clara asked, 'Your family stayed throughout the entire hunt?'

'From the first day to the last,' Naxos confirmed. 'We were Miles's men. Still are. He asked, we went.'

'It's good to have you on board,' Clara said.

Adrian asked, 'Did you have wizards with you?'

'Always,' Miles replied. 'My cousin has the gift. Her daughter is showing the signs.'

Jonah spoke for the first time since their departure. 'So why come to us?'

'My father already told you why. He searched and was pointed directly at you two.' Inyana showed them open palms. 'Aren't you lucky?'

'Luck doesn't have anything to do with it,' Malik said. 'The far-seeing has never been clearer.'

Adrian asked, 'Back to my question. If you had wizards and you didn't find anything, why stay so long?'

'An excellent question,' Naxos replied. 'The answer is, they kept getting mixed signals.'

Katarina said, 'Hunting for minerals isn't like a precise, go to this exact spot and dig.'

'It can be,' Jonah replied.

'Rarely. Almost never,' Katarina said. 'You get a signal.'

'A taste,' Jonah said. 'A hint of the scent on the wind.'

'You travel in ever-tighter circles,' Katarina said, sketching the air before her. 'Finally, if you're lucky and there's actually a vein of what you're seeking, you stop and say, dig here.'

'Luck.' Jonah snorted. 'Ha.'

'Even then it can be a waste of time,' Katarina said. 'A rich vein half a mile down smells the same as a weak vein just below the surface.'

'Two miles,' Jonah said. 'Ten.'

She added, 'Which is when things can get very rough indeed for the wizard involved.'

'It wasn't your fault,' Jonah said. 'I checked the site. You were right on the money.'

'Ten miles down is nine and a half miles further down than anyone has ever gone.' She told the others, 'I cost a mining family everything. They were coming after me. Jonah saved my life.'

Her brother repeated, 'It wasn't your fault.'

Katarina went on, 'My big mistake happened just as the flood of wizards showed up from the city.'

'Sis, come on. It wasn't a mistake.'

Jurgen asked Katarina, 'Where were you located?'

'Site Nine.'

Naxos nodded. 'Out west. Furthest site from the city. Rich pickings, is what we've heard. A lot of major veins.'

'Which only made it worse when I came up blank.' Katarina reached for her brother's hand. Only this time it was for support. 'The clan I served put out the word I was a fraud.'

'There were a lot of those,' Naxos said. 'Wizards from the city, people with families, on the brink of starvation. They'd say anything to get a job.'

Jonah said, 'Before, we were princes of the mining realms. Suddenly we're a dime a dozen. Anybody who has a bad day gets chopped off at the knees.'

Katarina pointed back in the direction of Vivianaville. 'We came here, trying to find a place where we could both work.'

'And stay safe,' Jonah added. 'Don't forget safe.'

They continued on, mile after empty mile. Every four hours they stopped for a meal and changed drivers, Franklin and Naxos and Clara. Adrian found it very touching, how Naxos remained so patiently caring for Meishi. The woman who would become his superior once they left Mars. She remained silent, thoughtful, bruised at some very deep level from her time behind bars. When night fell, the two of them shared a bunk. Meishi drew on Naxos and his love like a fragile Oriental hummingbird. Adrian spent a long time studying the two of them, wondering what it would be like to maintain a loving relationship within the strict confines of a crew in space.

He had a rough time falling asleep. When he did, his dreams

were terrible. Fleeting images of failing everyone. Coming up dry. The whole affair a giant waste of time and resources. Miles Lambert being wheeled out of his domes. Left to fend for himself in Marsopolis. Easy pickings for the regime, who appeared in the form of giant vultures. Miles fought futilely, but in the end they overwhelmed him, pinned him to the hard Martian stone and began picking at his flesh, tearing him apart . . .

A warm body nestled into Adrian's bunk. A deeply caring woman fitted herself to his troubled form. Strong arms wrapped themselves around him.

He sighed. Slept and did not dream any more.

FORTY-TWO

When Adrian next opened his eyes, the others were all awake and moving about. The crawler was filled with the fragrances of a hot meal. Chris brought over a steaming mug, waited for him to sit up, and greeted him with, 'Finally.'

Naxos said, 'I never knew a human could make such sounds.'

Chris stroked his face. 'Like a goose, this one.'

'Next sleep cycle, we're fitting you out with a pallet in the larder,' Clara said.

Chris continued her gentle stroking. 'Fine by me.'

'Such talk is not fit for young ears.' Malik cleared his throat. 'My daughter hears everything.'

Inyana rolled her eyes. 'Daddy. Pu-lease.'

Adrian used the fresher, joined the others, ate his meal in silence. When they were done, he stepped into the drivers' cubby and studied the terrain. The highest ridgeline he had seen on Mars rose directly in front of where he stood. Call it four kilometers away. The surrounding plain was scarred by remnants of crawler tracks, though most were now blotted by passing storms.

When he returned to the ready-room, they were all waiting. Ready.

He said, 'We might as well begin.'

Adrian asked, 'So we're clear. When they hunted around here, what mineral came out clearest?'

'We've been through this a dozen times already,' Inyana protested. 'More.'

'Daughter, enough.'

'Come on, Daddy. Really . . .' But a glance from her father stifled further protests.

Jurgen waited for the silence, then said, 'They found traces of everything.'

'Every mineral Earth demands from us,' Naxos confirmed. 'All here.'

Adrian repeated, 'Then they couldn't find a place to mine?'

'It happens,' Katarina said. 'More often than you think.'

Adrian sat at the narrow table's head, his back to the front window. 'And in Viviana's vision . . .'

'All the minerals,' Jurgen said. 'And something more. The place where we could build a city without domes.'

Clara added, 'Viviana insisted it was the most important element of all. Vital to the future of magic.'

'Over and over, she talked about this new city, there waiting for us,' Jurgen recalled, smiling sadly. 'Right to her very last breath.'

They had heard of this several times already. Adrian had mostly asked so they were all brought to the same point. The central question. 'OK, so we'll treat this as a trial run. What's the usual starting target for a new hunt?'

Naxos replied. 'Gold. Always gold.'

'And you do this by . . .?'

'We hold the sample,' Jonah said.

Katarina rose and went to her pack. She brought out a leather sack, not much larger than the one holding Odell's runes. She untied the leather band and upended the contents on the table. Thimble-size nuggets spilled out. 'Hunters carry this with them everywhere.'

'So you hold the item, and then . . .'

'We hunt. If we're lucky, we'll find.'

'So that's exactly what we'll do,' Adrian said. 'But as a team.'

Katarina pointed out, 'No one's ever tried that before.'

'Hunters are lone wolves,' Jonah said.

'Until now,' Adrian said. He pointed them into the empty benches running down both sides. 'Let's get started.'

'Bind yourself to Mars,' Adrian said.

Jonah fretted. 'What about with each other? I've never heard . . .'

Katarina took hold of his hand. 'Now is the time to follow orders.'

When her brother went silent, Adrian said, 'The joining spell, binding us with each other, that is my gig. Once that's done, I'll ask you to let me in. That's step one. Soon as you do so, I'll ask you to hunt.'

'Scary,' Jonah said.

Their gathering was indeed similar to the Circle, but just in two ways, both of which were superficial. First, they were all ages, races, and both sexes. Second, there was an undercurrent of antagonism. Only here, the friction was born more from uncertainty than genuine dislike. Maybe even fear. Though Adrian doubted even Jonah was frightened by what he wanted them to do, or what he might uncover at a personal level. No, these people had simply been afraid for so long, it had become part of their persona. A tattoo at heart level. Designed and put in place by the regime.

Katarina said, 'My brother will do fine.'

Adrian took that as his mark. 'Here we go.'

Soon as he began the process of bringing them together, right from that very first word, Adrian felt the bind take hold. All of them doing what now was natural. Firmly anchoring themselves within the planet they called home. And with each other.

To Adrian's mind, it seemed as though the next step had already happened. Chris held the rock of nearly pure gold in both hands. She reached out, positioning the sample at the table's heart. As if she sensed what was happening. And was part of it. A joining of forces. Including hers. The gifted healer.

'OK,' Adrian said. 'Now hunt.'

Soon as they started, Adrian felt himself journeying with them. He worked at a level beyond thought and individual control. As if the spell was already in place. As if it had been waiting for him. For them. For years.

He joined with them. Hunters and soldiers and merchants and healers. A motley crew, if ever there was one.

Together they reached out. Further and further.

What they saw . . .

The swirling energy faded. The Circle became just eight people.

Most of them sprang up and started babbling like excited children.

'Did you *feel* that?' Inyana.

Jonah. 'Feel? I *lived* it.'

Clara pointed at Adrian. 'What he saw—'

'Correction,' Jonah. '*We* saw it.'

Katarina nodded. 'We all did.'

'Even me,' Chris said. The only person beside Adrian still seated.

'Count me in,' Franklin said. 'Definitely.'

'All those elements,' Malik said. Inyana's father was not actually dancing in place. But close. 'All that *wealth*. If only we could find a way to make it happen.'

'Spread out,' Franklin said. 'Fine as dust.'

Clara said, 'No wonder they all came back empty-handed.'

'You can't mine dust,' Malik agreed. 'Yet.'

'But it's there,' Katarina said. For once she was as excited as her brother. 'All of it.'

Inyana looked at Adrian, the only one still seated. 'And that other thing. What you warned us about. Being able to turn your vision around and see us.'

'Yeah,' Jonah said. 'I felt that too.'

'I knew you could look inside me,' Inyana continued. 'But you didn't.'

'Thank you for that,' Jonah said. 'Very, very much.'

'Like he would ever have any interest in studying your innards,' Katarina said.

Clara said, 'Which brings us to the reason why we're all here today.'

From his place by the side wall, Jurgen confirmed, 'Viviana's quest.'

'If one part of this is real,' Malik said, 'the other is out there. Somewhere. Waiting.'

'Stands to reason,' Inyana agreed.

'I need to tell Miles,' Jurgen said.

Adrian spoke for the first time. 'Not yet.'

'He's waited for years,' Franklin agreed. 'He can wait a while longer.'

Jurgen shook his head, 'This would mean so much to the old man.'

'We need to be certain this is linked to what Viviana actually saw,' Malik said.

'It has to be,' Jurgen said. 'All right, yes, right now we can't mine this. But Miles has the resources to develop a new technology. Something to draw up the wealth here. Which can become the foundation for a new city!'

'Stop and think for a minute,' Clara said. 'What if someone else hears?'

'Oh, come on. We'll encrypt the conversation.'

'Of course we will.' Clara showed him only patience. Telling him in attitude as much as words to be calm and think this through. 'How would we set it up?'

'We'll have to make our connection via Vivianaville,' Naxos said. 'We're too far out. Unless we wait for a satellite to pass overhead.'

'Bad idea,' Malik said. 'Very bad.'

'Either way is bad,' Clara said. 'Either way the regime will be monitoring.'

'Not for us specifically,' Naxos said. 'For anything coming from or going to Lambertville.'

'So the alert sounds,' Clara said. 'They track us back to here. And start looking for themselves.'

'We can't risk that,' Franklin said. 'For Miles's sake.'

Jurgen knew he was defeated. And gave up in bad grace. 'I still say Miles needs to know.'

'He will,' Clara soothed. 'Just as soon as it's safe.'

Adrian waited until they had all settled. The energy was still part of them all, the fizzing power of expanding beyond known boundaries. When the chamber was quiet, he asked, 'Is there any chance I can speak to Odell?'

Malik was the first to understand, or so Adrian thought. He broke into a wide grin, glanced at the others, said nothing.

Jurgen demanded, 'What, now? Did you not hear a word of everything they just dumped in my lap?'

Malik offered, 'This is different.'

'Oh is it, now. What splendid news. Do please tell me how.'

'Lambertville wouldn't be part of this conversation. Which means the regime will most likely not be monitoring.' He glanced at his daughter, who now shared his smile. 'We can pipe this through the family of Naxos. If he agrees.'

'Long as it's safe, absolutely. Can I ask why?'

'I'll put it on speaker,' Adrian said. 'You will all hear the reason.'

'In that case,' Malik said, 'As far as any watchers are concerned, it is simply a communication between friends. One of whom is both old and very ill.'

Jurgen complained, 'And why, pray tell, can't we do this sort of legerdemain for *my* call?'

Clara said, 'Jurgen.'

'What?'

'You're not pretty when you pout.'

He glared at her. Or tried to. 'I'm not . . .'

'Miles should wait. For all the reasons we said. What's more, you know it. You're just riled because you didn't get your way.'

'I have every reason.'

'Of course you do.' Clara asked Adrian, 'Is this so important?'

'I'll only know for certain when we speak,' he replied. 'But I think this may bring us closer to reaching Viviana's true quest.'

She asked, 'Naxos?'

He rose, gestured to Franklin, headed for the driver's cubby. 'Let's set this up.'

FORTY-THREE

Odell's voice radiated through their living quarters. 'Hello, young man. How are you faring?'

Adrian sat in the second driver's seat, staring out the front windscreen, watching night gather. He had not realized how long their initial search had required until he came forward and saw the sun's last glimmer on the far horizon. He replied, 'So far, OK. I'm not sure about tomorrow.'

She offered an old woman's chuckle, wet and swift. 'Perhaps that's best. Not knowing.'

'Maybe so.'

'Is that why you wanted to chat?'

'Not directly. The others you've contacted. Reaching out. Across space.'

'Like you. Yes. Go on.'

'Did none of them survive?'

She answered without hesitation. As if she had known this would be the first point of their conversation. 'Not enough. Those who do, we can't discuss. Not even a whisper. You understand?'

'All too well.'

'So. We are done with the preliminary, yes? Now ask the real question.'

He found a distinct comfort in the two of them being in synch, a sensation so strong it defied the gathering dark. 'Did their spells follow a certain pattern?'

'Now that is an interesting question.' She paused so long, Adrian feared that would be all she said. Then, 'You understand, you are the first who prepared to become a wizard before arriving here. All the others required years of training. On Mars.'

'If they survived. If they managed to make it here.'

'Correct. And because they began their magic lessons late in life, they were immediately identified as coming from Earth. Which created very serious problems. Can you tell me why?'

'The old Wizards' Council,' Adrian said. 'They feared these people were spies sent from Earth.'

'And some were.' Odell was silent for quite some time. Then, 'Others remained deeply tainted by all it took to arrive here. You understand what I am saying, yes?'

'Not fully, no. And I hope I never do.'

'These poor souls remained mired in anger and attitudes that can only be described as self-destructive.' Another pause, then, 'But that is not today's issue, is it. No matter how important, how vital.'

Adrian asked, 'Did any of these other arrivals from Earth feel a genuine sense of purpose? Did they use their magic to reach toward a specific goal?'

'Now we arrive at the crux. Excellent. Do go on.'

'Once they identified what their personal spells were, could they say there was something definite they were here to accomplish?' Adrian felt as if he was wrestling with words that did not quite fit the way he wanted. He tried again, 'Did this goal, or whatever it was, did it come from you?'

'Young man, you do my heart good. The answer is most definitely not. My talent, my task, is to cross the impossible distance and *listen*. When I find an individual with potential, *I call*. I do this over and over. For years. The question is are *they* listening? If so, will they *act*? Will they travel here and join us?' A pause for breath, then she continued, 'And this time I will save you the need to ask why I did this. First, because every shred of my being remains convinced this is a vital task. Second, some of those gifted who arrive from Earth carry with them huge magical potency. Not all. But enough for my compatriots to put up with my duties and endless quibbling.'

The night was complete now, as dense as the mysteries Adrian feared he would never fully understand. The front windscreen reflected silhouettes now, all of them poised and silent and listening. 'So where did this concept of a goal even come from?'

'Assuming there truly is one.'

'I feel like it does.'

'Explain, please.'

'The first time I heard of Viviana's quest, it took hold of me. It's been growing stronger ever since.'

There was a stirring behind him. The silhouettes breathed, shifted position, looked at one another, then froze again when Odell said, 'Go on, young man.'

'I feel like everything that's happened since I left Earth has been connected to my arriving at this very point in time and place. The pattern of spells I've used, the crisis points where I had to act, the friends and allies . . .'

'Young man, do you recall what I told your lady here in the Circle?'

He nodded to his own image. 'Focus.'

'I suggest you do so now. Doubt has no place in our conversation.'

'The pattern,' he repeated. 'Drawing me closer and closer to a specific juncture. Where Viviana's final quest has become very real. But I am afraid it is also creating a huge new danger. One that threatens all our lives.'

'Adrian,' she said, using his name for the very first time. 'You do my heart good.'

'Is that your answer?'

'Look around you. We mages are *already* threatened on all sides. Unless the current situation changes, I give us very little chance of survival. The regime views the mages of Mars as a power they can never control. A few loyalists are being licensed to work the mines. For everyone else, unless something changes, it is only a matter of time.' She paused, then asked, 'Were you hoping for my permission to proceed?'

'I didn't . . . Well, yes.'

'Go and do. Find us a way forward. Stay safe. Survive. For all our sakes.'

FORTY-FOUR

Soon as the connection ended, they started jabbering. Inyana demanded, 'Just exactly when were you going to tell us?'

'This is real what you said?' Jurgen demanded. 'You understand what Viviana was after?'

On and on and on.

Adrian's response was the same to them all.

One word.

Tomorrow.

Actually, though, he figured it would take two days more. Perhaps three. Then they would be ready.

Adrian waited through a meal that felt as if it lasted forever. He helped clean up, waiting for the chance to speak with Clara alone. Finally, as they were setting up for the next morning and waiting turns for the fresher, it was just the three of them, Clara and Chris. He said, 'You need to get word to Odell. There's a spy in the Circle.'

Chris demanded, 'You think or you know?'

'I'm as certain of that as I am what's happening out here right now.'

Clara said, 'We've suspected for months. Can you say who it is?'

'Not yet.'

'Try and find out. Also, we need to know if they're spying for the old Wizards' Council, or Earth, or the regime. You understand?'

Adrian nodded. 'If it's the council, you may want to leave them in place.'

'There you go.' She offered one of her very rare smiles. 'It's been a long time since I've looked forward to anything as much as tomorrow.'

The next morning there was a new energy to their gathering. An almost childlike intensity filled the living space. Breakfast was not so much cheerful as electric.

Adrian took his time, gathering himself. Going through mental points. Readying himself.

They must have understood, or at least sensed the reason. No one pressed or even questioned. Adrian wondered if perhaps there was a lingering bond, even when they were not actually connected. A link that, once forged, remained and grew. If so, Adrian decided, it felt almost natural.

When they were seated around the table, empty save for the gold nugget Chris would soon be holding, Adrian started in. 'We begin with the spell that brought us together before. That is our jumping-off point.'

'Let's hope it's more like our launch pad,' Clara said.

'Jumping off portends a drop, a fall and a bad landing,' Malik said.

'Flying good, falling bad,' Inyana said. 'For once I agree with my father.'

Malik smiled. 'This is indeed a day for wonders.'

Adrian waited until the table was quiet, then continued, 'The spell I want to try, this will be the first time I've ever cast it. I mean, here on Mars. I practiced it like all the others back on Earth. Where it didn't matter. Not like now.'

Jonah asked, 'How many spells can you claim?'

He liked that. *Claiming* a use of power. 'Seven.'

'This is, what, the last?'

'Yes.'

Jurgen said, 'Back up a minute. Your connecting with Viviana's quest. Can you unpack that for us?'

'I will if you insist. But I'd rather wait until after today's hunt. See if it becomes clearer for everyone. More well-defined.'

'We can wait,' Katarina said. When Jurgen started to protest, she said, 'Jurgen. We *wait*.'

'Who made me the bad guy here?'

'Nobody made you anything,' Inyana cooed. 'You were just born that way.'

'Daughter, stop.'

'Just saying.'

Adrian said, 'The primary task today is to gather gold.'

'Hello. Mars to Adrian,' Inyana said. 'Dust, remember? Scattered, like, everywhere.'

'Which brings us to the seventh spell,' Adrian said. 'I call it a spell of *refining*. I'm not going to try and explain. We'll just see if it works.'

Jonah asked, 'Why are we still sitting here?'

'Because I want to see if this sharing element of the joining spell works both ways.' Adrian slowed his words, punctuating each in turn. 'I'm going to try and open myself. Invite you in.'

Jonah said, 'Whoa.'

'I see your call and raise it,' Inyana said. 'Double whoa.'

'The goal,' Adrian continued, 'is for at least one of you to be able to do what I do.'

Jurgen was still put out enough to demand, 'Do *what*?'

'You'll see soon enough, I hope.' Adrian rose to his feet. 'Let's get started.'

There was an element of disbelief to their preparations. Which was hardly a surprise. What Adrian proposed seemed impossible. Even to him. Which was not the best way to encourage the group. But in the end, he decided to go with honesty. Which had them all moving at half speed.

Eventually, though, they were ready.

Their version of the Circle gathered at the table, just like the previous day. What was different was how the others – Naxos and Meishi and Jurgen – were now suited up and standing alongside the three ore carriers. Which were, of course, empty. Because there was – in effect – no ore to mine.

They joined.

The link was easier now. Not natural, that would have been expecting too much. But there was a ready willingness to push through each individual's natural reserve, and accept that a degree of openness, of vulnerability, would result.

Chris held the gold nugget, just like the previous day. Adrian waited as the encircling tempest of energy grew in force. He endured the curious internal glances cast his way.

Not yet.

This time, the extended awareness that defined a wizard's ability to hunt came far more swiftly. They knew what was expected.

Or so they thought.

Once again, the surrounding plain revealed how gold lay in abundance, spread across the entire expanse, call it nine or ten kilometers to a side, perhaps more. The minerals were all there. Just below the windblown dust. Embedded in the surface material. Fine as milled flour. Impossible to mine.

Until now.

Adrian's final spell had been the weirdest of all. Found in just one location, an Aramaic scroll he happened upon while traversing the main Jordanian museum. Impossible to even touch, much less unfurl and read in full. Just the same, he was drawn to the glass-topped case. A magnet blasting his heart could not have been any more potent. He stood there for hours. Two full days, from the main doors opening to closing bell.

On the second day, portions he could not actually see had gradually been revealed. As if his concentration was enough to unfurl the scroll and grant him entry. Just for fragmentary moments, which was why he remained there so long. Then other tourists would crowd in around him, or the security staff would come by and insert themselves into his field of vision. He would move away, stop in the restaurant for tea he didn't want and food he couldn't eat. Then he would return, and try again.

He named this spell, *Refine.*

Like several of the others, the purpose was a mystery. Just the same, he memorized. At least, he hoped what he had visualized was actually the correct spell, and it did what he thought. Aramaic was considered by some experts to be mankind's oldest written language. But this was hotly disputed, as was the claim made by some that it formed the root structure used by Persian, Hebrew and Arabic. So little was known about Aramaic itself, including where it came from.

Adrian could not have cared less. The only thing that interested him was how many spells were unique to this tongue.

Including this. The mystery of refinement.

There were all sorts of hand motions and such. Which he performed. Sort of. Mentally. Internally.

At the same time, he did his best to reveal his incantation and the mental motions, sharing them with everyone else in the Circle.

Not spoken, yet mentally scripted within the encircling power. There for all to see.

When he was ready, he reached out. Following the hunters.

He became poised over this huge territory. It was impossible to determine size. Such things as physical measurements belonged to a different realm.

As he began the spell's final elements, the ones he had never actually been able to read . . .

The gold dust lifted from the earth.

Somewhere in the far distance he heard a cry. A shout. Something. The swirling bond of power began to fracture.

Then another of those within the power Circle demanded not just silence, but intent focus. He thought it was Chris, but couldn't be certain. In any case, the bond reknit. Adrian continued his spell.

The cloud of gold condensed. Tighter and tighter. But he couldn't seem to bring it together as he wanted, he couldn't . . .

Chris reached over and gripped his wrist. She turned over his hand so that it was palm up. And settled her other hand on top of his. With the gold nugget now inside their unified grip. Sealing it to him as firmly as she knew how.

The cloud froze. The dancing particles melted, condensed, then reformed. And gathered by the trio standing outside the empty trailers.

Then gold rained from the sky.

FORTY-FIVE

When they finished the final meal, excited and exhausted in equal measure, Katarina asked the ones who had not been part of the Circle what had it been like.

None of them spoke. Not Jurgen or Meishi or Naxos. Instead, they stopped in the process of clearing the table and filling the recycle bin. And shared a smile.

Katarina went on, 'I'm mostly interested in that moment when gold started pouring down.'

'We were all part of Adrian working his spell,' Naxos said. 'In a very strange way.'

'For the first time in my life,' Meishi agreed, 'I experienced magic from the inside.'

'That sensation of joining began long before the gold appeared,' Jurgen said. 'When the cloud rose up, and coalesced, it was a confirmation that what we witnessed was real.'

Meishi slipped back into her seat. 'One minute we were just standing there. The next . . .'

'I wish Miles could have witnessed what we did today,' Jurgen said.

Naxos stepped over to where he could settle a hand on Meishi's neck. 'You know the feeling before a thunderstorm strikes?'

'There was an energy in the air,' Meishi said. 'A current I felt inside my suit.'

'The very air you're breathing felt charged,' Naxos said. 'Dense with power.'

Inyana asked, 'Was it scary, feeling that?'

'If it hadn't been you people, friends we could trust, absolutely,' Meishi replied. 'It would have been terrifying.'

'We knew it was you,' Jurgen agreed. 'There was a definite signature to the force. Mind you, this is coming from a man who has spent his entire life wondering what it felt like to work magic.'

Inyana said, 'This is just the coolest thing ever.'

'We joined with your work,' Naxos said. 'Connected so tight, we might as well have been in here. Part of the Circle.'

'Chills,' Inyana said.

'And then this cloud of particles just rose up,' Meishi said. 'Slightly higher than our heads, shimmering and sparkling like fairy dust.'

It was Clara who said, 'This just keeps getting better.'

'When it started taking shape . . .' Jurgen shifted so he was looking at the other two. 'I thought . . .'

Naxos smiled again. 'You too?'

'Oh, definitely,' Meishi said.

Jonah demanded, 'Talk to us.'

'It looked like forms began appearing inside the cloud. Not human, maybe not even alive. But that's how it felt,' Jurgen said. 'What they were exactly, I can't say. Definitely not human.'

'Artwork,' Meishi said. 'Sculptures that moved.'

'Then zap,' Naxos said. 'One second to the next.'

'The beings or whatever they were vanished, the cloud condensed,' Jurgen said. 'And started raining gold.'

'But nothing touched us,' Meishi said. 'We stayed totally safe.'

'Beautiful is the only way to describe it,' Naxos said.

That was precisely the word Adrian held in his mind. Seeing the three of them share that smile, that spark to their gaze and faces. Even Meishi. Beautiful.

They held to an easy levity as they prepared for sleep. The sense of happy accomplishment defied their exhaustion.

Then came the dreams.

None of them slept well. They all shared similar bad dreams. Terrible, near suffocating nightmares.

There was very little conversation about this, even from Jonah and Inyana. There was actually no need. They all suffered. And they knew why.

The power emanating from the Circle was a dominant force in all their lives now. Extending the hunt outwards in every direction, drawing up clouds of gold flecks, molding and shaping and refining this into tons of pure alloy, they were all exposed to the force. And the aftermath to their deeds.

Just the same, no one felt any need to ask the obvious. Was it the spell-casting, the refinement of gold, causing their fragmented nights?

At the level of binding to the Martian magic, far beyond any normal human confines, they all knew the answer.

Yes and no.

FORTY-SIX

With each passing night, they all grew increasingly reluctant to give into sleep.

The swirling force continued to fill their nights with fragments of doom. To Adrian it felt like cinders from some unseen fire. Danger lurking and ready to rise up in an all-consuming blaze. And destroy them all.

But for Adrian there was also something else at work.

Each of these intense moments offered an unspoken challenge. *Endure*, the storm seemed to be telling him. Look *beyond*.

Every time he woke, Adrian fought against the tremors and the fear. And used his second spell's capacity to look *beyond*. Only now he was no longer seeking to delve into another person's secret realms. Instead, he asked the same question Odell had posed in his first Circle. Back in Marsopolis.

Would this one survive?

In response, he glimpsed fragments as harsh and confusing as the dark dreamtime cinders. The answer, he decided, was only, perhaps.

But gradually something else began to take shape there on the Martian plain. Something else mattered far more.

He glimpsed the true answer to Viviana's quest.

And that answer changed everything.

They needed four days to fill all three lagers.

That was how miners referred to ore wagons, by their German name. Mobile lagers. These particular lagers were rated to hold five tons of ore each.

Which meant they would return to Vivianaville with fifteen tons of refined gold.

They had no way of gauging their product's actual purity. They had not brought proper assaying equipment. Why should they? Miles Lambert had sent out highly skilled teams for years and found nothing.

But Naxos and Jurgen and Malik all thought their gold came very close to pure.

In between the Circle hunts, they suited up and helped load the gold. The unending work left them exhausted. The gold was not shaped in anything like a regular form. To Adrian's mind it resembled the salt-water taffy of his childhood, standing in the fairgrounds with his mates and watching as the sticky mess was stretched and pulled and prodded into the oddest possible forms.

At first they tried to stack it. But exhaustion and the sheer volume soon put paid to that. With each gathering of their new circle, the amount they generated continued to grow.

Once the lagers were full, they still kept at it. Joining in the Circle. Casting the spells. Gradually the others began reaching a distinct harmony. Not actually doing the work. Just the same, their increasingly intense joining magnified the result. Then, before the fifth and final hunt, Jonah and Katarina and Inyana all declared they'd like to work the spell with him. Not take control. None of them was ready for that. But actually work with him in casting. Magnify the effect.

They left five lager-loads there in the plain. A great hulking hill that glinted in the day's final light. Jonah then revealed one of his own individual spells, something that heightened his value to any miner's clan. But unlike his normal task of scooping out the surface dirt to reveal where the actual mining should begin, Jonah piled massive loads atop the gold, until there was nothing to see except just another hill protruding from the empty plain.

As they prepared their evening meal, there was none of the friction or backbiting one might have expected from eleven exhausted near-strangers crammed into a miners' carry-all for eight hard days. Instead, they moved in silent harmony. All of them intent upon what they had accomplished, and what lay ahead.

Adrian knew Jurgen wanted to say some things. Bring the risk out in the open and discuss next steps. Twice he had shot Adrian a hard look, asking in silence if it was time. Adrian had responded with a minute shake of his head. Not yet.

By the time they finished cleaning up, there was less than an hour left of daylight. They had no intention of making the return journey at night, and no need to hurry back. Meishi and Katarina started another game of chess. Franklin settled into his bunk and read. Jurgen retreated to the drivers' alcove, stared at the gathering dusk, and made notes on his tablet. The others tried to teach Clara a new card game, but Inyana cheated outrageously and changed the rules every time she risked losing a hand.

Adrian motioned to Chris and held open the rear door leading into the larder. It was the only really private space they had, other than the fresher, which was cramped even for one. The others pretended not to notice as she stepped inside and he closed the door behind them.

He said, 'I need to tell you what's probably going to happen.'

She had clearly been expecting this, and used the tone she had last employed in the ship's sickbay. 'There's only one question I want you to answer.'

He nodded. 'Will I survive?'

'And?'

'Chris, I want to love you all my life long.'

It seemed to Adrian as if she had been saving up tears since those first dark flecks began staining their nights. 'That is not the answer I want. Or need. And you know it.'

'What I know,' he replied, 'is that I won't lie. Not to you. I can't.'

'Is there any chance?' A hard swallow, a struggle for control, 'For us?'

'Yes. A big one.'

She raised one fist, like she intended to strike him. But then it simply dropped to her side. 'Why didn't you say that first?'

'You know why.'

She wanted to deny it. He watched her struggle. Aching for her. And for himself.

Adrian said it for her. Wanting it clear and out there. In words. 'The risk is as big as our chances. And something else. As soon as we return to Vivianaville, I'm going to be arrested.'

'You think or you know?'

'This is a certainty.'

Chris stared at the room beyond the closed door. Clearly thinking of Meishi, who still had not fully recovered. 'I'll be there for you.'

'Thank you, Chris. So much.'

She started to say something more, but in the end she reached for the door, paused another long moment, then opened it and stepped into the ready-room.

All eyes were on her. Including Jurgen, who had swiveled the driver's seat around so as to stare down the central aisle. Everyone saw her tears.

Their gazes swung to Adrian as he entered and closed the larder's door. Blank expressions to match their gazes. Disappointed and accusing, some trying to mask it, others not bothering.

Abruptly Chris spun about and flung herself at him. Wrapped her arms around his neck, pulled him down, and kissed him hard. And then held him there, face to face. Adrian tasted the salt of her tears, felt the wetness smear her face.

Chris said, 'You have to survive. You just have to.'

'Chris, you're breaking my heart.'

She released her hold on his neck, wrapping her arms around his chest. Nestling herself close. Adrian straightened and kept his arms tight around her. He looked down the central aisle to where Jurgen stood, watching him.

Adrian nodded. 'It's time.'

'Finally.' Jurgen stumped down the passage, past the fresher and kitchen and bunks. 'Places, everyone. There's work to be done.'

Jurgen did not cloud his description of next steps with unnecessary detail. They already had a lot to think through. Decisions to be made. By everyone involved.

They left when dawn was a faint smudge on the eastern horizon. None of them had slept much – a few hours at most, and those tainted by the same nightmares.

Adrian assumed the hard night was why no one demanded answers from Jurgen. Or pushed forward with agendas of their own. Everything the attorney had told them carried an immense weight. His words had solidified the dark swirling flecks, the images staining everyone's nights.

They took the return journey very easy. They had to, pulling three lagers holding fifteen tons of gold over mostly uncharted terrain. Especially where the going got rough, the dust blown free, the uneven shale exposed. The last thing they needed, the very last, was to break an axle on one of the lagers, or worse, fracture a link connecting the containers to the main crawler. They couldn't risk some relief driver catching wind of them returning with this particular load. There was no way they could allow anyone outside their group to glimpse what they carried. Their tracks laid out a very clear destination point, back to a hill of pure gold.

But that was nowhere near the greatest danger.

They had not yet discussed the full meaning of their cargo, what it represented, how it might impact their futures. So far Jurgen had just mentioned the issue, then assured them the answers would come. In time. Once the steps were in place for them to survive. And that was what he had covered in greater detail. The roles each of them must play, so that all might stay alive.

And Adrian had still not revealed the other thing. The secret he knew he had to share. In case he didn't make it back from the cage that awaited him. At the end of this unmarked road.

When light dimmed and they stopped for the night and finished their meal, Adrian asked if he could have a word. Chris and Clara and Jurgen rose without question and followed him into the larder. He found it interesting, how none of them saw any need to question. Especially those who were not included. They simply continued with cleaning up and preparing for sleep.

Soon as the door closed behind Chris, Adrian launched straight in. Told them the answer he had divined to Viviana's quest.

Their response was curious and reassuring both. They took a few moments to absorb, then Jurgen said, 'You were right to tell us.'

Clara asked, 'And the others?'

'They should know what we know,' Adrian assured her. 'But I thought it might be better if right now they focused on next steps. Unless you disagree. In that case—'

'No.' Clara nodded. 'It's already complex. There's no need to add another burden.'

'We'll tell them soon as we're safe and the way ahead is clear,' Jurgen assured her, and reached for the door.

When they emerged, Adrian offered the others as much as he felt it was safe to divulge. Of course they deserved to know. But they had to follow a precise and invisible path, each step set in place at the right moment. This new revelation, and what he thought the quest actually meant; all that could wait.

Plus he wanted to honor the old man and his late wife's legacy. Miles Lambert should be informed. And given a chance to add his voice to whatever came next.

Adrian would have vastly preferred to tell Miles himself. But that was not possible. And the reason why was what he divulged when they returned to the ready-room. It was what he had told Chris in their earlier private moment. The news had made her cry. Hearing him say it again had the same effect.

What he told the group was, 'As soon as we get back, I'm going to be arrested.'

Meishi moaned softly. Jonah demanded, 'You think or you know?'

'The last three times we joined, the dark elements we've all been experiencing at night have coalesced.' Adrian settled back into his seat. Chris moved up behind him, draping both arms on his shoulder and neck. 'These nightmare warnings never last long. Quick flashes. Hard images. But I'm pretty sure that's what I'm seeing.'

Naxos took hold of Meishi's hand. 'But you get out of this?'

Clara was the one who replied, 'So long as we do our job right. All of us.'

Inyana said, 'Wouldn't it be better if we do whatever it takes to keep you free?'

'No.' This time it was Chris who replied. Resigned. Sad. But still. 'This needs to happen.'

Clara said, 'I hate to say it. I really do. But they're right.'

'We have a way through this,' Chris said. 'It's what keeps me going.'

Jurgen nodded. 'The multiple steps we need to set in place. This is part of what is about to unfold.'

Inyana asked, 'We don't know everything, though, do we?'

Adrian found himself pleased that this remarkable young woman had sensed the unspoken. 'Not by a long shot.'

Malik asked, 'Will you tell us the rest?'

'In time,' Jurgen replied. Definite. 'Absolutely. In time you will know everything.'

When Meishi looked ready to object, Franklin spoke for the first time since they had emerged. 'What you're seeing here, this is how a good command structure works. We're about to become very busy. Getting things right is a life-or-death issue. Looking too far down the road risks losing track of the here and the now.'

'Up ahead is a danger zone,' Clara agreed. 'We trust our officers. We do our job. We watch each other's back.'

Franklin nodded. 'That's how we all get through this alive. The only way.'

It said a lot about them, this unity they were forging, in how no one protested further.

They dimmed the lights, took turns in the fresher, stretched out for what rest they could muster.

The dreams were as hard and dark as ever. Flashes of danger and enemies with evil intent. Adrian slept and jerked awake and tossed and turned.

Chris slipped into the bunk.

They clung to each other. Breathing together. Merging in ways beyond the reach of all those outside forces.

They remained like that until Clara rose with the dawn and announced, 'Time to move out.'

Too soon. Far too soon.

FORTY-SEVEN

L ate that afternoon, they swung past the final ridge and the Vivianaville domes came into view. The lengthening shadows were so deep they could tuck a crawler hauling three lagers in close to the ledge and go unseen until night fell. Naxos assured them that no one in Vivianaville had a reason to look in their direction. Years of searching, countless miners and wizards taking the old man's coin, all had ended in futility. There was nothing out their way except shale and dust.

They were close enough in for Malik to reach his office by encrypted comm-link, a straight connection, no satellite linkage, just the boss checking in as usual. He spent over an hour dealing with items that had arisen during his absence. Jurgen was clearly worried, until Inyana said, 'Pop disappears all the time. Relax. We've got people who know how to handle things.'

Somewhere in that lengthy conversation, Malik casually inserted the initial step that was absolutely required. Finally he cut the connection, rose from the co-pilot's chair, and nodded. 'Everything is set.'

Once the meal was done and they had cleaned up, they gathered. Everyone resumed their places at the table. Malik and Naxos and Clara brought tea and little honey-cakes that they had all become addicted to, finger-sized delights that were baked every morning and left out for all to savor.

Soon as they settled, Jurgen launched in. 'I am very grateful for your not asking the most evident question. It represents a huge amount of trust. It gives me hope that we can make this work.'

Jonah opened his mouth but hesitated. Adrian had seen this same uncertainty numerous times. This evening, though, Katarina said it for him. 'Just the same, we need to know. What is our share, and when do we get paid?'

'Let me make one point. And then I will offer what I can. What I hope will satisfy.' When no one objected, he continued, 'What we have here is not fifteen tons of refined gold. It is power.'

'It's a death sentence,' Clara said.

The attorney bobbed his head from side to side. 'Yes and no. Those of you who are actually part of this new magic Circle, the regime will definitely want to keep you alive.'

'Inside their version of a gilded cage,' Clara replied. 'Wealth, a good life; everything but our freedom. Which we'll never have again.'

Jurgen nodded. 'But the others here, those who witnessed the event but don't share the magic, I doubt we'll survive.'

'Secrecy,' Malik said. 'The lesson my family has learned and practiced for generations beyond count.'

Jurgen went on, 'The regime contains a select number of cronies and wizards made rich by their grip on power. The lies they tell to the common man are simple enough. They have wrested control from Earth. Which is both true and not true. Day-to-day operations are now handled here on Mars. As they should be. But *real* control is the same as it has always been.'

Meishi said, 'The monopoly controlling the ships and their pods.'

'Precisely. These pods are transported from all over Earth. The monopoly portrays this as part of the new global order, how the Mars colonies are good for everyone on Earth. It's the same lie they've been telling since they realized Mars held a wealth of gold and rare earth minerals.'

Malik was nodding now. A slow back and forth, marking time to Jurgen's words. 'The pods are the only way to ship the ore.'

'There you go,' Jurgen said.

'Which is why our current rulers want the technology to refine here on Mars,' Naxos said.

'Want isn't strong enough,' Clara said. 'It's their rallying cry.'

'The one point Earth will never give in on,' Malik said. 'They can't.'

Jurgen spelled it out. 'Only a ship as big as one holding multiple pods can economically transport raw ore back Earthside. But if Mars develops the ability to refine the ore here . . .'

'Any ship can carry it,' Malik said. 'Any nation on Earth, any company, any group, they'd all be able to make a profit on these shipments.'

'And there's more,' Meishi said, eyes gleaming. 'We'd have the riches to buy our own ships.'

'There you go,' Jurgen said.

'Mars would have true independence,' Naxos said. 'At long last.'

'Earth won't allow this to happen,' Clara said. 'They can't. There's too much wealth at stake, too much power.'

Katarina said, 'OK, so you've managed to frighten us. Now answer my question.'

But it was her brother who said, 'Any sign we've come into more money than usual miners' pay, alarm bells sound inside the regime.'

'We'd raise the red flag,' Clara agreed. 'The regime would do whatever it takes to find the truth.'

'Which is why it's vital you trust Miles Lambert,' Jurgen said. 'He will pay you what you are owed. As soon as it is safe. I offer you my personal guarantee, based on years of serving the man.'

'My family's done well standing with Miles,' Naxos said. 'I see no reason to change.'

'I second that,' Malik said.

'Here is what I propose,' Jurgen said. 'You are paid full hunter's rate, plus bonus, for every day we've been together.'

'The same Miles has paid to all the other hunters who came back empty-handed,' Naxos said.

'That's all the watchers observe,' Jurgen went on. 'All they need to see. But in addition to this, Miles will secretly deed you owner-ship of executive quarters in Lambertville. And a credit ring intended to cover all expenses that might come your way.'

Jonah looked at his sister. 'That's as close to true freedom as I'd ever hope to come.'

Clara said, 'He's not done.'

'What we don't know, what we can't say, is how much of the gold we carry will go toward changing the current power structure. Sealing our way to fair elections. Finally ridding ourselves of the cretins currently holding power. Creating a democracy, and after that, making Mars a true and independent nation.'

Malik covered his eyes with one hand. Inyana reached for the other, held it in both of his. Blinked her eyes fiercely. Clenched her jaw. Stayed silent.

Naxos said, 'I've just glimpsed my family's secret dream begin to awaken.'

'At long last,' Clara said.

'We won't take any step regarding the parceling of this and future gains without your full approval,' Jurgen said. 'It has to be unani-mous.'

'Tell us what you're thinking,' Katarina said. 'Please.'

'Ninety percent of everything we reap goes into what will become the new federal treasury. The other ten percent will be divided equally.'

'To all of us here,' Clara said.

'With two shares to Miles,' Jurgen said. 'One for him and his investing in our quest.'

Inyana was the one who said, 'And one for Viviana.'

FORTY-EIGHT

When it was time, they set off. Trundling over the final kilometers, taking it very slow in the dark, making it safely to the main airlock of Malik's warehouse dome. The late-night security guard was both a relative and highly trusted. He let them in, closed the interior airlock door and, at a wave from Malik, walked back to the offices and cut off the interior security cameras. They eased themselves out, stretching and marveling at being freed from the crawler's tight quarters.

They unhitched the lagers, then connected them one by one to a forklift used to shift ore containers. The dome's western wall was lined with storage units holding miners' loads until the next ore train left for the capital. The containers were eased inside, the doors shut and locked and sealed.

Their work held a weary ease. They were friends now, bound together by far more than a new find. Knowing what was coming added a certain formality to their parting. Adrian shook hands, accepted embraces, then – when it was time – he walked with Chris back down the connecting tunnel. Into the clinic's dome, into their cubby, sealing the door, together.

The day after their return, Franklin drove the ore wagons back to Lambertville, a trip he had made countless times before. He traveled fourth in line of nine vehicles, a standard-size ore convoy. There was just one outrider serving as guard detail. Ore bandits were rare along this route. It was well known the Vivianaville miners needed Miles's support to maintain a decent living. The bandit gangs focused on richer prizes elsewhere.

Jurgen rode with Franklin. He was listed on Malik's manifest simply as 'Guard One'.

Adrian was more than content to wait out the days in the clinic's apartment. He found a simple pleasure in almost every hour. Even when the nightmares persisted, at least for him. At his first restless stirring, a single fretful murmur, she was there. Offering comfort with her arms, her warmth, her love.

He and Chris settled back into more or less the same routine as before they trekked. A few people at the clinic asked how it had gone. They all knew Miles Lambert had asked the same favor of Chris and Adrian that he had of so many others. Go out and see if they could uncover the reason for Viviana's final quest. Everyone knew Miles was both old and ailing. They were all worried about their future, what might happen to Vivianaville once the old man passed. This was their home. They felt safe here. When Chris said they had not found anything worth mentioning, the others accepted it and went on with life. They had expected nothing more.

Their days held to a steady routine. Chris restricted herself to an eight-hour daytime shift. She was volunteering her services – no way was the clinic going to argue. Before she left each morning she gave Adrian a preliminary list of patients who could use his care. He left about an hour after she did, cleaning the place and taking his time, allowing her to complete her initial rounds. When he arrived at the clinic's front desk, he was usually presented with a second list – new patients he should add to those he was already seeing.

He was done in around three hours, sometimes less. If Chris wasn't too rushed, they shared a quick meal in the clinic's canteen. Then she resumed caring for her patients, and he went out exploring. These days, Clara was always the one to escort him on his jaunts through the town. Sometimes Inyana joined them, and those were the best times of all.

As the days progressed, Adrian felt as though the very air he breathed became condensed. New forces aligned against him, the dream's dark fragments merging into his tomorrow.

Despite this new reality of threats beyond the horizon, he experienced hours of a joy so intimate, so unique, they left him breathless. He tried to tell Chris one evening, but she broke down and wept long before he had fully explained. She ordered him to stop, saying it sounded too much like a final farewell. 'When you're back. When you're safe. When we're together. Tell me then.'

So he shaped the telling in his mind.

He had never fully understood what it meant to fit in. To be part of something greater than his own self-centered aims. To feel as though he was healing. Becoming a whole person. As if the worst elements of his past might fit themselves into a new today.

At long last.

The others must have felt some of this, both the danger and the formation of a group taking aim. On the eighth day, Clara arrived with Malik and Inyana and Naxos and Meishi in tow. Clara waited until they were seated in Inyana's favorite tea-stall, then did her best to try and express what she sensed. Becoming part of a new Circle, and beyond that something she could not even define, much less describe. The others listened in silence. In harmony. Glad this iron-hard woman could strive to speak for them, as unseen clouds condensed so tightly he suspected they almost tasted the coming storm.

When she was done, Inyana pulled an amulet from an inner pocket and set it on the table between them. She told Adrian, 'I want you to wear this.'

'At all times,' Malik agreed. 'Next to your skin. Heart is best, but bound to your wrist will also do.'

'My mother gave this to me,' Inyana went on. 'I don't actually remember, but Daddy says it is so. She died when I was two.'

'My beloved wife bound inside that amulet her own life's energy, her passions, her love,' Malik said, watching his daughter. 'A keepsake to help our beloved child stay safe through life.'

'Inyana, Malik, no, I can't—'

'Bring it back to us when this is over,' Malik said.

'When you are safe,' Inyana agreed. 'Please.'

FORTY-NINE

Nine days passed without any word from Jurgen. Clara remained calmly confident. Whenever the others pressed, she reminded them that Jurgen was a champion at putting plans in place. They needed to give him time. He would come through.

But on the tenth day, the same two agents who had tried to arrest Adrian outside the quarantine zone were waiting when he arrived at the clinic.

This time they were accompanied by four uniformed militia. They jammed the small lobby and kept Chris from approaching.

Riggins, the tall inspector, had a receding hairline and pockmarks from some childhood disease. Gupta, agent in the new magical division, was low to the ground and carried himself with a quiet menace.

Riggins actually smiled as he said, 'You're under arrest. Again. And this time you're coming with us.'

Three of the electric inner-dome vehicles waited in the clinic's ICU parking area. They formed a silent parade through tunnels and domes. As they passed the central market, Adrian thought he heard a young woman shout his name.

As far as he could tell, they used the same elongated police vehicle that had been parked outside the Q to haul him back.

They left by way of the township's central warehouse, with guards' outrider vehicles before and behind. They loaded him in the rear cage and sealed it shut. Through the small wire-mesh window, Adrian spotted Clara come racing into the main hall, shouting furiously as the airlock door closed.

In a strange way, Adrian thought Clara's anger formed a beautiful farewell. Less than two months before, he had arrived here a stranger. Now he had a lover willing to weep in public, a young friend who froze the market with her scream, a senior Justice agent who shouted and gestured at his departure. Friends.

* * *

They kept Adrian locked inside the rear cage for several hours. Long enough to travel beyond the township's reach. His cell contained a bench just broad enough for Adrian to stretch out on, a steel toilet, and nothing else. A polished metal door connected the cage to the rest of the vehicle. There was no handle, at least on Adrian's side. He sat on the bench, his back to the frigid wall, and listened to the big tires hum across the Martian landscape.

Finally the door clicked open and the inspector stood there. Riggins demanded, 'You need the fresher?' When Adrian nodded, he took a step back. 'Let's go.'

The interior was lined up pretty much like Miles's mining crawler, minus all the luxury and most of the comfort. A large ready-room also saw duty as a sophisticated comms station, with an array of electronic equipment lining the wall beside a central table. On the opposite wall, above the steel utility kitchenette, was a weapons cabinet fronted by a wire-mesh screen.

The fresher was no better. When Adrian emerged, the two agents were joined by a third man. Silver-grey hair, neat Van Dyke beard, extra layer of flesh beneath a tailored outfit. The same seal Adrian had studied in years of dreams was sewn into the fabric above his heart. 'Sit down, young man. May I call you Adrian?'

'If you like.'

'I am Gerritt. Head of the Wizards' Council.'

Riggins slipped into the bench directly opposite Adrian. Gupta remained standing, his hip touching the table, holding Adrian with a gaze as hard as the steel cage. Adrian said, 'I thought the council had been disbanded.'

Gerritt's smile was a meaningless rearrangement of his features. 'Perhaps I should say, the new council. Sanctioned by our leaders. Loyal to the cause of Mars and its future. The question, young man, is whether you share that same loyalty.'

Adrian saw no need to respond.

'I intend to question you. Your answers are vital to any hope you might have of a future. These responses will determine your fate. Refuse to answer, offer us anything less than what we need to know, and my associate Gupta will ask you again. The agent's methods are far less polite, I assure you.'

This was a man, Adrian decided, in love with his own voice. Like Jurgen, only minus the charm, the character, and the spine.

'My associates have made a careful inspection of the planetary records. As my own aides have at council headquarters. We find nothing that indicates a man with your fingerprints or DNA registered as a wizard on Mars. We can only come up with one possible answer to this mystery. You have traveled here multiple times as a crew member on the pod ships. Every time you landed, you continued your training—'

'I've never been on Mars before.'

'I personally find that very hard to believe.' He glanced at the tall man seated opposite Adrian. 'Inspector?'

'He's lying.'

'Last and final warning, young man. The truth, or you face a very brief and painful time in Marsopolis—'

'I've been training for this since I was a child. On Earth.'

Riggins laughed out loud. Gerritt offered another empty smile. 'Come now. A childhood fantasy hardly—'

'I've spent my entire life studying. Ancient texts, spell-casting, languages. I have a working knowledge of Sumeric, Sanskrit and Archaic Chinese. I did my masters in Aramaic.'

Gerritt said, 'Doesn't matter. Earth has no magic.'

'They did. I'm certain it existed. The similarity in spells between ancient cultures with little or no communication links is too precise. There's no other explanation I can come up with.'

On and on the questions came. Gerritt playing the good cop, Riggins the angry inspector, Gupta the silent menace. Pestering, probing. How he found his seven spells. Linking to Mars while still on the ship, they spent hours on that. Repetitive and eventually boring.

Three times they stuffed him back inside the cage. Feeding him ready packs that were beyond bland. He spent a lot of time asleep. Enduring the nightmares was marginally better than the boredom.

On the final approach to Marsopolis, they were back at it again. The three men took up the same positions as before, the wizard and Riggins seated while Gupta stood where Adrian had no choice but see him. The agent glaring and promising worse to come.

Through the front window, down the long aisle and between the two drivers, Adrian watched their approach. The dome above the airlock bore the same shield as the inspector's singlet. He continued responding to questions he had answered dozens of times before. More. Bored and resigned both.

Gerritt offered a theatrical sigh. 'I fear I'm not satisfied with these responses. How say you, Inspector?'

'Disgusted, more like,' Riggins said.

The outer airlock swung back, and they drove inside.

'Young man, I urge you to be frank with us. What does Miles Lambert and his minions plan?'

'I have no idea what you're talking about,' Adrian replied.

Riggins snapped, 'Another failed insurrection? A miners' strike?'

'Surely you've heard something,' Gerritt insisted.

'You said it yourself. I've just gotten here. Why would people in power discuss their plans with me?'

'Then I fear we must turn you over to our compatriot.' A gleam of bitter pleasure tightened both their gazes. 'I regret to inform you, young man, it is unlikely you will survive the asking. So very few do, you see.'

'And no one survives intact,' Riggins added.

'This is your last chance,' Gerritt said.

Adrian watched the inner portal swing open. 'I can't tell you what I don't know.'

Riggins said, 'You'll be wishing you had listened better and seen more. Oh yes. Soon enough . . .'

The driver shouted, 'You need to get up here!'

The three of them crowded into the driver's cubby, effectively blocking Adrian's view. Gerritt demanded, 'Who are *they*?'

'Justice militia,' Riggins replied.

'Why weren't we *warned*?'

The driver inspected his controls. 'All comm-links are open and active.'

'Radio for backup!'

'Can't sir. They've apparently jammed our signals.'

'There's the reason.' The inspector pointed at an upwards angle. 'Check out the office railing.'

Gerritt squinted through the front windscreen. 'Who is that?'

Riggins replied, tight, furious. 'Jurgen Roth. Legal adviser to none other than Miles Lambert.'

Gupta said, 'Roth should have been erased months ago.'

Gerritt looked back. Nervous. 'Careful.'

Riggins said, 'He deserves nothing less. Roth thwarted us the first time we tried to arrest this one.'

Gupta said, 'Then what happens, but the culprit here renovates

MarsPort.' He marched to the gun cabinet and searched his pouch for the keys. 'I should have done this when we left the miners' camp.'

Riggins yelled, '*Wait!*'

Gupta was so enraged he fumbled the keys. Dropped them to the steel floor. Picked them up. 'Crushing this one will be a pleasure.'

'I'm ordering you to *WAIT!*'

It was Gupta's turn to shout. 'What can he possibly offer we don't already know?'

Riggins rushed over and took hold of the agent's shoulder. Said, 'Look at our captive.' Riggins shook his shoulder. Or tried to. He might as well have tried to rock the crawler. '*Look.*'

Gupta glanced over. Then turned fully. 'Is that . . .'

'Someone is shielding him.'

Gupta slumped. Defeated. 'I told you before we picked this one up. Let me get to it on the way back.'

'Be glad you didn't!' The wizard kept his gaze fastened on something beyond the front windshield. 'Look at who is there by the portal.'

The pair stepped back, crowded in again. Riggins asked, 'Is that . . .'

'The chief justice.' Gerritt actually smiled. 'So the old man has finally declared himself.'

Riggins now shared the wizard's satisfaction. 'We've been looking for a reason to disband the Justice Ministry's militia.'

'They've handed it to us on a silver platter,' Gerritt agreed. 'Wait until the prime minister hears about this.'

But Gupta wasn't so easily pleased. 'So you're going to let this one go a second time?'

'He's not going anywhere,' Gerritt replied. 'Not for long.'

'You're the high wizard! Can't you dissolve this shield?'

Gerritt stepped between the agent and Adrian. 'Think for a minute. If I did that and you eliminated him, we would be handing the enemy the chance they've been looking for.'

'We'd be the ones arrested,' Riggins agreed. 'Brought up on charges. Publicly shaming the PM. Think he'd be pleased with you?'

'I still say this filth should die.'

'And so he shall,' Gerritt replied, smiling down at Adrian. 'Just not today.'

FIFTY

When the vehicle's dual airlock system opened, Riggins was first out, followed closely by the portly wizard. Adrian would have been worried about them leaving him alone in the crawler with the drivers and the still-furious Gupta. But the shield was a comforting presence, a crystalline energy that sharpened his vision.

Through the open portal, Adrian heard Jurgen declare, 'We are here to retrieve an individual you have unlawfully detained. Again.'

Gerritt replied, 'Adrian Capstan is under arrest!'

'That would be something the chief justice should decide, wouldn't you agree?' Jurgen shouted, 'Adrian!'

He rose and started for the portal, doing his best to ignore Gupta's scowl. 'Here.'

The chief justice was an elderly gentleman who bore his years with stern determination. His features were sharply defined, his gaze hard as a raptor's. He asked the pair, 'What charges do you intend on leveling?'

'Articles 1148 and 1149 of the new wizard's code of conduct.' Riggins glared as Adrian walked around the pair and stood beside Jurgen. 'Operating without a license is unlawful.'

'This criminal has repeatedly broken regime laws,' Gerritt said.

'Punishable by imprisonment without right of parole,' Riggins said.

'For as long as the regime deems the mage to be a threat to society,' Gerritt added.

'Threat. Ha,' Jurgen replied. 'Listen to you. That mage healed MarsPort!'

'Indeed,' Gerritt said. 'And did so without proper—'

'Enough.' The chief justice watched as Gupta appeared in the doorway. He told Jurgen, 'I see your warnings were justified.'

Gerritt demanded, 'What poison has that one been spouting?'

Jurgen replied, 'My far-seer—'

'You mean a mage in the employ of another man of questionable loyalty.'

Jurgen waited until the wizard was silent, then said to a young woman standing to his left, 'How did they put it?'

She replied, 'They intended to ask questions until the plaintiff was no longer breathing.'

'Do you deny it, Inspector?'

'That criminal mage hiding behind you is a *menace*,' Riggins snarled.

'That is for the court to decide,' the chief justice replied. 'And since there is a definable risk this young man would not survive in your care—'

'Your Honor, I strenuously object to any insinuation—'

'I was speaking.' The chief justice did not need to raise his voice to silence the wizard. 'Since it is unlikely the mage would not live to face trial, I declare it necessary to confine him in what all parties deem a safe and neutral territory.'

Jurgen made no attempt whatsoever to hide his smile. 'Your Honor, I know just the place.'

FIFTY-ONE

They squabbled over everything.

Jurgen treated it as a series of motions before the court. The chief wizard and Riggins had no choice but to respond in kind. Especially with the Justice Ministry's militia surrounding them, arms at the ready.

Location of Adrian's confinement until trial. Feeding. Guards, numbers and positioning and rotation. Dates for pre-trial motions and the court hearing itself. On and on . . .

Adrian knew his life and future both hung in the balance. Just the same, he felt the journey, the tension, the hours of interrogation all taking their toll.

The chief justice finally halted their arguments with a tight glimmer of humor directed in Adrian's direction. 'These proceedings are hereby closed.'

Gerritt had been forced to give ground at every turn, causing both him and the inspector no end of discomfort. He almost whined in response. 'Your Honor, please—'

'We will continue this in due course. Meanwhile . . .' He motioned to his militia chief. 'See this young man to his new quarters.'

'Sir, I object in the strongest possible terms!'

'Noted. But for the moment, you are all dismissed.'

They sequestered him in the high wizard's official residence.

The whole thing – where he was, how he got here, what it meant – would have been almost humorous were it not for all the baggage.

As in, two rings of guards. Solitary confinement. Nothing to do for hours on end.

The Wizards' Council building was a two-story structure that had not been used in over a year. Downstairs were the general meeting rooms, training halls, library, all formerly open to the general wizarding public. Upstairs were the council's chambers, a second library, and two apartments – one for the top mage and another for his deputy. Gerritt, the new senior wizard and head of the regime's replacement council, had not yet moved in. There was still foment among the magical community, mages who teetered on the verge but had not yet declared themselves for the opposition. Having a boss who was appointed by the regime, and not voted on by the wizards themselves, and then move into the apartment while the former council was still under house arrest, would have been a step too far.

The apartment was grand, high-ceilinged and empty of everything except the temporary furnishings brought in for Adrian to use – pallet, table, one chair, and so forth.

He missed Chris terribly.

Just the same, he stayed busy.

That night, the dark-flecked dream clouds coalesced once more, dominating his internal world. And yet . . .

None of this was directed at him.

He rose with the dawn, ate the ready meal delivered by his guards, exercised, paced, ate a midday meal, exercised a second time. He felt as if he could actually taste the storm just beyond the horizon. A brooding menace that threatened them all.

Nothing about this new version of reality was clear. Just the same, by sunset Adrian was convinced he was headed in the right direction. He spent an hour seated by the parlor's front window, looking out over the broad plaza and the thoroughfare beyond. Adrian wondered at the absence of other people. This was the only section of Marsopolis where he'd seen no crowds. He took that as a very bad sign. A regime where people avoided the seats of power was one ruled by fear and dread.

When night descended, he left his perch and went to bed.

The dream might as well have been hovering above his pallet, waiting for him to fall asleep. It seemed as if he had scarcely closed his eyes before he was once again standing in the soft light of another Arizona dawn. Looking out over the high desert. He stood there for a time, waiting for a word, a sense of why he had returned, what it all meant. Nothing. The dream ended, he slipped into deeper sleep, and woke hours later, filled with the same questions as before. Certain of just one thing.

He had to get this right.

FIFTY-TWO

The next morning Clara arrived just as he finished breakfast. She handed him a fresh set of clothes and said, 'We need to be leaving.'

It was not much of a greeting, but all the woman allowed herself. For through the open front door, Adrian caught a glimpse of two sets of guards. Clustered by the entrance were the Justice militia. Beyond them were four more, only these bore the same shield as the investigator and Gupta.

Adrian changed and followed her down the main staircase, flanked by the Justice guards. They crossed the tiled foyer, passed through the double doors, and proceeded down to where Franklin waited in the lead vehicle. There was a brief flurry, another quick argument, silenced by Clara when two of the regime's militia clambered into the vehicle with them.

They did not travel far. Around the central plaza, down the main avenue, halting before a stodgy square building with a different seal or symbol above the entrance. More guards.

As they climbed the front stairs, Clara spoke, her words clipped. 'They've tried to keep you out.'

'I don't understand.'

'The regime's representatives didn't want you to attend the tribunal. They claimed the risk of your using magic to influence the outcome was too great. No one knows your abilities. They used the transformation of MarsPort as evidence against you.'

The militia guards remained tight around them, determined to catch every word. Adrian slipped through the Justice building's front doors and replied, 'I hate to say it, but that actually makes sense.'

'Jurgen objected, of course. The judges offered a compromise. The trial is far enough along now that outside viewers can study the proceedings and check for magic. If you try something, it will go hard.' She glanced over. 'You can't, can you?'

'No.'

'Good.'

They traversed a broad corridor and entered a sizeable courtroom.

The chief justice sat behind the dais, flanked by two stern-faced women. All three wore the formal black robes of office.

Everyone tracked his progress up the central aisle, past a dozen or so rows of carved stone benches. Every seat was occupied. More people stood along the rear wall. The chamber was so quiet Adrian heard their footsteps scrape along the tiled floor, loud as drumbeats. The high wizard sat at the front table to his left, with two berobed figures Adrian had not seen before. Inspector Riggins and Agent Gupta sat directly behind them. Jurgen was alone at the right-hand table. Behind him were Captain Otieno, Meishi, Naxos, Lars and three other crew members. Captain Otieno did not look at all well. Frail, favoring his right side, hands gripping a cane set on the floor between his legs. Chris was seated in the witness stand to the justice's right. She maintained a professional calm as Adrian was led up front and locked inside a plexiglass cage to the right of the judges.

Once Adrian was seated, the chief justice said, 'Proceed.'

The high wizard shot Adrian a venomous look, then continued, 'I say to you, Doctor Leighton, that the infected crew were scarcely served at all by this charlatan and his noxious potions.' He paused, then added, 'The very idea of a mere trainee binding himself to Mars across deep space is ludicrous! It's *absurd*!'

Chris merely sat and waited.

'Well?' His voice was thunderous. 'Do you have nothing to say for yourself?'

She held to an icy calm. 'I didn't hear a question.'

There was a good deal of tittering, stifled when the chief justice lifted his gavel. He told Chris: 'Nonetheless, the court orders you to respond.'

'What about his repairing of MarsPort?'

The wizard huffed a pretend laugh. 'Who can say if the plaintiff did what these others claim? Or if the attorney seated at the opposing table simply chose to fabricate an absurd lie?'

Chris did not respond.

The high wizard glared at Chris a moment longer, then muttered, 'No more questions.'

'The witness may step down.' The chief justice looked at Jurgen. 'Defense may call your next—'

'Just a moment.' The woman to the chief justice's left was massive, almost twice his size, her robes big as a circus tent. Tight silver-grey curls layered her head like a helmet. 'I fail to see why we continue to waste the court's time.' She pointed at Jurgen. 'Even the defense counselor agrees that our statutes have been broken.'

'As the defense has repeatedly stated,' the chief justice replied, 'there are extenuating circumstances.'

'Granted. But how many more witnesses do we need to hear from if the core issue has already been accepted by the court?' She looked at Jurgen. 'Counselor, who is your next witness?'

Jurgen rose to his feet. 'If it please the court, Vincent Otieno, Captain of—'

She waved Jurgen to silence and turned back to the chief justice. 'And what will he tell us? The young man ministered to the crew. Correct?' She motioned for Jurgen to sit down. 'Let's cut to the chase. A crime has been committed. Sit *down*, Counselor. Adrian Capstan broke statutes from the moment he set foot on Mars. Even before he landed, if the previous witness is to be believed. The accused is guilty. Enough of this nonsense.'

Jurgen remained standing. 'Your Honors, please, if I may—'

'No you may not! Nonsense I said, and nonsense I meant. The defendant is guilty. Finished. This court needs to proceed to cases where there is at least a question of innocence.'

The chief justice turned to the woman seated on his opposite side. When he received a grave nod in response to his unspoken question, he said, 'Very well. It is the opinion of this court that articles of the wizards' code have been repeatedly violated. The fact that the defendant has only just arrived on Mars, and has done considerable good with his talents—'

'With respect, those claims are far from proven,' the high wizard insisted.

'—are indeed mitigating circumstances. He is, nonetheless, found guilty as charged.'

Adrian heard Chris and several others among the crew shout a loud protest. Otieno, however, merely looked his way. Somber. Stern. His warning clear enough.

The chief justice rapped his gavel, called for silence, then: 'It is customary to grant the guilty party an opportunity to address the court before sentence is passed. Adrian Capstan, do you have anything you wish to say?'

He rose to his feet. 'Thank you, Your Honor.' This was the moment he had been working toward, part of what had solidified during his solitary hours. 'It seems the best way to resolve this is for me to leave Mars and never return.'

'*No!*' This time the protest came from Jurgen Roth. The attorney rose to his feet. 'This is an *outrage!*'

Adrian directed his words to the lawyer. 'They don't want me here. They're calling me a criminal for doing what comes naturally.'

'Your Honor, this young man had done nothing, not one solitary thing, but serve the common good. He has sheltered, protected, healed, revitalized—'

'Jurgen.'

'We should be thanking him! He deserves a medal!'

'Stop. Please. If they don't want me here, I have no place. No home. It's the right move. The best for everyone.'

Jurgen stared at him a long moment, slack-jawed, defeated. Finally he slumped into his chair and muttered, 'I protest in the strongest possible terms.'

The chief justice glanced at the women seated to either side. When he received nods from both parties, he proclaimed, 'It is the decision of this court that you, Adrian Capstan, are banished from Mars. Never to return. You will remain in protective custody until your ship departs. If you dare use any further magic during this sequestration, you will be imprisoned.' He banged his gavel. 'Court is adjourned.'

FIFTY-THREE

Adrian spent another three and a half days inside the high wizard's empty apartment, enduring a rather grand version of solitary confinement. He came to loathe the lofty chamber, the silence. Most of the time was spent going back over his experiences since first binding with Mars. Wondering if he could have managed things differently. Not taken such an arrow-straight approach that led to him being in this state. Isolated in the place he had dreamed of and yearned for most of his life. Waiting for his banishment to take effect. Never to be on Mars again.

In the end, he decided that given the chance to do it all over, he would have taken pretty much the exact same steps.

His nights were disturbed by more dreams of the Arizona high desert.

They came with awful regularity. Three times each night.

Yet they never offered a message. Which at first only added to the dread of coming to full alert while dreaming, staring at the painted mountains, the desert shrub, the silent reaches, the hot wind he could not actually feel.

On the fourth morning, it all came together. The realization was so potent he lost all bitterness over his state, at least for a time.

Which was when he stretched out again. Needing to be there. Right this very moment. See if his idea actually held up in dream-time reality.

He rarely took siestas. His work schedule back on Earth had not permitted such indulgences. They had occasionally been part of a lazy Saturday afternoon, a punctuation to end a hard slog of a week.

This was different.

Adrian did not feel all that tired when he lay down. But soon as he was prone, the fatigue swept over him, a great wave of everything he had endured, all he carried. Three breaths, and he was gone.

There he was. Standing on the same empty path, high above the high desert town of Sedona, staring over the mountain peaks, the pale wash of dawn. A new day.

It was all his to claim.

Now that he had made the decision, it all seemed so incredibly straightforward. There was no message *given*. He had to make the choice. Decide which path to take.

He spoke the words aloud, at least in his dream. 'I want to serve the cause of magic. Wherever I am.'

The dream ended.

Adrian opened his eyes.

Captain Vincent Otieno was seated on the room's only chair. Hands resting on the curved handle of the cane between his legs. A thermos and mug rested on the table beside him. 'You're awake. Good. We need to have a word while there's still time.'

'The doctors insist it would be best if I remain here on Mars,' Otieno began. He lifted the cane and continued, 'There are issues related to an irregular heartbeat. And my legs are not back to full strength. Both of which would be helped by more time in low gravity. Miles Lambert has kindly offered me the use of an apartment. His personal medical team will supervise my recovery.' Otieno gave that a long beat, then continued, 'All because of their high regard for you.'

Adrian had no idea how to respond. Part of his being, mind and heart both, remained captured by the dream and the emotions he had carried back to full wakefulness. A bone-deep satisfaction. Regret too, of course. There was a very real chance he would never again walk the Martian reaches. Just the same, the decision and the declaration that followed left him with a sentiment far too strong to be contained in one simple word, like harmony.

Otieno continued, 'There has been a series of communications with our headquarters on Earth. I have been appointed representative of the space consortium. The former so-called ambassador is traveling back on our ship, something to do with a family emergency. In regards to your own situation, the consortium has now certified you as a full lieutenant. Your official duties on this return leg will be as liaison to the pod crews, a position I have fought for years to establish. Upon your return to Earth, you will of course be required to go through standard pre-flight training. But as you've already passed the pod exams, I think we can assume you will do well. As to your future prospects, your records now hold commendations from Commander Meishi, Flight Communications Officer Naxos, Doctor Leighton and myself.'

Adrian rose and stepped to the table and poured himself a mug of tea. He stood for a moment, sipping the still-hot brew and coming to terms with the realignment of his internal universe.

'Commander Meishi visited me in the hospital, where I've been under the care of Doctor Leighton,' Otieno went on. 'Following that, I have interviewed several others among my crew.' He fiddled with the head of his cane. 'Sometimes it is only in a situation like this, where a captain realizes just how isolated he is. No officer is perfect. There are always questionable elements to every individual's character, their methods . . .'

Adrian walked back and seated himself on the pallet. He did not want to stand over the captain, and there was nowhere else to sit. Plus there was a certain rightness to this situation, looking up to the man who had granted him his chance.

Otieno said, 'The crew have made it known – in no uncertain terms – that they will not serve under Harrow as their captain. I have now informed him of this. Harrow has not formally responded. But I have heard rumors that he has been offered a post as director of MarsPort.'

The news effectively sealed off any chance he might have of returning. Adrian watched the steam rising from his mug. Holding fast to the dreamtime declaration. Trying to, anyway.

Otieno must have seen the concerns raised by this news, for he added, 'Regardless of Harrow's decision, know this. You have earned the respect and the gratitude of any number of people here on Mars.'

'I'm banished,' Adrian replied. 'Permanently barred from returning.'

'So long as the current regime remains in power,' Otieno pointed out. 'If or when that changes, and a ship lands here with you serving as crew member, you will be greeted by any number of allies.' He thumped the cane once, twice, then added, 'And friends.'

FIFTY-FOUR

When they emerged from the apartment, Clara and Naxos and Meishi were all there, waiting. Adrian's departure was slowed by how Clara and Naxos settled Otieno into a wheelchair and carried the skipper down the central staircase. Every time Adrian glanced over, Otieno was watching him. The captain's message was clear enough. Life did not always offer what he might want or wish for himself. Deal with it.

The vehicle waiting for them was similar to the one that had transported Adrian to the courthouse. Justice militia stood at the top of the stairs, marched them down, and settled them inside. There were no chains, no sense of danger. On the contrary. All this was done to shield him. What was more, Adrian knew why. The real threat now had a name.

They took the main thoroughfare as far as it ran, away from the government buildings and the empty passageways. Clara drove. The lanes became crowded, dense with throngs of people. The shops along the broad avenue had illuminated glass fronts and bore names that Adrian recognized from Earth. People were well dressed, chattering, easy, happy.

When Adrian realized where they were headed, he could have laughed out loud. Despite everything.

The name above the entryway was suitably discreet. The structure itself was low-slung, enormous and elegant. The large entry was flanked by discreet bronze plaques, both bearing the name, Ritz-Carlton.

The hotel where Adrian had hoped to work. Back before he left Earth. All those many eons ago.

When their vehicle entered the semicircular forecourt, Otieno said, 'I am required to leave you here.' He offered Adrian his hand. 'You will remember what I said, yes?'

'Every word,' Adrian replied.

Another pair of Justice militia flanked the entrance. Adrian was effectively surrounded as they ushered him through the frozen lobby, past throngs of hotel staff and wealthy tourists, up the central staircase, and through the Ambassadorial Suite's double doors.

Where Chris stood waiting to greet him.

Clara remained by the entryway until the militia stepped out and the door shut behind them. 'Your ship lifts off in nine days. In the meantime, you are restricted to quarters. You are granted one visitor per day.'

Chris did her best to smile. 'Not counting me.'

'Indeed so. And I have been appointed head of your security detail for the duration.' Clara offered a warrior's smile. 'You have Chris to thank for your change of quarters.'

Chris corrected, 'Actually, it was the hospital director. And the deputy prime minister. Who is scheduled for surgery tomorrow. By me.'

'The good doctor refused to serve another shift until you were released from the council building,' Clara said.

Chris remained standing well apart. 'Don't forget the role Miles played.'

'He did and he didn't,' Clara replied. 'Miles simply offered to pay for your room. Funds which he will take from the sum he owes you.'

Adrian replied, 'Miles Lambert doesn't owe me a cent.'

'Funds already banked in your name,' Clara insisted. 'For repairing MarsPort.' She offered a rare smile. 'And other services.'

'What about the cost of keeping me safe?' Adrian protested. 'The transport. The court costs. Jurgen . . .'

Clara showed him an open palm, effectively silencing further protests. 'The funds have been transferred to an Earthside account. Acting Captain Meishi has the details.'

When Adrian continued to struggle over his response, Chris said, 'Now is the moment when you thank him.'

His voice sounded weak to his own ears. 'Please thank Miles on my behalf.'

Chris continued, 'And Clara.'

He thought he sounded like a petulant child. 'Thank you, Clara.'

'Good boy,' Chris said. 'That wasn't too painful, was it?'

The Justice agent offered them another tight smile. 'My staff will be on guard round the clock. Let them know of anything you require.'

When they were alone, Chris led him into the suite's bedchamber, closed the door, and said, 'The parlor and kitchenette are wired for sound. Actually, the entire suite is supposedly under surveillance.' She lifted a handheld device from the bed's side table and showed him a green light. 'This blocks all monitoring equipment.'

'You arranged this as well?'

'You bet.' She replaced the device and studied him a long moment. 'How are you really?'

The distance between them seemed immeasurable. 'Healing.'

'Truly?'

He nodded. 'We're together.'

'That's right. We are.'

'I can't see much beyond that right now.'

'And after? When the newness wears off?'

It was a valid question. 'I think I know what I'm going to do.'

'You mean, back on Earth.'

'Yes. A purpose. Something that makes all this worthwhile.'

'I'm so glad.'

'Thank you, Chris. For everything.' He knew the words were inadequate. Perhaps they always would be. Just the same, they had to be said. 'Most especially for—'

That was as far as she let him go.

FIFTY-FIVE

The next morning, Jurgen Roth arrived with breakfast. Chris had left for an early shift, warning she would be late getting back. The deputy PM's procedure was scheduled for midday, and Chris would hang around the hospital until he was through recovery. The procedure involved a tricky micro-surgery that none of the local doctors wanted to risk taking on themselves.

Jurgen was dressed in new tailored singlet, his hair perfectly coiffed, cheeks freshly shaved. The successful attorney off on just another day's business.

The breakfast trolley was rolled in by Clara herself. But the woman refused Jurgen's invitation to join them. Protocol, was her one-word response.

When they had filled plates and mugs, Jurgen placed a handheld device on the table between them. It was identical to the one by their bed, only the light on this one glowed red.

As they ate, Jurgen offered a brief overview of Mars's colonization. Most of it Adrian knew from his earlier research. But this was different, and not merely because of the listening ears. Jurgen did not connect the dots leading to the current crisis. Nor was it required. Everything he said now filled in the gaps, bringing the two of them to this point. Preparing for Adrian's banishment.

Eight days.

'It all began with what early expeditions found on the lunar south pole – the Aitken Basin, to be precise. Two and a quarter billion tons of metal, stretching over hundreds of square miles, running down three hundred kilometers into the moon's crust.' Jurgen showed the remarkable ability to eat at full speed, while talking at almost the same rapid pace. 'When NASA's Gravity Recovery and Interior Laboratory satellite first sent back details, scientists thought perhaps there had been an error in their calibrations. Further studies confirmed this wealth of metals was the result of a massive meteorite strike. But when they started mining, the problems they encountered were huge. The rare earth minerals were there, yet buried so deep it was impossible to reach them.

'When the Mars survey began in earnest, the scientists knew what to look for. Meteor strikes that were smaller in scale. Resulting in the same sort of mineral deposits. Not as large, of course. But also not as deep.' He paused to apply the napkin. 'You of course know where the largest deposits closest to the surface were found.'

'Right here. Marsopolis sits on them.'

'Correct.' He rose from the table, brought over the thermos. 'More coffee?'

'Please.'

Jurgen plied the jug, set it down, and hit the button on the jamming device. 'Which ends today's lesson. We can only do this for a few minutes each time. I have insisted on this as part of attorney–client privilege. Clear?'

'Yes.'

The attorney settled back in his chair. 'As Clara mentioned, you are allowed one additional visitor each day. They must be part of the ship's company. I will accompany them.' He pointed to the device, now green. 'Again, you will have a few minutes. If that is actually required.'

'It will be.'

'I was hoping as much.' Jurgen smiled. 'We need to talk about the gold.'

'Not yet,' Adrian replied. 'First we need to talk about my night-mares.'

Jurgen's response surprised him.

The lawyer studied Adrian, just for one quick moment, then he rose and walked to the suite's front door. He unlocked, opened, and gestured. 'Inside, please. Now.'

He pointed Clara to the table, but the agent refused to sit down. She noted the device's green light, then demanded, 'What's going on?'

Jurgen seated himself. 'Adrian wants to talk about his dreams.'

Clara snapped, 'For the nth time, they're not dreams.'

Adrian took an easy breath. Hearing he was not alone made the next steps much easier. 'Have the others experienced them? I mean, those who were with us—'

'I know what you mean. And the answer is yes. All of us. What about Chris?'

'I didn't ask. But this morning she . . .' He shrugged. 'Neither of us had an easy night.'

'Chris is operating on the deputy PM today,' Jurgen offered.

Clara pulled out another chair. 'OK, so talk.'

Adrian gave it to them in tight bursts. As close to a step-by-step procedure as he could manage. Call it three minutes, start to finish.

Clara gave it ten seconds of silence, then said, 'I totally agree.'

Jurgen asked, 'You're certain?'

'As I can be of everything.' She was not so much grim as battle-ready. 'Soon as we go public with the gold, they're going on the offensive. We hoped they wouldn't respond with an outright assault. Adrian is correct. It was a futile hope.'

'But you weren't sure of their meaning, those dreams.'

'I am now.' She pointed to Adrian. 'Hearing him is like watching unfocused images all snap into total clarity.'

Adrian said it again. 'The dreams were never about us. That's what I think has slowed us down, looking at them as if they were *our* warnings. As if what *we* did was at risk.'

'He's right,' Clara muttered. 'He's so right.'

'Soon as I started thinking about everyone on Mars, all this came together.' He gave Jurgen another chance to object, but when the attorney remained silent he continued, 'This ability to purify metals is a power they can't afford to leave in Miles's hands. Once the regime catches wind of this, they'll be forced to act. Immediately. Before word reaches the general populace.'

'We should have seen this,' Clara said. 'While we were still out there on the plains—'

'No looking back,' Jurgen said. 'No time.'

Clara looked ready to argue, but in the end she merely nodded and told Adrian, 'Your next steps are solid.'

He breathed marginally easier. 'I was worried. I don't have any experience in tactics.'

'I had better get started putting things in place.' Jurgen sighed himself to his feet. 'So now we're committed.'

'No,' Clara replied. 'We've been committed since gold rained from the Martian skies.'

FIFTY-SIX

The dark-flecked dreams returned that night. Yet there were significant differences to the sweep of threat and peril. Adrian's sleep was not disturbed. Instead, he remained merely an observer. Yet still involved. Viscerally connected by the role that took shape in the minutes after he woke.

He rose from the bed, walked into the suite's parlor, and watched it all coalesce. The steps he had outlined, the plans he was trying to help put in place, became crystal clear. Fueled by an urgency that tasted visceral.

Chris emerged from their bedroom a few minutes later. Her movements were unsteady, her eyes encircled by plum stains. He waited until she had finished her first silent cup of coffee. Then he took her by the hand and led her back into the bedroom. Where they could talk. In as few words as possible, he laid out what had to happen next. Adrian kept it to the issues that Chris needed to handle. The bigger picture could wait.

As he talked, he saw this woman he had come to love undergo a seismic change. She brightened. Straightened. Breathed easy. Almost smiled. As if he was passing on the best news possible.

When he was done, she said, 'I'll take care of everything on my first break. You're not in any danger? I mean, a new threat to your life.'

'Nothing that's come to me suggests anything like that.'

'Just say no, Adrian. I need to hear that.'

'No, Chris. The danger isn't . . .'

She sighed, kissed him, then held him tightly. 'I've been so afraid. I thought, you know, the dreams were about you.'

'I'm as certain as I can be they're not. Not any more.'

She nodded against his cheek. 'That's how it felt. As you talked, all the dreams and fears, they shifted.'

'I'm glad. That is the finest confirmation I could have this is all correct.'

She leaned back far enough to study him, eyes bright with tears she would not shed. Not now. 'Is this part of your far-seeing?'

'I haven't even thought about that.'

'Think about it now.'

'I didn't cast a spell.'

'No surprise there. You were asleep.'

'Is that a smile?'

'A little one. Maybe.' She kissed him. 'All night, every time I woke up, all I could think was, I can't go through the fear of losing you again. I just can't.'

Their moments together always seemed too brief. Each time it was harder to let this amazing woman go. When she rose from the bed and entered the fresher, Adrian took a pad and pen from her pouch and started writing. Now and then, Chris paused in preparing for the day ahead, returning to where he sat, closing the distance momentarily.

When she declared, 'I need to be going,' Adrian was ready.

He rose to his feet and handed her the pages. 'Can you give this to Clara?'

'No problem.'

'Tell her it's another part of what we discussed yesterday.'

She kissed him a final time, gave him another dose of those incredible eyes, and was gone.

Lunch was brought by one of Clara's minions, which Adrian took as a good sign.

Dinner the same.

Adrian was asleep when Chris finally returned from the hospital. He woke to the sound of the shower. A warm and slightly damp body slipped into bed. They nestled together without Adrian coming fully awake.

He woke early, as refreshed as he had been since renovating the Q's lone chamber.

No dreams. At least none that he could remember.

Chris had left a note by the coffee-maker, asking him to wake her as early as possible. He poured her a mug and walked back into the bedroom. Watching her moan her way to wakefulness, playing the fretful child over being woken too soon, fastening her gaze on him, made it very hard to rise and step back and let her begin her morning routine. Very hard indeed.

Jurgen Roth joined Adrian for lunch. It was his only break to the long and lonely hours. While they ate, Jurgen offered a smattering of information about his own background. Born and raised on Mars. One of the first students to attend Georgetown Law's new online program for Mars residences. How tough it was to study a legal structure that was still taking shape, twice undergoing fundamental changes since he entered practice, first when Earth removed its all-powerful representative and shifted to an ambassador, and now with the current regime. About the new political and legal structure, he said nothing at all.

In return, Adrian answered the lawyer's gently probing queries into his own past. Describing the hard early days, the incredible gift of those first dreams, entering the foster program, being held to a stable course by messages that a better life was ahead. Believing it because he had nothing else. Jurgen was visibly moved by the telling, which left Adrian feeling even closer to the man.

As they rose from the table, Jurgen touched the jamming device, waited for the light to go green, then said in a rush, 'Everything should be in place tonight. We intend to put your plans to work tomorrow at dawn. Five o'clock. Be ready.'

Adrian had two questions that could not wait. First, 'I have no connection to an unlock spell.'

'We've been through this,' Jurgen replied. 'Several times.'

'Who will work the spell for us?'

'Malik.'

Adrian wanted to press. So much was riding on their having an unlock-and-open spell at their disposal. In the end, though, he just moved to his second question. 'Miles is with us?'

'So many preparations are happening, I couldn't begin to tell you. And he is behind them all.' Jurgen touched the button a second time, offered his farewells, and departed while Adrian's heart was still near redline.

FIFTY-SEVEN

Before retiring Adrian wrote Chris a note and left it in the parlor with all the lights on. He had no idea when she finally arrived. Late. He simply woke hours later to find the lights off and a warm body breathing deep sleep breaths beside him.

He feared waking her would be nigh on impossible. But when his clock chimed at half-past four and he turned on the lights, he found her eyes were open, watching him. 'Five o'clock? Really?'

'How do you manage on such little sleep?'

'It's something every doctor learns during residency. If not before.'

'You look incredibly alert.'

'I am. And excited. But I am also in desperate need of coffee.'

He plied the coffee machine, brought her a mug, used the fresher, dressed, then joined her. She took the bedroom's only chair. He sat on the bed. 'What's with your crazy hours?'

'The question every lover of a doctor asks. Mars or Earth, no difference.' She sipped from her mug. 'How much time?'

'Four minutes, give or take. There's every chance this won't work.'

'Don't say that. It will. It has to.'

'Where are the runes?'

'Runes. Right. I hope I haven't lost them somewhere.'

'Chris. Please. Give me a break.'

She grinned, pulled them from the bedside table. 'Ta-dah.'

'That wasn't funny.'

'Oh, come on. It was a teeny bit funny.'

He checked the clock. 'It's time.' But when he reached for her hand, Adrian found himself frozen with fear. 'I have no idea this will work.'

Chris was beyond calm. 'Everything is good. It's better than that.'

'So much is riding on—'

'Sweetie, look at me. You think you're the first to handle impossible responsibilities? The first to feel afraid? Today, when we're done here, I'll do three surgeries. Each time, the lives of my patients hang in the balance.'

'How do you manage that stress?'

'You don't allow yourself to dwell on the risks. Do your job to the best of your ability. That's all there is.' She gave that a beat. 'Now take a deep breath.'

He did so.

'Fine. Another. Ready?'

He wanted to deny. Run screaming from the room. Admit he was a coward. Anything but . . .

She asked again, 'Ready?'

'OK. Yes.'

'Tell me what to do. Don't guess. Don't flail around. You *have* this.'

Another breath, then, 'Take my hand not holding the runes. Now reach out and bind. First with the planet.' He did the same. 'OK?'

'I think . . . Yes.'

'Good.' He began casting the joining spell. Then, 'Now reach out to the others. They're gathered inside a Rolligon, right in the middle of the plain where we—'

'I have them!'

Her excitement shimmered the air around them. Because he had them too.

The bond was as fiercely intimate as if they too were standing in the vehicle's ready-room. It was so good to be back among them all, Adrian could have wept. If only they had the time.

He experienced a series of impossibly warm greetings. Clara and Malik and Inyana and Franklin and Jonah and Katarina. All smiling down deep. Where it mattered most.

A moment for reveling in the togetherness, then, 'OK, Chris. Cast the runes.'

As she did so, Adrian shouted in his mind and voice both. 'Show us the opening!'

The rune's response was almost identical to what Adrian had felt during their first hunt, out there on the Martian plains. And every hunt that followed.

It was the same, only more precise.

Before, he had known it was there, the answer to Viviana's quest. A new city without domes. The impossible made real.

Now, he saw precisely *where*.

The answer lay inside the ridgeline marking the mineral plains' furthest boundary.

He and Chris remained linked while Franklin drove the others across the expanse. With each passing kilometer, the destination became more precise, the magnetic force binding them to this event all the stronger.

One hour and seventeen minutes later, they arrived. What was more, the Circle remained intact.

It did not matter to any of them how the vehicle now faced just another Martian cliff. They all knew.

This was it.

Jonah was the one who asked, '*Malik?*'

In response, the merchant lifted his hands high overhead, and screamed the word so loudly that the air around Adrian and Chris shimmered. '*OPEN!*'

Where before there was only rock, now there was . . .

The tunnel was mammoth. The spaceship's entire cockpit could have fitted inside. The largest of Vivianaville's domes. A flat stable floor of Martian rock joined with curved walls and a ceiling lost to shadows. The vehicle's lights did not reach that high.

Inyana cried, '*ILLUMINATE!*'

Adrian had not even known this was one of the young lady's spells until that moment.

Even though they viewed this from a vast distance. While their only connection came through a Circle that should not exist. And they viewed this through the eyes of others. Even so. Chris and Adrian both cried aloud at the sight.

A brilliant off-white illumination shone from the walls and ceiling. It was not exactly constant. More a pearlescence, one shade flowing intimately to the next. The effect was . . .

Welcoming.

They drove and drove and drove. Descending at such a gentle pace they could easily have thought it was a level journey. Finally, several kilometers in, the tunnel ended at another wall.

Malik shouted another command. The wall vanished.

They entered . . .

FIFTY-EIGHT

ive days later, Adrian was transported to the waiting ship. He traveled under the supervision of Inspector Riggins and Gupta, the glowering agent. From the moment they entered his parlor, to depositing him inside the cockpit's connecting tunnel, neither man spoke.

Clara and six members of the Justice militia tracked their every move.

The ensuing period had been far easier than Adrian had expected. Jurgen appeared just once, while Clara only reappeared on this final day, there to serve as official guard and escort. Adrian had little to do, and no involvement in everything that urgently needed to be put in place.

Just the same, he didn't mind.

Four or five times each day, he bonded with some of the newly formed Circle. Twice Chris joined him, breaking off from her final shifts to bind with the group and witness the frantic unfolding of so much, so fast. Those two events were the most special of all.

The other times, he observed.

His primary conduit was Inyana, the effervescent sprite who willingly allowed Adrian to piggy-back.

What he saw . . .

At the tunnel's end opened a cavern. The size was very difficult to gauge, especially at first, because Inyana's illumination spell resulted in the same pearlescent light shining from walls and ceiling. The effect was a gradual merging together of the seamless enclosure, far, far in the distance.

The cavern was eleven and a half kilometers long. Six wide. Four high.

The cavern's walls and ceiling formed a nearly perfect oval. The floor was polished sandstone, slightly graded except for a deep bowl-shaped depression at the cavern's center. The cave was large enough to swallow Marsopolis. Larger.

The cavern was also a hive of non-stop frantic activity.

The two times Chris joined them, the Circle used these moments of completion to hunt.

Only they were not after minerals. They searched for something far more valuable. They were after water.

For both of these hunts, Chris held a mug half-filled with the precious liquid.

Scientists had known since the early satellites surveyed the Martian surface that water was abundant. But it remained hidden deep in the Martian shale, tiny molecules that had waited millennia for this very moment.

After the second foray, the central bowl had become a lake. Call it sixty meters deep, a kilometer to a side, the water so clear the bottom appeared close enough to touch.

The drivers maintained a speed that Adrian thought borderline suicidal. He would have complained mightily if he had thought it would do any good. In truth, the response to his unspoken complaint was there in Clara's tense features. And the inspector. And Gupta. All of them locked in a tight intensity that made their silence almost welcome.

Adrian knew why, of course. Since there was nothing he could do about it, and watching the scenery blur to either side threatened to make him carsick, he did the only thing that came to mind.

He took a nap.

When he woke, the windows were dark. As far as he could tell, they were actually driving faster now. He refused Clara's offer of a ready meal and settled at the central table. He remained there, willing himself not to think what might happen if they struck a rock.

Finally, at long last, he felt the vehicle slowing. Clara announced, 'We're here.'

A collapsible tunnel snaked out from the cockpit and connected to the vehicle's airlock. The inspector refused to meet Adrian's gaze. Gupta formed a gun of his thumb forefinger and shot Adrian.

'Careful,' Clara warned. 'That's bound to be a felony. Even with this regime.'

Gupta snorted and turned away.

Adrian was mildly shocked when Clara remained standing in the vehicle's airlock. Then he felt foolish for not realizing she could go no further. He stood there in the collapsible tunnel, searching futilely for words.

She offered another of her sniper's smiles. 'Go.'

'Clara, thank you. So much. For everything.'

'My thoughts exactly.' She gave him a two-fingered salute, said again, 'Go.'

The ribbed tunnel made the surface uneven. Meishi waited by the entry, Chris two steps behind her. Adrian said, 'Captain.'

'Inside, Lieutenant.'

He embraced Chris, then nodded to Lars standing by the airlock controls. When the tunnel was retracted and the portal sealed, Adrian asked, 'How is Otieno?'

It was Chris who replied, 'Stronger with each passing day. He sends his regards.'

Meishi led them to where Naxos waited by the inner lift. They rose to the bridge, where their new skipper commanded, 'Prepare to raise ship.'

Seven hours later, they linked to the mother ship.

Adrian's first duty as pod liaison was to confirm that the pod pilots had all returned to Mars.

He then relayed Meishi's orders to the pod chiefs; they were holding in stationary orbit, awaiting crucial information before making way for Earth.

It was a tense time, and not just for the four who knew precisely what lay in store.

Naxos and his family had been instrumental in preliminary work in the as-yet-unnamed new city. Every miner and their team who could be trusted had been enlisted.

'Rumors' swirled that minerals were now being refined in Vivianaville. Nothing more, and no one who knew said anything. All the enlisted miners knew was that payment had been guaranteed by Miles Lambert, the unseen guiding hand behind everything that was taking place.

These newly arrived miners did not in fact work as miners. They became skilled contractors. Building new residences. Getting the air filtration systems up and running. Constructing three warehouse-size hydroponics plants. Support structures. Laying out preliminary designs for roads and districts and piping and everything the new city required.

Those people who worked in the new development effectively vanished. That was part of the arrangement. They came to work and to establish what would be their new homes. But for the moment, all contact with the outside world was stifled.

So many miners and their families suddenly disappearing from regular duties only stoked the rumors. Which worked in their favor, so long as the truth did not emerge. Which meant speed was everything.

The schedule was set. The whirlwind of force and dark images had been clear enough.

The moment their ship left Mars, Jurgen Roth approached the prime minister on behalf of Miles Lambert. He confirmed the rumors were true: a new method of refining and purifying all rare-earth metals had been perfected. One that required none of the heavy equipment and water used in Earthbound procedures.

On Jurgen's signal, Clara led the convoy carrying fifteen tons of refined gold to the regime's treasure house.

Jurgen received both a certified receipt and payment in credits and bearer bonds. The threat was there, and never spoken outright. Agree to Miles's terms, or they would turn around and ask if Earth would prefer to do business with Miles directly.

The result was inevitable.

The regime could not allow their strongest opponent to hold such power.

It was only a matter of time.

As soon as the declaration was made and the purified gold transferred, Lambertville went into lockdown. All passageways between Miles Lambert's domes and the rest of the city were sealed. No incoming traffic of any kind was permitted through the outer airlocks.

Far-seers in the employ of Miles had identified everyone in Vivianaville who took the regime's coin. While Miles informed the regime of his new source of wealth, every one of the regime rats were expelled from the mining community. Transported in three crawlers back to the main Marsopolis airlock.

Vivianaville itself remained isolated by an all-channel blackout. The entire region was muffled by a non-stop barrage of jamming signals. The regime's spy drones lost contact with their controllers and simply wandered about until they ran out of fuel and dropped from the sky.

All satellites were controlled by Earthbound companies. Despite numerous urgent requests for surveillance over the mining town,

Earth simply remained silent. Both Meishi and Otieno had informed their superiors of their treatment at the hands of the regime. Crucial decisions were to be taken with regards to future relations. All of which would wait until the ship's return Earthside. In the meantime, Earth's only communication with the current Mars government was to confirm Vincent Otieno as their new representative.

The message could not have been clearer. The rumors were true. The new refining technology was located in Vivianaville.

Six long days after they connected to the main ship and entered orbit, Naxos announced, 'We have movement. Multiple vehicles departing from Marsopolis.'

Meishi settled into the skipper's chair. 'Destination?'

A pause then, 'All appear headed for Vivianaville.'

'Satellites in place?'

'Two in stationary orbit.' A pause, then, 'Our watchers have seen the invasion force. The jamming signal is now shut off.'

Meishi nodded. 'Activate cameras.'

Throughout the blackout period, volunteers had planted cameras around Vivianaville. Surrounding the community. Now that they were activated, their images were fed into two outlets.

The new underground city.

And the satellites. The ones which the regime could not access.

'Split the front screen,' Meishi ordered. 'How many can you give us?'

'As many as you want,' Naxos said. 'But it's better if I hold them to, say, six, and rotate.'

'Very well. Do so.'

During the time it took for the regime's convoy to reach Vivianaville, the cockpit maintained its standard watch system. Just the same, few of the crew left the bridge for very long. Rotations were set so those not assigned bridge duty could also witness the events. And Naxos shared the camera feeds throughout the cockpit.

The bridge was as full as Adrian had ever seen when mid-afternoon the next day, Naxos announced, 'They're spreading out.' A pause, then, 'Standard military tactics. OK, they're unloading weaponry.'

'Are they offering any warning to the inhabitants?'

'Negative. They're holding to strict radio silence.'

Lars was seated to Adrian's left, Chris to his right. The medic reached for his hand as Lars said, 'Unbelievable.'

The murmur of near rage carried around the bridge until Meishi ordered, 'Hold fast.'

A long silence, then Naxos rose to his feet. 'Are you seeing this?'

Meishi stood with everyone else. 'What are they?'

It was Adrian who replied, 'Sand giants. Battle magic.'

The massive beasts of rock and dust marched upon the township.

And began tearing apart the domes.

Shouts rose all around the bridge. This time, Meishi did not silence her crew.

Soon as the interior structures were revealed and breathable air was denied everyone inside who had not suited up in time, the regime's militia attacked from all sides.

The sand giants collapsed into mounds of rubble.

The militia began tearing Vivianaville apart. Searching for what was not there.

No minerals refinery.

What was more, no inhabitants.

Those on the bridge could actually see the militia's building rage. Once the invaders realized their aims had been thwarted, they entered into full destruction mode.

Within hours, Vivianaville was nothing but a smoldering ruin.

Adrian let the crew vent for a time, then called, 'Can I please have your attention?'

Meishi clapped her hands. 'Silence!' Then, 'Go ahead, Lieutenant.'

'All of this was carefully planned out.' Adrian pointed to the destroyed township. 'Convoys have stripped Vivianaville to the metal bones.'

Chris added, 'Over fifty convoys have traveled from Vivianaville to the new city, all shielded by mobile jamming equipment.'

Another silence, then someone demanded, 'What new city are we talking about?'

'Somewhere safe,' Chris said.

Naxos added, 'We've been a part of this.'

Meishi nodded, 'Myself, Naxos, Chris, Adrian. And many others.'

Chris said, 'Every night, convoys have also left Miles Lambert's compound for the new city. Loaded to the gills.'

Meishi said, 'They have successfully dismantled and transported an entire township in a matter of days.'

Someone asked, 'So . . . they're safe?'

'They're more than that,' Adrian replied. 'They're getting ready to start over.'

'All right, everyone. Back to your stations.' Meishi seated herself, surveyed the bridge, then, 'Pilot. Chart a course for Earth.'

EPILOGUE

Twelve days after the ship entered Earth's orbit, six days after the crew made landfall, Adrian took an early morning flight from Annapolis to Phoenix. Earth's gravity left him continually exhausted. But he could not put off this trip any longer.

A limo met him at Arrivals and drove him into town. Chris had wanted him to fly by private jet. But Adrian was still not used to money no longer being an issue. The numbers in his new bank account were dizzying.

He was early, so he had the limo stop for lunch at a Denny's. Chris had warned him that his system was not accustomed to meat, and meals heavy on carbs like wheat and corn also required some getting used to. A lot of the recently arrived crew ate at Denny's, she told him. Their menu offered an astonishing array of gluten-free dishes. He ordered carefully and missed her while he ate.

His destination was a brightly colored single-story building in the medical park. The Phoenix children's hospital rose above the pines separating the park from the main facility. It was as cheerful and welcoming as any place that dealt with sick children could be.

When it was time, he entered through the main doors and approached the receptionist. 'May I help you?'

'I'm here to see Doctor Barnes.'

'I'm very sorry. She's with a patient.' She typed on her keyboard. 'Are you the parent of a patient?'

'I'm not. No.'

'Can I ask what this is about?'

Adrian wondered if this would ever become a normal part of his life. 'Actually, Doctor Barnes is expecting me. It has to do with her current patient.'

A PA with a stethoscope slung around her neck walked over. She asked Adrian, 'You're here for Debbie Barnes?'

'Yes ma'am.'

'Your name?'

'Mars.'

'First or last?'

'Just Mars.'

The two women studied him a long moment. Then the receptionist asked, 'Should I call security?'

The PA continued to watch Adrian as she lifted the phone and punched in a number. Then, 'He's here.' A pause, then, 'Mars. Right. Like the planet.' She set down the phone. 'OK, buzz him through.'

Odell was working with seven other far-seers now, and it wasn't just because of her age and failing health. She was still the only one capable of identifying the new candidates, though there was one young man who showed considerable promise. The others focused on intensifying the contacts. Offering more than the single message that had guided Adrian, yet had missed helping so many others. Following that, they began identifying cases where his direct intervention might help.

Today was their first trial run.

The PA led him down a side corridor and knocked before a closed door. She opened, but used her body to block Adrian from entering.

Or rather, she tried.

A boy of eleven slammed into the PA, using all the strength in his slender form to shove the woman aside. He flung himself at Adrian. Wrapped his arms around Adrian's waist. 'You came.'

'Let's go inside.'

Adrian pried himself free and followed the weeping child into the room. The setting was designed to be soothing, happy, pleasant. Dr Debbie Barnes, experienced child psychologist, sat in a padded rocker separated from the empty patient's chair by a table piled with coloring books and toys and a chess set. She stood and watched uncertainly as Adrian pulled over a second chair and said, 'We don't have much time.'

'This is most unusual. Unprecedented, really.' She was a heavy-set woman in her fifties who clearly disliked having her control over the situation shattered like this. She waved the PA out, waited until the door closed, then demanded, 'Is Mars your real name?'

'No. But before I say anything else, I need to know that the confidentiality you grant your patients extends to this conversation.'

'There is no way I can confirm that.'

'Then for the moment what I can tell you is highly restricted.' Adrian turned to the child. 'Can you tell me your name?'

'Craig.'

'Wait just a second. You mean to tell me you didn't even know this patient's *name*?'

'I know enough. I know Craig is here because his parents fear his hold on reality is fracturing. That he is paying more attention to these dreams of his than his schoolwork or his family or his friends.' Adrian gentled his voice. 'Craig, I need you to stop crying and get control of yourself.'

'Th-They're real, aren't they? The dreams. Mars. Magic.'

'All of this and more. Now I want you to pay careful attention. Ready? Good. These dreams have been inviting you to examine different branches of magic.' He heard the woman's intake of breath, and halted her next comment with an upraised hand. Adrian's attention remained fastened on the child. 'Did any of them—'

'Far-seeing. Did I say that right?'

'You did. And it's an excellent answer. So here is what will happen now. I am going to email a series of spells to the good doctor here. She needs to see that what I am sharing with you, what I represent, is very real.'

'But there's no magic here.'

'Just the same, it's possible that one or more of these spells will resonate with you. It's important . . . Craig, please. We don't have time for tears. That's it. Good man. You need to begin practicing these spells. See this time with your therapist as an opportunity to step away from your outside life and begin preparing. And something more. Pay careful attention, because this is important. You must maintain a new balance. Show your parents what they need to see. Engage with the outside world more. Keep up with your studies. If necessary, only discuss this alternate reality here. With Doctor Barnes. Where it's safe.'

'I can do that.'

'Of course you can.' Adrian rose to his feet. 'May I trouble you for a card?'

She did not move. 'I must communicate all this to Craig's parents.'

'Are you sure that's what is in your patient's best interests? Say this is real. That Craig holds magical ability. If so, he will most likely emigrate to Mars. And become a wizard. And he needs you to make it happen. What's more, he can only connect with the real world when he has you and this room as a haven where he can express his *other* life. His one true calling.'

The doctor moved in slow motion. Taking a card. Writing. Handing it over. 'I will think about what you say.'

'Craig and I are both very grateful.' He offered the child his hand. 'I can't tell you what a pleasure it is to meet you.'

'Will I see you again?'

'Perhaps. But I can't say for certain. Once you start moving down this new course, we can try to arrange face-time via computer. If the good doctor agrees.'

'But when can we *meet*? I mean, in person. Like this. Together.'

Adrian tried to be as gentle as possible. 'Perhaps when you turn eighteen.'

The news actually calmed Craig. 'You're going back, aren't you? To Mars.'

Adrian nodded. News had reached them soon after they passed lunar orbit. The dictatorship formerly known as the regime had been overthrown. Laws governing magic and the Wizards' Code of Conduct had been rescinded. The agency put in place to restrict the use of magic had been abolished. Gerritt and Gupta and Riggins and a number of other regime henchmen were in custody awaiting trial.

Adrian's banishment had been rescinded.

Jurgen Roth, on behalf of the new democratically elected government, had formally requested Adrian's return on the next possible transport.

Harrow had returned to Earth and resigned his commission.

Adrian and Chris had of course discussed this at length. For the moment, his return would be a temporary assignment. He and Chris would remain official members of the flight crew. In time, however, that too might change. Someday there would be others helping with this vital task. For now, though, there were too many Earthbound mages like Craig who needed his personal intervention.

Adrian replied, 'I leave in nine months.'

'That is just so totally cool.' Then, 'Why can't I see you before you go?'

'There are others like you,' Adrian replied. 'All over the globe.'

The doctor asked, 'Are they all children?'

Adrian faced her. 'Confidentially?'

She hesitated, then nodded. 'All right. Agreed.'

'They are all ages. My job is to reach out to those who are most vulnerable, those facing some form of threat or danger.'

She studied her patient. Thinking. 'This is a lot to take in.'

'I understand better than you will ever know.'

She breathed. Again. Then, 'I accept your request for confidentiality, and will abide by these precepts. You may use me as the conduit for these spells.'

Craig said quietly, 'Yay.'

'Thank you so much.' Adrian rose to his feet. 'Study hard,' he told the child. 'More lessons will come. Prepare. Be ready. I'll see you on Mars.'

On his way back to the airport, Adrian asked the limo to stop in a highway rest stop. His legs felt leaden as he crossed the small park and stood staring at the mountains.

He was tempted to go. Speak the words aloud while actually standing among the painted hills. That he wanted to serve the cause of magic. Wherever he was.

But there simply wasn't time.

A young woman in Calgary who had been repeatedly treated for depression was next on his list. Then Boston, train down to Baltimore, and finally home.

Besides, he really wanted to make that Sedona trip with Chris.